IMAGINARY FRIENDS

Other books by Arlene F. Marks

Adventures in Godhood

SIC TRANSIT TERRA
(Edge Science Fiction and Fantasy Publishing)

Book 1: *The Genius Asylum*

Book 2: *The Otherness Factor*

Book 3: *The Relativity Bomb*

Book 4: *The Genome Rally*

Book 5: *The Cockroach Crusade*

Book 6: *The Identity Shift*

IMAGINARY FRIENDS

Arlene F. Marks

Milton, Ontario
http://www.brain-lag.com/

Brain Lag Publishing
Milton, Ontario
http://www.brain-lag.com/

Library and Archives Canada Cataloguing in Publication

Title: Imaginary friends : stories / Arlene F. Marks.
Names: Marks, Arlene F., 1947- author.
Identifiers: Canadiana (print) 20220157618 | Canadiana (ebook) 20220157634 | ISBN 9781928011712
  (softcover) | ISBN 9781928011729 (ebook)
Classification: LCC PS8561.R2868 I43 2022 | DDC C813/.54—dc23

Contents

Bemused.............................9

Comfort Food.............................15

The Witch in the 'Hood.............................23

Candles.............................35

Freudian Slip.............................55

Business is Business.............................69

Maury and Shred Go Ballistic.............................79

Doubling Back.............................95

Mightier than the Sword.............................113

The Best Defence.............................119

Manua's Children.............................133

Introduction

Every time an author writes a story, an imagined world enters our own. The plot is a journey of exploration, and the characters are the guides who lead the expedition, first taking the author by the hand…

Wait a minute. That can't be right. Doesn't the author create the characters and orchestrate the plot?

The answer to that is yes and no. Yes, characters spring to life in an author's mind, but they bring their stories with them. They confide their back story, smiling at remembered details while the writer records them. They chat easily about their family relationships, their goals for the future, and what they would do if presented with particular choices. Then they say, "Let's go on a trip. There's something I'd like to show you." And the wise author realizes that the characters are in charge—because it is, after all, their story—and goes along.

When I was a child, my imaginary friends were characters from books I'd read and television programs I watched. They were the product of someone else's creativity, and that was all right. I just needed them to follow me around and be witnesses to my life—to let me feel that I was in some small part in charge of *my* story.

Now that I'm an adult, our roles are reversed. My imaginary friends are my own creations, and I follow them around, sharing their adventures and bearing witness to their lives… and in some instances, as in this book, introducing them to others.

I hope you enjoy the trips they'll take you on, and that you'll want them to be your friends as well.

Arlene F. Marks
October 2021

The inspiration for this story, believe it or not, was a dictionary definition. I'm a logophile—a lover of words and wordplay. So, when I read in my Collins dictionary that "bemused" was a synonym for "bewildered", my brain went automatically to other "be—" words such as "bedevilled" and "besieged". Hmm. Bedevilled by a muse? What might that be like, I wondered… and my imagination responded with this.

Bemused

Originally published in:
Polar Borealis Magazine #17, February 2021

Danna Olsen sensed the familiar gloomy presence in her room even before she opened her eyes and saw the dark cloud hovering over the foot of her bed.

"You again," she moaned. "What is it this time? Somebody sprained an ankle three farms over? A soup pot boiled dry on some unattended stove?"

The cloud did not reply. It did, however, scud over to the window when she threw back her blanket. She couldn't decide whether it was protecting her from curious eyes as she dressed or simply moving to get a better view.

"Why won't you go away?" she demanded. It was a rest day, a day of freedom from the clutch of children she normally taught and cared for while their parents worked the various farms in the area. Danna loved being a schoolteacher, but it was demanding in ways that made her cherish her personal time. Today she had hoped to spend it immersed in a book, not running around investigating alleged portents.

I'm your muse, the cloud replied inside her head, in the voices of her brother and her cousin Becky.

"Whoever told you that was lying." Danna aimed the toes of her right foot into a sock and shoved, extra hard. "Muses are made of light, and they help people. They inspire them to create, or they guide them to safety, or they strengthen their bodies as they strive for excellence."

So I've heard. A new voice this time, belonging to Mr. Carmichael, the egg man from down the road. Memories of his overturned cart last week splashed across her mind.

"All you ever do is bring me bad news and send me on fool's errands."

Yes. It still doesn't change what I am. Three familiar voices, one after the other.

"What you are is a nuisance," she declared, pulling her favourite slacks out of the closet.

Your uncle named me. A child's voice this time.

Yes, he had, she recalled, right after dropping his tea mug on the floor and uttering something in the sort of language that children weren't normally allowed to hear.

It had happened eight years earlier. Danna had been twelve, two years past the age by which most of the children in the colony acquired a muse. No one knew exactly where these tiny luminous beings came from, but they were intelligent, they were generous, and they seemed to gravitate toward the young. Once paired with one of the alien creatures, a human was "bemused" for life.

That Danna wasn't came as no surprise. Her only demonstrated inclinations to that point had been a dogged curiosity, a love of reading, and a bossy attitude toward her younger cousins.

By her twelfth birthday, Danna was telling herself that not everyone needed a muse. Perhaps it was better not to rely on another being for inspiration. Perhaps she was fortunate to be able to find it within herself.

Nonetheless, when a small fluffy cloud materialized in her bedroom early one morning and addressed her by name, relief flooded her body. She felt as though she'd reached the top of the mountain and could finally stop climbing. The fact that she'd been chosen by a cloud and not a light was of little concern to her. Danna hummed happily as she came downstairs for breakfast that day, with her new friend trailing behind her.

Uncle Mats was standing in the front hall, sipping his customary tea. He turned at the sound of her footsteps, a smile on his lips. An instant later the mug lay in pieces and the tea in a puddle on the hard wooden floor, and the shock stamped on his weathered features stopped her in her tracks.

"A harbinger!" he rasped, pointing excitedly with rapid jabbing motions at the cloud. "Danna, it's not—you've got to—!" Then his mouth snapped shut and he fled out the front door.

Drawn by the commotion, Aunt Suzanne emerged from her studio. She'd been painting—the glow of her muse illuminated the slice of room visible through the doorway. Suzanne cast a regretful look back over her shoulder. Then, with a confirming glance at the mess in the hall and a curious one at the cloud coming down the stairs, she went to fetch a broom and some rags. It had been another full day before Mats could bring himself to look his niece in the face.

According to the colony's common lexicon, a harbinger was a warning, foretelling the later arrival of something big and important. Danna had to admit, the cloud had been looking much more threatening lately, like one of the thunderhammers that built up in the sky before a heavy storm.

On the other hand, the "portents" she had already witnessed—eight years' worth of minor annoyances—hardly added up in her mind to a major disaster.

Danna stood in front of her closet, choosing a top to go with her dark green slacks. Pulling on a matching tunic, she fastened a belt of woven leather strips around her waist and stepped in front of the mirror to adjust the drape of the cloth.

Green was the colour of Earth's oceans. Perhaps she would read *Moby Dick* today. Or *Twenty Thousand Leagues Under the Sea*. Her father had loved the classic novels of their home world. Now, reading them always made her feel as though his spirit was nearby, sharing them with her.

Downstairs. The voice was her uncle's this time.

Danna whirled to stare at the cloud. "What about downstairs?" she demanded.

Bad news. Downstairs.

"Danna, we have a guest who wants to meet you."

It took her a moment to realize that her aunt's voice was real and coming from the other side of her door. There was a visitor. Bearing bad news? Or perhaps bad intentions? In the mirror, the cloud hovered black and roiling behind her. Danna drew a deep breath and left her bedroom.

Sitting in the front room was a plain-faced woman wearing

city-made clothes—tailored, with gem-shaped buttons that glittered in the light. She stood up as Danna reached the bottom of the stairs. The woman's dark eyes shifted to register the storm cloud floating just behind. Then she turned to Uncle Mats and said quietly, "That's it?"

He nodded.

"And she doesn't know what it signifies?"

"She was just a child when it first appeared. It would have been cruel to tell her then. Now it would be cruel *not* to tell her."

"So you believe she's ready?"

All this urgent muttering about her as though she wasn't there was making Danna impatient. "Ready for what?" she chimed in.

Aunt Suzanne put a soothing arm around her shoulders. "Do you remember the very first time a cloud came to you? You were quite young."

"I was twelve," Danna corrected her.

Suzanne threw her husband a pleading look. "Maybe it's best if we just—"

"No," Mats declared. "If this is her lot in life then she needs to know everything."

Bad news, the cloud confirmed.

"You'd better sit down, girl," he told her. Uncertainly, Danna lowered herself onto the sofa beside him. "When you were just four years old, your parents went on a sailing expedition, leaving you in our care. Two weeks later I found you on the back porch, talking to what appeared to be a puff of smoke. You were reciting numbers. Every day for the next week, you sat on the porch reciting numbers, a different string of them each day. I thought it was curious, so I wrote them down. Then the wrecked hull of your parents' boat was found washed up on a beach on the southern land mass. No bodies were recovered. But all at once the numbers made sense. We checked. They were coordinates, changing each day as the ocean currents moved the wreck closer to shore."

Something inside Danna was spinning like the useless wheel of Carmichael's overturned cart. "So the harbinger came to warn me that my parents were dead or dying. It told me where to find them so that I could tell you," she said numbly.

"Darling, I'm so sorry! We didn't understand—"

"Hush, Su!" Mats commanded her.

"When the harbinger returned eight years ago," said the visitor from the city, "your uncle informed us immediately. We've been on high alert ever since."

"And does your presence here today mean that you know what it's been trying to warn me about? Because I honestly have no idea."

The woman's expression softened. "It's taken eight years for the message to arrive here from Earth, but yes, Danna, we finally know." A pause, then, "There has been a war. Nuclear weapons were involved. The Earth we remember, that you've been reading about in your father's books… that planet no longer exists."

Comprehension broke over Danna in a suffocating wave. The harbinger could assemble brief verbal messages using the voices stored in her memory, but new information had to be communicated in symbols. Injured limbs, crashed vehicles, sudden fires—it worked with whatever was at hand, pointing her at clues and hoping she would be able to solve them in time to sound a warning.

No, she corrected herself, it wasn't the harbinger's hope, it was the colony's.

Uncle Mats was gazing at her with pain in his eyes. Danna swallowed hard, but the bitter taste in her mouth persisted as she recalled his earlier words. This was her lot in life, he'd said. To be tormented with riddles and vague premonitions, understood only in hindsight. To pass them along to others if asked. Like an ancient Greek oracle. That wasn't so bad. There was a reason seers were elderly. Eventually, she would learn to interpret the harbinger's language, but only if…!

As though through a veil, Danna watched the cloud grow pale and dissipate. *Don't come back,* she begged it.

I am cursed, it whispered sadly in her own voice. *I have no choice.*

The opening sentence of this story was a writing prompt that I composed for an exercise, to see how many different story ideas it would spark in my imagination. There were several. The mysterious door showed up in a laboratory as part of a teleporting experiment, in a rainforest where explorers discovered an ancient temple, and in an artist's studio where a picture began painting itself. I may write those other stories one day, but none of them burrowed into my mind and demanded to be told the way this one did.

Comfort Food

The door was the first thing to appear. One day, the corner lot was its usual tangle of crab grass and thorny shrubs, and the next morning a shiny metal door was just standing there as though it had sprouted up through the hardscrabble overnight. It had strange symbols engraved on it and a recessed handle halfway up its left side.

We looked for any wires that might be keeping it erect but found none. When I bent to peer behind it, the door seemed to disappear. When I straightened up it came back. I had a sudden urge to bang on it, but I didn't dare. It was almost nine o'clock and Dad depended on me to get my little brother Willis to school on time. He'd be madder than hell if he found out we were late because I couldn't resist daring a disembodied door to fall on me. So we kept walking.

After dinner that night, I said, "There's a really spooky door sitting in the vacant lot at the corner."

My father looked up from his newspaper and said grimly, "Half of Manitoba is under water. It's the worst spring flooding they've ever had. Doors aren't spooky, son. It's the possibility of not having one that should be scaring the bejeezus out of you."

Next morning was Saturday. I left the house early to go check on the door. A metal frame had materialized around it, and the engraved symbols had somehow transformed overnight into English words: "Receiving entrance. Please knock and wait."

At breakfast I said, "I think the door in the vacant lot belongs to some kind of business."

My father had been watching the news on TV. "Tornado season is starting early this year," he commented, shaking his head sadly. "Biggest twisters in history. They're sucking whole towns into the air and dropping them in pieces all over the countryside. Maybe that's where your door came from."

When Dad works weekends, Willis is my responsibility. That afternoon, we found some paint and a flattened cardboard carton in the garage and made a sign to put in the vacant lot, like the ones we'd seen on empty buildings:

COMING SOON

"What do we put underneath it?" Willis wanted to know.

"Let's find out," I said. And we walked down the street to the vacant lot and hammered on the big steel door as hard as we could.

After a moment, the door made a popping noise and slid sideways a crack, and an almost-human face appeared in the opening. Its large eyes blinked curiously at us a couple of times. Then its extra-small mouth curved into a smile. Then the face disappeared and we heard its owner say to someone inside, "Papa, it's children."

Willis stood at attention beside me, his eyes almost as wide as the alien's. I grabbed his hand in case he panicked and tried to run. Meanwhile, a wonderful spicy aroma was wafting through the open doorway, carrying with it a voice that I could swear tasted equally delicious.

"Well, don't just stand there, Gretti. Give them each a sample."

Gretti reappeared holding a tray of small cookies. The door opened wider, and for just a moment I saw a shiny metal room behind her. Then another, larger alien appeared, blocking my view. He wore a flour-dusted apron and a grin as wide as his extra-small mouth would permit. "Please," he invited me, "try one."

They smelled like wishes coming true. I took a cookie and

popped it into my mouth… and remembered with perfect clarity the soothing music of my mother's voice and the adoration in her eyes as she hovered over my crib. For as long as I kept chewing that cookie I felt completely safe and secure and cherished. When I swallowed it, the feeling faded almost immediately; but the memory of it remained sharply etched in my mind.

Tears were sliding down my cheeks. I didn't care. Willis was staring fearfully at me. That didn't matter either. "What's in the cookies?" I demanded.

"Comfort. This is Bloom's Bakery. I am Bloom. And you are…?"

"Jonah Reid," I told him. "This is my brother, Willis."

"Papa, we have customers in the front," Gretti reminded him.

"I have to go," said Bloom, still smiling. "Come back tomorrow."

Next morning at breakfast, I told my father, "There's a bakery coming to the vacant lot at the corner. Bloom's Bakery."

"Their cookies make you cry," Willis chimed in.

Dad had worked all night. A freak hailstorm had knocked out a power station at the other end of the city, leaving a thousand homes without electricity. "That's nice, guys," he sighed wearily.

Sunday was his only chance to get some sleep before his next regular shift, so I took Willis to Bloom's Bakery right after breakfast. As we approached, I could see a thin margin of wall around the metal door. Gretti answered our knock and greeted us by name, then held out a tray with some buns on it.

They smelled like daydreams. I had to nudge Willis twice before he would take one. After a single bite, he smiled. After a second bite, he laughed.

"What's so funny?" I asked him.

"The circus. The clowns."

I already had a perfect memory of that day, our last happy day as a family before Mom got sick. Willis had been just one year old when it happened. I was nine. Six months later she was gone.

I stared uncertainly at the bun in my hand.

"It's all right," said Gretti. "Papa bakes only happiness into these."

But I couldn't take the chance. After five years the pain of loss had dulled to an ache but it was still there, wound like a parasitic vine around every moment of my life, including the ones I'd forgotten. "Maybe later," I told her, and stuffed the bun into my pocket.

Gretti studied me for a minute. Then, "Wait here, Jonah," she said.

"Can I have another bun?" Willis piped up just before the door slid closed.

I gave him mine. One bite later he was chortling to himself again.

Right after that, the door opened a crack and Gretti's father was eyeing me through it. "Gretti tells me you don't wish to remember being happy."

I shrugged. "Happiness doesn't last. It only makes the sadness that follows it feel worse."

"But when things are at their worst, isn't that when you need to recall happy moments, to lessen the pain?" He reached behind him, then handed me one of those buns. "For you," he said. "For later. But it doesn't come free of charge. Do you bake, Jonah?"

"My mom used to let me help her make cookies when I was younger. Does that count?"

He smiled. "Cookies always count. Did you enjoy spending time with your mother?"

"Yes, a lot."

"Then here is what I want you to do. You will make a batch of cookies like the ones you made with your mother, and you will bring me three of them to taste. But before you finish preparing the batter, you will add this." He reached back once more and produced a tiny vial of transparent liquid. "As you empty it into the mixing bowl, think about how you felt when you were younger and you watched your mother's cookies come out of the oven."

"And all you want from me is three of mine? How will you know whether I used your 'secret ingredient'?"

"I'll know," he assured me, "and so will you."

"Are you going to do it?" Willis asked me as we were walking back to the house.

I patted the small bulge in my jeans pocket and consciously

slowed my steps. "Dunno," I replied. "It depends on what we have in the house."

"Can I help?"

I gazed into his face and saw myself at his age, all wide-eyed and eager to try, and something stirred inside me, like a knot in my stomach struggling to work itself loose.

"Sure, you can," I told him.

I found Mom's recipe box shoved to the back of a shelf in the pantry and riffled through the cards, searching for one in particular. We'd made these cookies many times, the cinnamon-laced ones with crackly sugar crusts. I checked that Dad was still asleep. Then I stuffed the card into my pocket and took Willis grocery shopping. Nothing unusual about that. Getting the groceries was my weekly chore. But today it felt like an adventure. It was as if we were on a secret mission or something.

When we got back, I preheated the oven and set up the ingredients on the counter, just like Mom used to do. Then we followed her recipe, somehow managing to get flour and sticky spatter all over the kitchen in the process. It was worth the mess to clean up, though. Baking with my little brother was the most fun either of us had had in a very long time.

I mixed Bloom's secret ingredient into the batter before spooning it onto the cookie sheet, but I didn't have to remember how it felt when I was young. All I had to do was look at the anticipation on Willis's face. I knew he was imagining how good these cookies were going to taste.

Dad wandered in as they were cooling on a tray. They smelled like a welcome-home hug. He took one still warm and bit into it. His eyes widened, then closed as his features relaxed into a gentle smile.

"I don't know what you put into these, son, but they're perfect. Absolutely perfect," he declared, and helped himself to two more.

Later that afternoon, Gretti's father bit into one and smiled that same way.

"What exactly did I bake into these cookies?" I asked him. "Was it happiness?"

"No. It's something much better—optimism."

Hesitantly, I began, "I realize it's your secret ingredient, but—"

"—but you're going to need more of it. I know. Do you still have the vial?"

"Yes." I reached into my jeans pocket and dug it out. I'd brought it with me, hoping to get it refilled, but when I looked at it, I realized with a start that it was no longer empty.

"What—? How—?"

"As long as you keep using it, it will never run dry. You do intend to keep on baking, yes?"

"Oh, yes!" I replied, tucking the vial safely away again.

"Every day!" Willis chimed in. He'd polished off four cookies and was optimistic as anything.

Ten years have passed since that conversation. The door to Bloom's Bakery disappeared from the vacant lot shortly afterward. I have no idea where it went, or even where the bakery was while the door was here. But I honoured my promise to Gretti's father. I baked something every week. Right after high school, I turned professional. A couple of years ago, I started my own bakery company and named it after him.

He was right about the importance of optimism, by the way. We're currently in the middle of a pandemic. Climate change is in full swing. Half the world is teetering on the brink of all-out war and much of the rest is either burning up or under water. Dad moved to the west coast last year to help fight the wildfires, and Willis went with him. There's a tremendous demand for comfort food right now, and thanks to the web site and social media presence I've set up, I'm able to provide it. Bloom's Baked Goods are being sold and shipped all over the western hemisphere.

My cookies smell like the beginning of an adventure.

My pastries smell like coming home to family.

And I've figured out what the 'secret ingredient' is. It's love.

The Beatles had it right all along.

They say that everything is fodder for the writer's imagination, and they're right. In the case of this story, it was a stubborn headache. Pain pills had reduced it from a roar to a mutter, but it was still hanging on after 36 hours. Finally, I shared it with a character who'd been at the back of my mind, patiently waiting for the right role to come along. The resulting tale turned out to be therapeutic for both of us. By the time I'd finished writing it, the headache was gone.

The Witch in the 'Hood

*W*hip-thin and tough as leather, old Mrs. Albert stretches lazily and steps outside, onto her wide front porch. The entity inside her has been sensing the approach of its old foe, making her bones itch night and day. Lately, it feels as if they're about to burst her flesh.

Her previous battle with the Healer was costly. It ended with both her sons dead and her husband infected with a cancer that took its own time killing him, as though he was a fancy buffet and it wanted to sample and savour every dish. It has been a year since his funeral. Now the enemy is returning to the neighbourhood, in search of another victim.

Mrs. Albert hasn't the power to destroy the darkness, any more than it can annihilate the lambency that dwells within her. Nonetheless, for as long as she has lived, she has been putting herself in the Healer's way. They've been locked in a stalemate, this dance of yin and yang, life and death, for almost two thousand years.

Healer is what the enemy calls itself, as though evil can be transformed by simply giving it a virtuous name; for this 'healer' doesn't end pain—it feeds on human suffering. It prowls battlefields, whispering in soldiers' ears, reminding them of the innocence they lost forever the first time they stilled another beating human heart. It places images in their minds of the loving family left behind, and asks in a voice that rustles insidiously through their thoughts, Do you really deserve them, now that you have killed? *Sometimes the Healer follows a soldier home, feasting on a trail of misery and self-*

loathing. All your friends are dead. Why are you still living? It drowns hopeful dreams in blood-soaked memories, suffocates happiness beneath a smothering blanket of guilt, until one day life itself is too much for the soldier to bear; and then sirens and flashing red lights converge in front of a house, marking another tragic loss for an already wounded family.

Now there's a soldier down the street, recently returned on crutches from the fighting far away, and Mrs. Albert's bones are itching more fiercely than ever before.

~

I woke up this morning with the worst headache yet, like a white hot spike being driven into the side of my skull. Popped four pain pills at once and they're not even making a dent. The Healer must already be in the 'hood, tracking down my brother.

My name is Dorene Gunn, and I'm sixteen years old. I'm recording this blog in case the witch woman's spell fails and everything goes sideways. The headaches are coming closer together now and stronger, like baby-birthing contractions, and it's getting really hard for me to think straight, but people need to understand what's been happening.

Before I knew what she really was, I thought she was just a crazy old woman who didn't like kids. Every day she would stand on her porch with her long bony arms crossed over her chest, scowling us past her scrubby front lawn as we walked to and from school.

One day as we were passing her house, she arched her back and sniffed the air, then turned her smoky eyes slowly over the group of us and let her gaze settle on me. I shuddered a little, feeling her interest like the soft brush of a hand on my skin. Later, she had some words with my mother at our front door, and next thing I knew I was being asked to go down to the corner house two or three times a week to "visit with nice Mrs. Albert, who's all alone."

I was about to say no way. But then my mother made a point of telling me how Mr. Albert had passed away from cancer just last year, and how the Alberts had lost both their sons in a tragic accident three years before that, and how good it would make me feel to bring some companionship into that poor old woman's life. When she put it that way, how could I refuse? Meanwhile, recalling conversations I'd overheard when I was younger between my brother and his friends about "that wack job on the corner", I figured it would be a good idea to tuck a blade down my sock before going over there.

The inside of Mrs. Albert's house is pretty much what you'd expect from a lonely old lady. It's a maze of burrow-like hallways lined with tiny rooms. Every window is shaded, and every cubicle is cluttered with random furniture under heaps of junk, some of it spilling out of odd-shaped wicker containers. The whole place is dim and dusty and has an old-person smell to it, like a museum that's been boarded up for a long time.

Except for the front room.

That's where we sit whenever I visit her. It has a green and gold sofa and matching chair, with carved wooden feet and narrow wooden armrests, and a couple of small round tables with starched lace doilies on them, and pale green wallpaper with bouquets of yellow roses rising in staggered rows from floor to ceiling. There's never a speck of dust in that room. Everything smells freshly cleaned.

Each time I arrive, the window blind is raised halfway; but she pulls it all the way down after we've had our tea. That's when the lesson begins. She's teaching me spells.

That's my word for them, not hers. Mrs. Albert calls them 'commands'. She also gets upset if she hears me use the word 'witch' to describe her, so I don't call her that to her face, even though that's what I think she is. She says that there are people like her all over the world, and none of them use magic. But they can still recognize one another just by looking, and that was why she singled me out that day. She says I'm full of light, like her. When she saw that, she knew I would be her successor.

I'd been having the headaches for weeks at that point, and my parents were talking about taking me to a specialist to find out what was causing them. When I told Mrs. Albert about them, she nodded knowingly. She said it was no coincidence that they'd started up shortly after my brother Damian got back from Afghanistan. The headaches were a warning from the light inside me that the Healer had caught Damian's scent again and was on its way to finish what it had begun on the battlefield. The Healer was a kind of parasite, she told me, only it got into people's minds instead of their bodies. Sometimes it did that by infecting someone they might go to for help, like a social worker, or a medical doctor, or even a pastor, and making them give bad advice.

A lot of what she said made no sense to me at first. I thought she must be sick in the head, from loneliness or grief. I hoped that I was having the headaches because of an allergy, and that they were worsening because of something inside her house. I thought a hundred times about begging off from going to visit her. But then something strange happened.

One afternoon I was sitting with her, sipping ginger tea in her front room, and she was going on about how an alien life force was living inside me, keeping the darkness out, and I would soon have the power to protect my brother from the Healer's touch. All at once, everything went out of focus for just a second and then sprang back sharp and clear, and I could see something flowing out of her chest and entering mine, like a ribbon of light connecting the two of us. Its rich, warm glow filled the space between us. While I was wondering at that, an answering warmth kindled inside me. And then, as though a switch had been flipped, a wave seemed to break over me, drenching me with ease and contentment.

I know now that it was her life force, throwing a shield around me. At the time, all I could think was, *Damn! This magic stuff is real!* Since then, I've decided that I will do whatever it takes, learn whatever I need to learn, to make Damian feel as safe and complete as I felt at that moment…

…because there's an emptiness inside my brother, one that I can finally understand. He never smiles anymore, and rarely speaks. Sometimes I catch him staring out the window with eyes I hardly recognize, they're so bleak and hollow, the eyes of someone who's already accepted death and is just marking time until his grave is ready. He's on the edge, about to fall. If the Healer touches him, Damian will be lost to us, gone forever. And I cannot—will not!—let that happen.

❧

Mrs. Albert makes no sound as she walks. She gathers up the cups and saucers and puts them on the tea tray, along with the honey and the half-filled milk pitcher and the small plate of golden brown sugar cookies. Smiling to herself, she carries the tray into her tiny kitchen and deposits it noiselessly on the counter. Sheer yellow curtains swell and hollow in the breeze sifting through the window screen over the sink. A warm baking aroma lingers in the air as the cookies are tipped into an airtight plastic container and pushed to the back of a cupboard.

The clutter is, of necessity, more controlled in the rooms where she actually lives, but she knows she won't be here much longer. Plain brown cardboard cartons occupy the space under the round kitchen table. One, half-filled, sits open on the spindly wooden chair beside it. This carton bears the girl's full name, printed in red marker in large block letters: Dorene Rachelle Gunn.

Mrs. Albert reaches into a drawer for a small item wrapped in a red and white tea towel. A braided lock of long dark hair fastened at one end by a scrap of red cloth, it's all that remains of her long-ago youth. She has pared away other parts of herself over the centuries, careful to preserve and conceal them as each encounter has taught her what she dares not carry into battle again. Empathy made her hesitate. Uncertainty crippled her. Innocence was the first thing to go, of course. Even at a tender age, she understood its dangers.

Fortunately, it shouldn't be a problem for her successor.

As if my head didn't hurt enough already, Mrs. Albert has been stuffing it full of spell words. She says they're instructions to the life force inside me, in its own language. I've been practising shield-casting, sitting in her darkened front room and repeating the phrases over and over. By now they're burned so deeply into my mind that I swear I can taste ashes in my mouth.

I've also been formulating some strategies of my own.

Damian began teaching me how to fight when he was jumped into the local gang. He was fourteen then and I was eight, just old enough to get myself into serious trouble. By the time he signed up with the army four years later, I could handle myself pretty well on the street. I'm not jumped in, but I know who is and how to be when they're around. And I know how to use a blade. I've been carrying one pretty much 24/7, as a fall-back in case the shield spells aren't enough.

I'm glad today is Saturday, because there's no way I could concentrate on schoolwork with this freaking headache. Nothing turned up on X-rays or an MRI, so the doctor prescribed some heavy-duty pain pills and told my parents to keep an eye on me. He has no idea what's going on, and I'm not about to tell him. Meanwhile, for the past few days, I've been drooling spell words whenever I try to sleep. The Healer is getting close.

I have a hunch about who may be bringing it into the neighbourhood, and I hope I'm wrong. There's a new pastor conducting services tomorrow in the church at the end of our street. My parents got real tight with the Lord when Damian came home minus a leg four months ago. They've been dragging both of us to services every week to 'refresh and renew our souls'. According to the church bulletin board, tomorrow's sermon is going to be about the healing powers of love.

Healing powers? Sure sounds like a shout-out to me.

I asked Mrs. Albert whether she would be attending the service, and she scowled at the floor for a moment. Then she changed the subject. I really hope the magic she's taught me works. I don't know whether it's in me to shank a pastor in front of the whole congregation.

❧

Mrs. Albert moves on slippered feet from room to room inside her house. She has been busy all night, gathering items, reviewing their contents, deciding their fate. Most of them have been fed to the flames crackling in the old stove in her basement. The rest have been carefully packed and sealed inside the labelled cardboard cartons in her kitchen. The girl's box is still open.

The life force and the Healer are both very old. They came to Earth millennia ago, the symbiote and the parasite, two living clouds of energy, each made up of many separate entities. They spread themselves out to ride the air currents that flowed in every direction over the planet. They sampled Earth's energies, found them sufficient, and settled in to resume their ancient war.

Occasionally, a life force entity encountered a human that it could join with, and care for, and respond to. Mrs. Albert was such a human. So now is the girl. Mrs. Albert's symbiote is connecting them as it once tried to connect Mrs. Albert with her husband and their sons… but that was a mistake, and it will not be repeated.

Her packing done, she makes herself a cup of Earl Grey tea and eases herself onto the sofa with a sigh.

It is an hour before dawn. The itching in her bones has deepened into a ravenous ache. The battle will be joined today.

As Mrs. Albert waits for the darkness outside to lift, a pewter lamp on one of the circular tables provides a gentle illumination. When the time comes, she will utter her final command. The life force entity that has been keeping her mortality at bay will leave her body and seek out the girl's, giving her the strength she needs in order to prevail.

The Healer will be arrogant in its certainty of victory, but there is much about humans that it still does not understand.

The girl is young, but she will learn quickly, because she understands much more than she thinks she does.

And Frances Albert, who has answered to more names than she can remember and can no longer recall a time when she was not at war, will finally be able to rest.

❧

Dorene walks in front of her parents, pushing her brother along the sidewalk in a folding wheelchair. He has been fitted for a prosthetic limb but refuses to wear it. Now he slumps in the canvas-sling seat, indifferently studying the folds and creases in the dark blue lap-covering that conceals the absence of his right leg. Sunday morning is the only time he consents to leave his parents' house. Dorene knows that he is only humouring them. He may once have harboured hopes of finding salvation in the house of the Lord, but those hopes evaporated months ago. Now, struggling into his one good suit and tie and going to church is no more than a weekly concession that he makes in order to preserve his parents' illusion that he is still part of their world.

Hearing her sigh, Damian glances backward and notices a flash of metal against his sister's left ankle. He watched her swallow a huge dose of painkiller before they left the house. Now she's carrying a blade into a church. This unsettles him. That he can't explain the feeling unsettles him even more.

The Gunn family take their places in the short back pew, with Damian's wheelchair in the aisle. Dorene sits next to him, scouting the room with a grim, calculating expression on her face and muttering to herself. She reminds him of a soldier about to go into battle, and for a moment a chill settles over his shoulders. And then, suddenly, it lifts, taking with it the feeling of futility that has been haunting him ever since he returned home. For the first time in months, he can see a path in front of him. It's a reason to smile.

When the pews are three-quarters full, the new pastor emerges from his office with a sheaf of papers in his hand and tentatively, like a substitute teacher on his first day, takes his place behind the pulpit. He is young, round of face and body, with large soft hands that shake slightly, rustling the pages as he ensures that they are in the right order. Then he clears his throat and begins to speak.

Dorene gasps involuntarily as the world goes out of focus for just an instant, then springs back sharp and clear. Except for the pastor. Around his body there remains a blurred outline, a smoky double image that she recognizes at once despite never having seen it before. The Healer. She was right. The pastor is carrying the parasite. And there's still no sign of Mrs. Albert.

Dorene watches tautly as the young clergyman scans the congregation, his gaze leaping from face to face. When he gets to Damian's, his eyes blink and narrow as though he is struggling to make out her brother's features.

The shield spell must be working.

But it's not enough simply to confound the Healer. It needs to be driven away. Urgency tightening every muscle in her body, Dorene searches the room for the only person she knows with the power to do that. Then, all at once, a heat kindles deep inside her. It swells like a tide. It spreads along her limbs as though carried by her blood. It fills every cell of her body. Her brain sings with it. Her fingertips ache with it.

Dorene stares around her in wonderment, for the first time seeing as Mrs. Albert sees, through alien eyes. She realizes that people are nothing but shells. Some are empty and brittle, ready to shatter at the next glancing blow. Others are more robust, containing inner strength and substance; but every one of them harbours a deadly darkness—the shadow of mortality, writhing at the core of their being.

Dorene glances tentatively at Damian. His outline is blurred as well, but not by shadow. By light. The shield spell has driven the darkness right out of him.

In an instant, Dorene is on her feet, spell words spilling from her mouth. Curious excitement erupts around her. She shakes her head to block it out. Around the pastor's form, the dark outline has begun to shift and heave. His voice softens. It falters. His words resist being spoken aloud—he must push them one by one past his lips. He is blinking very hard and fast now, his eyes darting to and fro in confusion.

Dorene has instructed the life force within her to shield the pastor from the Healer.

A ribbon of golden light leaps from her chest, launching itself toward the pulpit. In a heartbeat, pastor and pulpit are engulfed by a maelstrom of radiance and shadow, a pulsating, violent, desperate battle between life and death. Dorene holds her breath, unable to tear her eyes away, willing the light to win, fearing it might not.

Then the pastor comes back into view. His cheeks are flushed. His breathing is a series of huge, ragged gasps. Finally, he can neither speak nor move. His eyes roll upward in their sockets and he drops to the floor, and as though blown away by a stream of fresh air, the final hazy remnants of after-image surrounding him dissolve.

Dorene feels the rush of warmth as her life force surges back into her body, and a wave of relief as she realizes that her head no longer throbs with pain. Light has won over darkness. The Healer is gone and, to her amazement, the witch who sent it packing was not Mrs. Albert.

Where was Mrs. Albert?

Gripped by a sudden unease, Dorene scrambles past her brother and races out of the church. Behind her, there is wondering talk of speaking in tongues, and of holy rapture.

❧

Dorene knocks gently on Mrs. Albert's front door, hesitantly trying the knob when there is no response. The door is unlocked. She enters slowly, all her senses alert.

The old woman is gone. An errant breeze whispers through the front room. It stirs what appears to be a pile of ashes on the sofa, in the space where Dorene has become accustomed to seeing Mrs. Albert sit while they drink tea together.

Frowning, Dorene wanders into the kitchen. On the round wooden table she finds a sealed envelope addressed to a lawyer, and a roll of heavy tape sitting beside a cardboard box with her name printed on it. She flings open the carton and finds a container of sugar cookies and a half-dozen jars of Mrs. Albert's special peach and raspberry preserves, labelled and carefully packed around a very old leather-bound book. She flips through its pages, realizes what it is, and puts it back. There are also six tall beeswax candles, an antique teapot, and a red and white dish towel. Dorene stares at this last item for a moment, then thrusts it back into the box. There will be time to figure out its significance later.

There are three other cartons, already sealed, with three different names on them. Family members, most likely, mentioned in Mrs. Albert's will.

Dorene seals her package and tests its weight. It is awkward but light enough to be carried out the door. She isn't certain where she'll take it, only knows that she's going to need somewhere private if she's to practise the spells in the book. Being able to shield people from the parasite was just the first step in her training. Now it's time to get down to business. Time to begin turning her life force entity into something a lot more soldierly, making the next battle more final, the next victory more decisive.

Making the next time the last time the Healer dares to enter this witch's 'hood.

I envision the Sic Transit Terra universe as a large and busy canvas, like a painting by Pieter Bruegel the Elder, containing literally hundreds of figures and dozens of stories, all happening at the same time. In a Bruegel painting, all the figures are about the same size, leaving it up to the observer to decide where to focus their attention. As the author of Sic Transit Terra, I get to make a similar decision, choosing which characters will take the stage and whose story (or stories) will be told in each book of the series. Rabbi Leon Goldman has so far been a minor character in these novels. He will have a more important part to play later on, as Humanity's future unfolds. Until then, here is a slice of his past.

Candles

The offices of the Relocation Authority in the Urban District of Lakeshore Ontario had been purposely designed to intimidate visitors. Walls of steel, doors of glass, floors of polished marble. Rabbi Leon Goldman's heart thudded into his stomach as the elevator doors glided soundlessly apart, depositing him in a place that was cold and shiny and apparently devoid of humanity. Nothing moved or breathed in this sterile maze, including, at the moment, Leon Goldman.

He was a few minutes early for an eight o'clock appointment with his relocation officer. The tone of the summons had been disturbingly formal, even distant, coming as it did from someone he'd known since they were both five years old, and Goldman couldn't help imagining the worst.

"Leon!" Goldman spun at the sound of his name and saw Josh Weinstein striding toward him, his hand outstretched for shaking. "So good of you to come!"

As if he'd had a choice.

Weinstein's forced heartiness making him even more nervous, Goldman followed the relocation officer down a long narrow corridor to an enclosed cubicle. It was spartanly furnished, just as blank and barren as the rest of the space on this floor, with a monolithic glass door that closed and latched behind Goldman with an ominously loud click.

"So, Leon, how have you been?" Josh asked once they were seated across the featureless expanse of desk from each other.

Unsure how to respond, Goldman shrugged. How had he been? He'd been comfortable. He'd been happy. He'd been feeling secure, perhaps too secure.

Josh pulled a compupad from somewhere behind the desktop and called up Goldman's file. "You've been deferred for relocation seven times now, correct?"

Goldman nodded, an icy knot beginning to form in his stomach.

Weinstein leaned back in his chair with a regretful sigh. "I'm afraid I can't defer you again, Leon. There's a posting available, as chaplain aboard the *Vasco da Gama*, and you're going to have to take it. I'm sorry, but the rules have changed. Neither one of us has a choice in the matter."

"The *Vasco da Gama*. It's a ship?"

"A star cruiser, explorer class." Weinstein leaned forward again and read aloud from his screen. "It has a crew complement of two hundred men and women."

"And how many of them are Jewish?"

Weinstein paused, then shook his head sadly. "None of them. I hate to tell you how few practising Jews there are out in space, Rabbi."

"And yet you think it's a good idea to rip me away from my congregation at Beth Avraham and transplant me onto this star ship where I would be the only Jew aboard." Goldman felt the blood rush to his face and saw his anger reflected in Josh Weinstein's darkening expression.

"Leon, please, don't make this any more difficult for yourself."

"Those people are like my family! They helped me get through the loss of my wife. We have a bond."

"You think I don't realize that?" demanded Weinstein, now on his feet and leaning across the desktop toward him. "Sarah was my friend, Leon. I miss her too. But her funeral was four years ago. It's time for you to put the past behind you and move on. Leon, I'm sorry, but it is what it is. You're Eligible and you're going off-planet, end of discussion." Weinstein sank back into his chair and busied himself with his compupad, refusing to make any further eye contact. "Your replacement at Beth Avraham has already been selected and notified. A week from Monday you begin three Earth months of orientation. That gives you plenty of time to prepare yourself for the transition."

As though summoned telepathically, a woman appeared on the other side of the glass door. "Ms. Ellis will walk you to the elevator," said Weinstein, in a voice as cold and impersonal as the decor.

And with that, the interview was over, along with a lifelong friendship. Goldman couldn't honestly say that he was surprised. The Relocation Authority tended to have that effect on people.

By the time he stepped through the front door of his apartment, Goldman's anger had mellowed. At his age, it was important to pick his battles, and this one was clearly unwinnable. At least they were letting him stay in the clergy. That option hadn't always been offered. So, he would bow out gracefully and let the congregation throw him a bon voyage party. He would be a model student at orientation. Then, if *Adonai* hadn't already struck him dead, he would go bravely out into the vacuum of space.

❧

"Here it is, Chaplain, your home away from home."

The young shuttle pilot who had walked Goldman from the landing bay of the *Vasco da Gama* to the ship's small chapel was what Sarah would have called an 'all of'. Lieutenant Greg Ostermeyer was all of 25 years old. He was also bright, earnest and respectful, with an air of smooth-skinned freshness that invited motherly kisses and grandmotherly pats on the cheek. Once, years ago, Leon Goldman had had a face like that. Now, however, he knew what the young officer was seeing—a man in his middle years, with thinning grey hair and large pores and a slight paunch, who ought to be reclining comfortably in an easy chair somewhere, not venturing out into the hostile vastness of space. And Leon would agree with him.

Orientation had prepared Goldman for the size and appearance of the multi-faith chapel. Still, as his gaze swept the interior of the tiny room, he couldn't help letting out a disappointed sigh. Artificial flowers, faux windows made of imitation stained glass, and a modest wooden cross mounted on the bulkhead behind a draped altar that held a featureless seven-branch *menorah* fitted with flame-shaped bulbs in place of candles. A podium sat beside the altar, looking down on just a dozen pews, six on each side of a narrow central aisle. Less than a quarter of the ship's crew would fit into this room. That was assuming any of them attended services at all. It was hardly what he would consider an auspicious beginning to this new chapter of his life.

Abruptly, he realized that he and Ostermeyer were not alone. Someone was sitting in the rearmost pew. Curious, Goldman stepped closer and saw a woman in an officer's uniform, wearing a gauzy white scarf over a tumble of short, fiery red hair. She looked up at him and smiled, and he felt his heart turn over. Sarah's eyes had been that same shade of green.

"I'm sorry," he said, his tongue stumbling over the words as though he were back in high school, asking the prettiest girl in the class for a date. "I didn't mean to interrupt your—I mean—"

What should he call it, Goldman wondered. Prayer? Worship? Meditation?

Seance?

Her smile never faltered. "It's all right," she assured him, and he heard its warmth in her voice. "I come here sometimes when I want to be alone with my thoughts. The chapel is usually empty."

That was what he'd figured. Goldman nodded philosophically.

After only a moment's hesitation, the woman extended her hand toward him. "I'm Luce Armendaro, of Stellar Cartography. I joined the crew about a standard year ago." Her grip was firm and welcoming, and Goldman had to remind himself that it was just an introductory handshake. A formality, nothing more.

"Lieutenant," Ostermeyer cut in, "would you mind seeing that Rabbi Goldman finds his quarters? I have to get back to the landing deck."

The green eyes twinkled. "Sure, no problem. So, the new chaplain is Jewish?"

"I'm afraid so," Goldman sighed, settling himself onto the pew across the aisle from her.

"My late husband was Jewish. Sephardic, from España. I always wanted to learn more about the rituals and holidays, but we kept getting posted to different ships and somehow there was never any time. Let me know when you plan to conduct Sabbath services, and I'll be sure to attend."

In that moment Leon Goldman knew he was in love.

Rabbi Goldman had just concluded a *Shabbat* sermon on inner strength, one of the best he'd ever delivered to an empty room. After five years on the *Vasco da Gama*, his congregation still numbered just one, and she had taken leave half a standard year earlier to visit family on one of the colonies as yet untouched by Angel of Death, and had promptly been trapped by a quarantine when the plague arrived right behind her.

He spent every day with an ache in his heart now. Standing in the chapel on *Shabbat* mornings, Goldman felt despairingly alone. And yet, continuing to hold services, lecturing himself about strength and hope and forbearance while visualizing Luce smiling at him from the front pew, was the only thing that seemed to ease his pain.

Goldman wasn't a recluse. He had many acquaintances aboard ship, and some very good friends, including Ostermeyer, the first fellow officer to shake his hand. They shared meals, they spent time together in the social sector of the ship, and over time they had built a foundation of mutual trust and respect. But none of them warmed his spirit, none of them made him feel *whole* the way Luce had done. Now she was gone, and all the old wounds were tearing open. It was like losing Sarah all over again.

Religion had saved him before. Sadly, there was precious little of it out in space, and even less when he was the only Jew for literally hundreds of light years. Of course, the captain and his bridge officers could be counted on to attend the generic Christian service Goldman performed at the end of every eight-day interval, but he suspected their presence was *pro forma* only. As for providing personal support and guidance to the crew, that role continued to be quite ably filled by the psych counsellor in Med Services. By now, it was blindingly clear to Leon that the *Vasco da Gama* had never actually needed a chaplain. The Relocation Authority had just needed an excuse to fling him into space.

Goldman cleared his throat and began the *kaddish* prayer. Rapidly he chanted, the old Hebrew words becoming a string of nonsense syllables as his tongue pushed them automatically out of his mouth. After all, who was there to care about the meaning, as long as the words were spoken? Would *Adonai* interrupt him and tell him to go back and do it again, this time with feeling?

Finally, the service was over. With a sense of relief, Goldman slammed his prayer book shut and walked out into the corridor. He stood staring for a moment at the door to the tube transit system. Strict orthodoxy demanded that he walk back to his quarters, a good half-hour hike through a maze of passageways. The tube car, on the other hand, could put him at his cabin door in twenty seconds.

Whose *Shabbat* was this, anyway? Rebelliously, Goldman pressed the call button.

In his quarters, the rabbi removed his prayer shawl and folded it carefully into its embroidered velvet case before storing it in the top compartment of his wardrobe. Beneath it hung the long black coat with its old-fashioned button closure. It was all he had left of his great-uncle Chaim. Leon's great-aunt Sophia had willed the garment to him four years earlier, along with several other family heirlooms and enough credits to cover the outrageous cost of having the parcel shipped to him out in space. Goldman fingered the coarse, heavy fabric thoughtfully for a moment, then swung the door shut with a sigh. His parents and all their siblings, his brothers and their families, all were far away. Sarah had died without giving him children. And now Luce was gone. How was he supposed to get through *Hanukkah*?

Hanukkah, a festival of lights, was traditionally a time for families to gather and celebrate the miracle of a lamp that had burned for eight days on one day's worth of oil. But the Relocation Authority had scattered his family across the galaxy, and the rabbi was alone now on a star ship where safety regulations prohibited the making of fire.

His first year aboard the *Vasco da Gama* he had simply foregone the holiday, telling himself that *Hanukkah* didn't define him as a Jew in the same way as *Rosh Hashanah* or *Yom Kippur* did. And then his inheritance from Great-aunt Sophia had arrived.

Luce had helped him unpack the shipping container. When she saw his great-grandmother's beautiful *hanukkiah* with its nine delicately sculpted branches, her eyes widened with delight. Luce asked him to teach her the prayers so they could observe *Hanukkah* together. That year, on each of the eight nights, they carried the *hanukkiah* into the chapel. After counting out and positioning Sophia's precious beeswax candles, they chanted the blessings and mimed lighting the *shammash* and using it to light the remaining candles. Goldman felt as though a window had opened, letting his soul breathe fresh air for the first time since Sarah had passed away. Each year since then, he and Luce had shared this celebration together. Just the thought of doing it without her this time was enough to drain all the warmth and colour out of his world.

Luce had completed that world. Not telling her he loved her when he'd had the chance had unquestionably been the worst mistake of Leon Goldman's life.

The wallcomm in his quarters buzzed loudly, startling him. "Rabbi Goldman, report to the captain in the strategy room." Struggling into his uniform jacket, Goldman was halfway out his cabin door when he realized he had to acknowledge the summons. Hastily, he reached back and thumbed the wall switch. "On my way," he stammered.

The strategy room was in the command sector of the ship. Senior ship's officers—*real* officers, unlike himself—met there to discuss ship's business. Braced against the motion of the tube car as it carried him toward the nose of the *Vasco da Gama*, Goldman could think of only two reasons for a chaplain to be ordered to a meeting of ship's officers. One was to bless a mission, and the other was to administer final rites to someone who'd fallen down dead.

In the five years that Goldman had been aboard his ship, Captain Nordstrom had never once asked him to bless a mission.

The tube car delivered Goldman into a broad, finished passageway, almost directly in front of the door to the strategy room. Nervously, he paused to inspect his uniform and straighten his shoulders before pressing the enter button. The grey metal door slid aside, and he stepped inside the room—and stood staring in confusion at the captain and three of his officers, all very much alive, whose abruptly halted conversation now hung in the air as they gazed expectantly back at him.

"Thank you for joining us, Rabbi," said Nordstrom, nodding curtly toward a vacant seat to his left. "If you'll sit down, we can begin the briefing."

Warily, Goldman sat, beside the Supervisor of Med Services and across the table from Watch Commanders Narampal and King.

Nordstrom was blond and powerfully built, like his Viking forebears. The set of his craggy features spoke of great determination. In a civilian, Goldman reflected, he would have called it something less flattering.

"All right," said the captain in a clipped, official voice, "I've received special orders from Fleet Control."

Goldman leaned forward curiously. Had he been brought here to bless a mission after all?

"Angel of Death appears to have finally run its course in our arm of the galaxy," Nordstrom went on. "There have been no new outbreaks of plague reported in the past standard half-year. So, every vessel in the fleet is being mobilized in a census, relief, and evacuation program. Those ships with chaplains aboard—all two of us—have drawn census duty."

Narampal settled back in his chair and blew out a disgusted sigh.

"Census duty?" Goldman repeated, puzzled. "Forgive me, Captain, but why would you need a cleric for that?"

Nordstrom smiled thinly. "Census duty, Rabbi, is a euphemism for body count. Diseased corpses are often burned and buried without ceremony. That's where you come in."

"Funerals," murmured Goldman.

"They're necessary," the captain reminded him sternly. "By law, these remains cannot be disinterred. Earth High Council must be able to assure the families of the deceased that proper rites were observed."

"But what about the victims whose families are still there, on the planet? And what about the local clergy? Surely they would have to be consulted—"

"You don't understand, Rabbi," King interrupted him. "We only do a census on planets where there are no survivors. We count them up, and you commit them to God. No consultations are required."

"And… are there many such planets?"

Grimly, Nordstrom thrust a compupad down the table toward him. "That's just our share."

There were twelve of them.

"*Oy, vey,*" breathed Leon.

As the captain went on discussing practical arrangements with his officers, Goldman scanned the list of planet names. His heart lurched when he got to number nine.

Luce.

For half a year he had been holding his breath. Now it was official. She was dead.

～

The Self-Contained Environmental Tester (SCENT) rolled smoothly through a sun-drenched landscape of bright emerald hills, broad shaggy meadows, and whispering streams. Passing cluster after cluster of thick-boled trees with funnel-like leaves, the small, barrel-shaped vehicle made its way slowly along the top of a slope.

SCENTs had been designed originally as drones, to gather information on planets inhospitable to Human life. This particular unit, however, was on a special mission… and it was manned.

"I'm sorry about the cramped space, Rabbi," Ostermeyer apologized for the hundredth time.

Goldman smiled faintly. He could guess what Ostermeyer was thinking—that a man his age, and in his deplorable condition, shouldn't be going on missions. Particularly not missions that required him to sit with his knees spread and bracketing his elbows like a frog's. And he was right.

"We're coming up on another homestead," said Ostermeyer. He called up a map on his compupad. "This must be the Dedrick place. Three family members, no livestock, no pets. If he was a crop farmer, he sure picked a good place for it… sort of," he added, tucking the compupad under his seat.

Rabbi Goldman stared bleakly out the cockpit window at the lush green growth all around them. Yes, this looked like an excellent place for crops. If only it hadn't been so lethal for people.

The Angel of Death plague was named for the deadly messenger God had sent into Egypt, to kill every first-born Egyptian child while sparing the homes of the Jewish slaves. In the ship's databank, Goldman had discovered how horrifically appropriate the naming was. On planet after planet, the virus had selected and then annihilated a single category of life. The old… the unborn young… the flora… the fauna… It was a biological Holocaust, the dead numbering in the many hundreds of thousands, and for months now he had been compelled to wallow in their ashes.

Adonai could be very cruel, indeed.

The SCENT came to a crunching halt directly in front of the blackened ruins of a small building. Behind and to one side, they saw a Quonset shed with blistered wooden doors.

"Let's see how long ago it burned," said Ostermeyer, keying an instruction into the cockpit computer.

Goldman heard the muted whine of a sampler claw unfolding from the hull. As he waited in uncomfortable silence for the automated chemical laboratory behind him to do its job, he studied the segment of yard visible through the cockpit window. His gaze came back to rest several times on an irregularly shaped pile of stones.

"There's a grave over there," he said quietly.

Ostermeyer peered out the window. "Where?"

"I think that's a marker."

Before the lieutenant could respond, the computer screen blinked to life, demanding his full attention. He studied the display for a moment. "Okay," he sighed, "this is the one. According to the computer, the Dedrick place and the Hammond place burned on the same day, one standard year ago. Whoever buried them and burned their houses down was the last one to die."

Last one to die. That meant another body hunt. Another hour or more in this sardine can while it sniffed out someone's decayed remains, gathering them piece by piece if necessary in its sampler claws. The SCENT had been specially modified for this mission. It could also dig and cover a shallow grave.

Ostermeyer made a face. "It was probably a Dedrick," he decided. "You figure that's a marker over there, Rabbi?" he said, nodding in the direction of the stones. "Let's go count up the bones and find out."

The SCENT ground to a halt less than a metre from the stone pile. Both men saw clearly that there were two graves here, the first unmarked.

With a sigh, Rabbi Goldman took out his copy of the omni-faith prayer book. It fell open automatically to the correct page. As the SCENT hummed quietly in the background, he began rapidly murmuring the generic burial service under his breath. He scarcely glanced at the text. After seven planets and more funerals than he could count, the book was little more than a prop. By now Ostermeyer could probably recite the words of the ceremony from memory as well.

The pilot waited in respectful silence for Goldman to finish. Then he typed rapidly on his keyboard, ordering sensor scans of the graves while the rabbi leaned back into his seat and once more attempted the trick of stretching his leg muscles without actually extending his legs.

The results came through in less than a minute. Only two Dedricks were buried here.

By now, the young pilot had evolved a standard procedure for the body hunt, which he preferred to carry out in silence.

Parking the SCENT directly on the foundation of the charred homestead, Ostermeyer ordered the unit to begin sifting through the rubble for Human remains. If none were found, he would program the scanning sensors to seek out whatever chemical processes were supposed to be going on in the vicinity of a year-old corpse exposed to the elements. So far, the longest time they had had to search a planet after locating the last-burnt structure had been three standard hours. By the time they'd returned to the *Vasco da Gama*, Rabbi Goldman had been sure his legs would never be straight again.

"Well, there's nobody home," muttered Ostermeyer. "Let's start over there. Maybe the last victim crawled out into one of those fields to die."

They found no body in the cultivated fields around the house, and no Human remains in the near woods or on the grassy slopes beyond them. Privately, Goldman thought it unlikely that anyone healthy enough to dig a grave and burn down a house would have stayed around long enough to die. But Ostermeyer was the pilot and ranking officer, in spite of his youth, and the rabbi had already discovered that it made the mission much less stressful if he let the younger man find out things for himself.

The light outside was beginning to fade. Soon the night would end their search, and Goldman could unfold his poor old body from this child-sized cockpit and stand in the heat room in Med Services until his limbs felt normal again.

Ostermeyer had also noticed that daylight was waning. "We're nearly at the perimeter of our last long range scan. Let's do one more before we leave. Maybe we'll be lucky and get a fix on someth—Huh? What the hell—?"

That got Goldman's attention. "A malfunction?"

"A large life form."

"But that's not what you were looking for."

"It's what the SCENT unit is hardwired to seek out."

"I thought they sensor-scanned these planets before declaring them plague-dead."

"They do, more than once."

"Then how did they miss this one?"

"I don't know."

"A new arrival, perhaps?"

"Impossible," declared Ostermeyer. "This whole system is under strict quarantine."

A convulsive shiver raced down Goldman's spine. Since losing Luce he had been praying without hope. And now... a life had appeared where before there had been only death. Could this be an accident? The timing, a coincidence?

In the dimly lit cockpit, two pairs of eyes stared widely at each other.

"We'd better get back to the ship and file our report," said Ostermeyer, licking his lips nervously. "See what the captain wants to do about this."

❧

Rabbi Goldman stood in the middle of his quarters, paging through a book of religious philosophy. Lieutenant

Ostermeyer had just buzzed him on the comm to deliver the jubilant announcement that an orbiting visual scanner had found their missing Dedrick very much alive. Somehow, she'd eluded the earlier sensor sweeps. The communications officer on duty had shown Ostermeyer a snap. The girl was a beauty: not quite a woman, but more than a child, with large eyes, a delicate, solemn face, and a thick fall of dark hair.

Goldman had immediately dropped to his knees to retrieve the old clothbound book from the bottom of his wardrobe. The picture was in here somewhere—he remembered being fascinated with it while still a student.

There it was. Goldman's hands trembled as the pages finally surrendered the long-remembered image to his hungry eyes— the slender, graceful body, neither male nor female, the face so finely etched and with eyes incredibly large and wise, neither child nor adult, but shaped by the purity of divine innocence and the knowledge of supreme power—it was her. It had to be. The Angel of Life, following after the Angel of Death, just as the rainbow had followed after the great flood.

Leon had prayed, and *Adonai* had given him a sign. And if this girl, this survivor, could be found on a plague-dead world, then maybe…

Sudden hopeful speculation flooded Goldman's mind, a rising tide of unthinkable possibilities. Perhaps, through the Lord's intervention, Luce could be found alive as well.

He closed the book slowly, reverently, and knelt to replace it in his wardrobe. As he stood up again, his chest patch snagged his attention, and he stared down at the black and gold rectangle as though it were an alien parasite clinging to the front of his uniform. His skin began to crawl under the smooth grey fabric.

Not like this, he thought. He had to make himself worthy to receive such a favour from God. He had to rededicate his body and his spirit to *Adonai*. He would take some water into the heat room to make steam for the ritual purification bath. After that, he would dress simply, with his head covered and his spirit bared. He would shed his uniform, a symbol of service to other gods, and learn innocence anew.

It would take time, but God would wait for him. The Lord had infinite patience. Like the rainbow, the Angel of Life was a promise. And *Adonai* always kept His promises.

～

As if Nordstrom didn't have enough to worry about.

According to Ostermeyer's latest report, Rabbi Goldman had stripped off his uniform, replacing it with a skull cap and a shiny scarf and very little else, and had then locked himself in his cabin. He was refusing to come out, even for meals.

Census duty was punishing work—long periods of boredom, interrupted at intervals by corrosive depression. Since the only reason the *Vasco da Gama* had even drawn the assignment was the presence of a chaplain on board, Nordstrom had requested that Med Services update the rabbi's psych profile to determine whether he would be fit to complete the mission. He'd passed easily. He was a rock. So why all of a sudden was the man apparently coming unglued?

As he sat at his desk staring his computer screen into submission, Nordstrom could feel the muscles across his shoulders drawing themselves into painful knots. At least he knew what was elevating *his* stress levels these days: Sven Nordstrom didn't enjoy waiting around. He'd joined the Fleet to get things done, not sit parked in orbit while Fleet Control waffled over what to do about the Dedrick girl and whether to send the *Vasco da Gama* on its way. The sooner he received clearance to proceed with the rest of the census mission, the sooner it would be finished. Then Nordstrom and his crew could get to work doing something more interesting and rewarding than tying up loose ends on plague-dead worlds.

With luck, it would turn out that Goldman was just blowing off some steam. Nordstrom sincerely hoped so, because the last thing he wanted to have to do was report to Fleet Control that his chaplain was broken. They would order him to abort the mission, and this Nordstrom absolutely refused to do. In more than thirty-five years of service, Sven Nordstrom had always prided himself on finishing any job he began. The *Vasco da Gama* had never once failed to complete a mission since Nordstrom had taken command of her, and he was damned if he would let her start now.

All at once, the comm unit buzzed. "Captain Nordstrom? We have a priority one Gate transmission from Fleet Control on Earth."

Finally!

❧

"He still won't come out of his cabin, Captain. I relayed your order, told him we were already in orbit around planet nine and it was time to go to work. But he says forget it—he's had it with meaningless funerals. His words."

Nordstrom stared for a moment, dumbfounded, at the apologetic face of the SCENT pilot standing at attention in front of his desk. Then, fighting to keep his voice low and under control, he demanded, "Who the *hell* does he think he is? Does he really believe he can just up and quit in the middle of an assignment? Does he *want* to be brought up on charges?"

"With respect, Captain, there's something you should know. We're orbiting Dervinco. That was where Lieutenant Armendaro went on leave, about a year ago. She's buried down there with some of her family. She and the rabbi were very close, sir."

Nordstrom cleared his throat uncomfortably. "Define 'very close'."

"I know he had strong feelings for her."

"And Goldman's eccentric behaviour began when the two of you returned from MF-307, correct?"

"Yes, sir. Right after I told him about the Dedrick girl being found alive."

Of course. Nordstrom didn't like the picture they were making, but at least the pieces were starting to come together in a way that made sense. Sometimes the cruellest thing you could do to someone was give them hope.

"Captain, should Rabbi Goldman be referred to Med Services for psych analysis?"

"No, I've got a better idea. The longer he delays going on-planet, the harder it will be to get him there. So here's what you're going to do: you're going to study the maps of Dervinco and find a logical place for Armendaro's remains to be buried. Then you're going to tell Goldman that the scanner found some of her personal effects in that gravesite and has positively identified it as Armendaro's final resting place."

Ostermeyer's eyes widened in horror. "Captain!"

"I'm giving you an order, Lieutenant."

"Yes, sir," he replied, discomfort in his voice.

"I guarantee you the rabbi will climb back into uniform and

come out of his cabin to give funeral rites to the woman he loved. And once you have him down there on the surface, you are going to get him to perform the other services as well."

"But, sir—"

"I don't care how you do it, Lieutenant. Just make sure he buries the whole damned planet before you bring him back to my ship."

❧

"This is the one, Rabbi," said Ostermeyer, clearing his throat for the dozenth time. "Her son's place was just over there."

Ostermeyer pointed, but Goldman paid no attention. His eyes were riveted on the mound of reddish-brown soil directly in front of the SCENT unit. Slowly, he took out his prayer book, opened it, then closed it again with sudden decisiveness.

"I'm going out."

"Rabbi, no," said Ostermeyer, alarmed. "This planet's atmosphere—"

"We're under a life support dome, Lieutenant," he pointed out gently. "The air may be a little old, but, trust me, nobody's been depleting the oxygen."

Goldman popped the hatch on his side of the cockpit and manoeuvred his body out of the cramped half-seat.

"Aw, jeez!" moaned Ostermeyer, tumbling out on his side of the SCENT unit as well. "They're going to clap us both into Isolation…!"

Goldman ignored the young pilot's fussing. The packed soil underfoot offered satisfying resistance to his boots. He stamped them a few times, noting how the thudding sound resonated beneath the curve of the dome. He noted also a peculiar, sweetish smell to the air, sharp but not unpleasant, like fermented fruit.

The rabbi stepped over to the gravesite. Turned soil lay like a scab covering a wound in the ground. And under it somewhere was Luce Armendaro, her lively green eyes and sweet smile and melodic laughter forever lost. Goldman called up her face into his memory, a happy, warm, loving face framed by flame-coloured hair, and he just let his soul sit and stare at Luce's face for a while.

If only he could have worked up the nerve to tell her how he felt. How a few words from her had always made his day complete. How no day would ever be truly complete again, without her...

There would be no generic funeral rites for this woman, he'd decided, no impersonal omni-faith recitations. The prayer book in his hands was printed in Hebrew. It had come from the inside of his wardrobe. This was what he was. This was how he would tell her goodbye.

As he ran his fingers along the edges of the clothbound cover, Goldman felt something stir deep inside him. It stretched as though awakening from sleep. Then it grew. It swelled slowly, like a rising tide, filling his heart with a pain so exquisite that it was beautiful beyond words. The pain of longing. The pain of loss.

When it became too much to bear, Leon Goldman opened his mouth, and words and music soared out of him, borne on a clear tenor voice that he scarcely recognized as his own, so long had it been since he had sung the Hebrew prayers with genuine feeling. The planet, the dome, the machine behind him, all peeled away like an old skin as the universe emptied itself of everything but this moment.

He sang her the songs of David and Solomon, the celebrations of a life together that they would never share. He sang until the air around her grave was heavy with his heartache and there was nothing left inside him but a pulsing void.

Tears were flowing freely down his face when he finished. Ostermeyer appeared at his elbow, murmuring, "Let's go home, Rabbi." And Goldman turned and saw that the pilot's cheeks were wet, too.

Ostermeyer escorted the rabbi slowly back to the SCENT unit. When they returned to the ship, he swore to the captain that Goldman had, indeed, 'buried the whole damned planet' that day.

❧

"He has to sit *where*?" thundered Captain Nordstrom.

Ostermeyer shifted his weight uncomfortably, but stood his ground. He'd learned a great deal from Goldman during their twenty-four standard hours together in Isolation. "*Shiva* isn't a place, sir, it's a time. Bereaved Jewish people get together after a funeral to comfort one another and say prayers. It helps them achieve closure. It's sort of like a wake, only without the alcohol."

"I see," growled Nordstrom. "And this *shiver*—"

"*ShiVA*, Captain."

"Whatever!" he snapped. "How long does this dry wake go on?"

"Eight days."

"So for eight whole days he sits in his cabin and prays? Again?" Nordstrom blew out his breath with a hiss of vexation. "Tell Rabbi Goldman that I intend to visit him this morning. And he'd better be in for company."

"Oh, he'll be in, Captain. He said to tell you that anyone who knew Armendaro is welcome to stop by."

❧

"Come in, Captain. I'm so glad you decided to join me. I'm sorry there isn't any honey cake, but perhaps you would care for a biscuit and some tea?"

Sitting on the edge of the bed, in accordance with ritual the lowest seat in the room, Goldman studied the face of the man who stood ramrod-stiff just inside his cabin door. He hadn't thought it possible for Nordstrom's features to become any more granitic, but they had. It was clearly not his custom to go to others when he wanted something done, and Goldman's refusal to appear when summoned must have first stunned, then angered him.

This was the first time in five and a half years that Nordstrom had even set foot in the ship's chaplain's quarters. Goldman watched his gaze dart uneasily around the little room, freshly tidied for the *shiva*. The tea tray that almost covered the desktop had been part of Leon's inheritance from Great-aunt Sophia, a very civilized and discerning lady. He had brought it out regularly when sharing refreshments with Lieutenant Armendaro, another very civilized and discerning lady.

"Won't you sit down?" Goldman invited, gesturing toward the chair.

Nordstrom's posture was naturally erect. In an instant he

drew himself up even straighter, as with a single explosive shake of his head he declared, "I'm not here to condone your insubordinate behaviour, Mister Goldman."

Of course, he wasn't. He was rigid and authoritarian, and Goldman would be forever grateful to him. By ordering the rabbi down to the planet that was Luce Armendaro's final resting place, Nordstrom had given Goldman the opportunity to say goodbye to her. Twenty-four hours in Isolation had provided him and Ostermeyer time to reflect, to regret, and to forgive. Goldman realized that it didn't matter whether he'd actually been standing at Armendaro's graveside when he performed the service. She'd been somewhere on the planet and he knew that she had heard him.

And Goldman finally understood something else now, too, something Luce had been slowly teaching him. It wasn't the candles that were important, it was the warmth and light and joyfulness they brought into the cold, dark vastness of space. Each Human aboard the ship had the potential to do that. Each of them was a candle, and Leon Goldman was the *shammash*, the worker candle, put here by *Adonai* to set them aflame. Some candles, like Ostermeyer, would light easily. Others, like Nordstrom, would be more challenging. But that was all right—Goldman liked a challenge.

Nordstrom didn't. "I'm here to order you back on duty, Lieutenant," he snapped. "Report to my office, in uniform, in one hour."

"Captain, as I know you've been told, *shiva* is eight days long. Every other officer on this ship has been given time to mourn the loss of loved ones, each in his or her own way. Why not me?"

Nordstrom's cheeks reddened. He clamped his mouth shut and swivelled his gaze to the tea tray. For a long moment, he stared at Great-aunt Sophia's cups and saucers, as though memorizing their elegant lines.

Finally, his expression relaxed. "Eight days of this, you said?"

Goldman nodded. "Traditionally, yes. But *shiva* can be shortened if the circumstances demand it. When will we be arriving at planet number ten?"

"About five standard days."

"I'll be ready."

With nothing left to say, Nordstrom nodded curtly and turned to leave. Goldman watched him pause at the tea tray and palm a couple of biscuits on his way out.

Challenging, yes, the rabbi reflected with a smile, but not impossible.

"The mass of men lead lives of quiet desperation, and go to the grave with the song still in them." (Henry David Thoreau)

And then there are the "model" suburban housewives, whose desperation simply refuses to be silent.

Freudian Slip

It was morning again. Feeling drugged and lazy in a cocoon of warm blankets, Marcie willed herself back into the dream that still clung to her thoughts. She had found herself blissfully alone on a picture-postcard island, strolling along a swath of silver beach that lay between a wall of brilliant green foliage and a lustrous gem-blue lagoon. The overhead sun gently warmed her skin. Floral fragrances carried on a tender, playful breeze stirred her hair and her senses as the forest shadows beckoned, inviting her to explore…

Not at all like the daily grind, was it? See what you've been missing by playing at being Mrs. Sally Suburban?

As if in response, shrill voices erupted downstairs:

"Let me do it, Brandon. I'm big enough."

"No, you're not. You'll miss the glass and make a mess."

"Give it!"

"No!"

Raising her head wearily, Marcie glanced at the digital clock on the nightstand. Behind her, Frank went on snoring softly.

Of course. He slept soundly through all those midnight diaper changes and three o'clock feedings. Why should he wake up now for a little spilled milk?

With an inward sigh, Marcie heaved herself out of bed. Obviously, her day had begun.

Angela Noyes, her neighbour from down the street, was always urging her to "get a job, take a class, anything to break out of that terrible rut you're in."

A rut? Marcie wondered distractedly. How could there be a

rut where there were three growing children—except perhaps on a direct path from the front door to the fridge?

"That's enough. Settle down," she ordered automatically, padding barefoot into the kitchen. Three startled young faces looked up, caught in the act, with smudges of brown icing around their mouths. So much for last night's leftover chocolate cake. At least they were all fully dressed, and the girls were wearing their own clothes. Now, if only Cathy would stop painting her face and calling it makeup… seven was way too young for blush and eyeshadow. All it did was make her look like a battered child.

Oh, come on! Let the kid play. If you're lucky, Children's Aid will come knocking at your door, making you the talk of the neighbourhood and sending Frank into a well-deserved apoplectic fit.

"As you were," Marcie sighed. Then she set about pulling bacon, eggs and whole wheat bread out of the fridge, pausing once to savour a delicious ripple of relaxation as the sunlight pouring through the kitchen window warmed her right through her robe.

Outside, the yard was a solid velvety green all the way to the back fence. Perfection, Frank called it, sometimes with a catch in his voice. From spring to fall, he spent every spare minute out there, feeding and grooming and admiring his wonderful lawn. Cherishing and preserving it. Mowing his way to nirvana.

That's just pathetic! You know what this yard really needs? A vegetable patch, tucked up against the fence. It'll give the lawn character, like an appliqué on a tea towel. Come on! Frank's had his fun—it's time for you to have yours.

"Is breakfast ready?" Frank had entered the kitchen and taken his usual place at the table.

In fact, it was. While Marcie had been woolgathering, her hands had busied themselves, buttering his toast, frying his bacon, breaking his eggs sunny-side-up into the skillet. Frank had eaten this same breakfast every morning for the last twelve years.

All that cholesterol and he's still breathing? Sweetie, you really need to use a faster-acting poison.

Mechanically setting her husband's plate down in front of him, Marcie brought the Corn Crinkles out of the cupboard for herself.

Corn, she mused, staring at the illustration on the cereal box. Wouldn't it be nice to eat corn on the cob, fresh-picked from her own garden? *Yesss!* She could visualize it now, growing tall and soldier-straight just inside the fence, and the bright green tufts of carrots or parsnips dotting the spaces between the rows, and shallots rising along the perimeter, to keep small animals away…

"See you later, honey," said Frank. He shrugged his suit jacket on, snatched up his briefcase, and deposited a hasty kiss on his wife's waiting lips, just as he did every morning before dashing off to work.

"You won't forget about our costumes, will you, Mommy?" whined Laura.

Like you did last year, forcing another parent to make them at the last minute and embarrassing the hell out of your kids…?

Marcie groaned and swore under her breath. Laura was a talented musician and Cathy wrote passable poetry. But that wasn't good enough for Mrs. Ruttenbach: 'Effrybawdy mosst go onstaich!' So, each year, the Hayward twins were part of the scenery in the school play.

Last year, they'd been trees. But not just any old trees would do for an Uplands Junior Academy of the Arts production. Laura had been a weeping willow and Cathy had been a birch. And they couldn't just *say* that they were a willow and a birch—with nonspeaking roles, they had to *look like* a willow and a birch. This year, Mrs. Ruttenbach had decreed, they would be a daffodil and a bluebell. And the costumes had to be made, not bought, from the patterns she had so thoughtfully specified.

"Mrs. Ruttenbach says all the costumes have to be at the school by Monday at the latest," chimed in Cathy.

Of course, so they can be minutely inspected for errors, giving the Hauptfrau yet another chance to make disapproving noises over that neglectful Mrs. Hayward: 'Effrything mosst be perfekt!'

So what were her imperfect 7-year-olds doing at that exclusive school? Oh, right—Frank's parents had picked it out and prepaid it, as a gift for Cathy and Laura's first birthday. Thank heavens, Brandon had been spared Mrs. Ruttenbach's tender ministrations! On *his* first birthday, Gramma and Grampa Hayward had made a reservation for him at Harvard Law School.

Marcie gave the front door a resentful shove closed and returned, tight-lipped, to the breakfast table. "All right," she said, forcing her lips to curve upwards. "Today is Tuesday. I'll get the fabric this afternoon and make those stup—make the costumes before Monday, I promise."

The children smiled at her across the table, but Marcie could tell they were unconvinced.

Are they really looking forward to being a backdrop for someone else's centre-stage performance? If so, perhaps there are things going on at that artsy-fartsy school that the parents need to know about... hmm?

At 12:45, as Marcie was gulping down a sandwich and a cup of instant coffee, the phone rang. It was Angela Noyes.

"Marce, make sure you watch the Suburban Living Channel at 1:00 this afternoon. There's going to be a segment on the *Today's Woman* show about the 'too-tired-to-get-liberated' housewife."

"What about the 'too-busy-to-watch-television' housewife?"

"Come on, girl," scolded Angela. "Drag whatever you're doing in front of the tube. This is *educational* TV!"

By the time Marcie had set up the ironing board in the family room and tuned to the right channel, *Today's Woman* was half over.

The hostess of the show was an impeccably dressed redhead with a sculpted hairdo and porcelain features. She was talking to a balding gentleman with hyperactive eyebrows about a book he had apparently just published, something to do with the powers of the subconscious mind. The id, he was saying, was a seething cauldron of repressed desires and socially unacceptable impulses, and like any container, it could overflow. "It's the people who are constantly forced to be on their best behaviour that we need to be concerned about. Society's helpers, for example. And the clergy. Have you ever wondered why serial killers are so often described by their neighbours as appearing quiet and pleasant?"

Actually, Marcie had never given that a second thought. She left the program on while she ironed and folded, listening with half an ear for the segment Angela had mentioned and mentally going over her schedule for the rest of the day. Or trying to. Her mind kept wandering rebelliously to the imaginary vegetable garden in Frank's perfect back yard.

~

"Marcie? Wake up."

She blinked violently. Was it morning so soon? Marcie groaned and snuggled deeper into the blankets. She'd been swimming in the sunny lagoon at the north end of her island. Its water had felt like warm silk sliding along her naked skin as she moved effortlessly, scattering schools of tiny fish. They studded the lagoon like living jewels, catching and reflecting the light that pierced the water in startling shafts from above…

"I have to go." Frank was bending over her, fully dressed and with an impatient set to his mouth.

"Got an early appointment?" she murmured lazily.

"Hardly. It's 8:45," he snapped. "You slept right through the alarm. I guess you wore yourself out making like a farmer the last couple of days. Anyway, the kids are on their way to school, and I have to leave now, too." He kissed her dutifully on the forehead. Then he was gone.

Marcie yawned. What had Frank said? Something about making like a farmer. His voice broke up like haze in her mind, and she wondered whether she'd dreamt it.

Then she glanced at the clock and came fully awake. Dream or not, he'd been right about the time.

As she moved to throw off the covers, every muscle in Marcie's body—arms, legs, back and stomach—protested in painful unison, sending her falling back with a gasp against her pillow. Only when the aching subsided, a long second later, did she become aware of her hands. Marcie stared incredulously at her palms, which were generously sprinkled with cuts and fresh blisters. What on Earth had she been doing? And why couldn't she remember doing it?

Carefully, she sat up and levered herself off the bed, doing her best to ignore the complaints of her poor strained body as she very slowly put on a pair of slacks and a peasant blouse. Then she hobbled downstairs to the kitchen.

Barefoot and in the kitchen again, huh? Get pregnant and you'll be Frank's perfect woman.

Marcie froze in the doorway and stared around her in horrified confusion. The sink overflowed with dirty pots and utensils. Crumbs and scraps of food littered the countertop. Moats of darkened grease surrounded all four stove elements.

The sunlight kept tripping on a puddle of something that had dried in the middle of the floor.

Was this unspeakable mess what happened when three children and a husband had to fend for themselves at breakfast? Marcie's stomach was churning as she stepped into the room. How could Frank have permitted such chaos to happen?

Since when does chaos ask permission, especially from a perfection-obsessed tightass like Frank?

Then she noticed the large, plump, white and purple bag from Fabric World sitting on the kitchen table. Costume ingredients, no doubt.

Well, first things first. Gingerly, Marcie reached across the table and switched on the radio, tuning it to an oldies station. As The Cars demanded in three-part harmony who would be driving her home that night, she picked her way over to the counter and tested her grip on a scrubbing sponge. Then she happened to glance out the window. Marcie dropped the sponge and just stood there, staring numbly at the large, dark brown rectangle of turned earth just inside the back fence.

'Making like a farmer,' Frank had said.

Marcie darted a confirming look at her trembling, blistered hands, then turned her awed gaze back to the garden—her garden—sitting like a blight on her husband's beloved back lawn. Poor Frank! No wonder he'd been so abrupt with her this morning. But when had she—?

"Time for a weather update," announced a cheerful voice on the radio. "We're going to have a beautiful weekend, with warm, dry weather continuing for the rest of today and all day Saturday. Twenty per cent chance of a shower Sunday night—"

Marcie couldn't hear the rest over the buzzing in her ears. Sparks danced in her vision like demented fireflies as she fought her way back across the tilting, heaving kitchen floor and sank down onto a chair.

Today was Friday. The words hit her like a battering ram. Somehow, Marcie Hayward had gone to sleep on Tuesday night and awakened on Friday morning.

But she hadn't just slept through Wednesday and Thursday. No! She'd dug herself a garden. If she needed proof, she only had to look at her hands. She only had to flex an arm or leg muscle. She'd obviously spent the entire two days working like a demon, and then blocked it out of her memory. For heaven's sake, why?

Why? You know the answer, girl. It's right here inside you.

It could be amnesia. Or, maybe—no, definitely not!

Hands shaking, she managed to punch up Angela's phone number. As soon as she heard her friend's voice, Marcie blurted out, "Angie, I'm not losing my mind!"

"Is that husband of yours still on your case because you tore up his sacred turf?"

"Oh, probably, but I don't really care about that right now—"

"Well, good for you! Lord, I loved it yesterday when you told him that if he didn't share the work he couldn't eat any of the crop."

Marcie's skin prickled icily. "I said that?"

"You didn't back down an inch. I was so proud of you," Angela declared. "It sure took Frank by surprise. And it's about time, I'd say!"

Marcie's darting eyes came suddenly to rest on the large paper bag on the kitchen table. She couldn't ask anyone else to make those costumes for her, not this late and not for a second year in a row. The weekend was going to be a nightmare.

Only if you decide to spend it sewing, honey.

❧

"Marcie, for God's sake!"

Her eyes popped open. Bewildered, she stared up into the strained expression on her husband's face.

"I've been shaking and calling you. Are you all right?"

She couldn't answer him. She'd had that dream again, the one about being shipwrecked on a tropical island. The first few times, the warm embrace of the lagoon, the silken caress of the breeze, and the blissful feeling of utter solitude had been a treat, a hedonistic vacation from reality. But now that she knew what would probably greet her when she awoke... Marcie's stomach tightened into a knot as she pulled herself slowly to a sitting position. Muscles complained across her shoulders and down her arms each time she shifted her weight.

Frank's lips clamped tightly together as he watched her ease back with a groan against the pillows. "You're not all right, are you?" he demanded anxiously. "Dammit, Marce, I told you the paint fumes were dangerous."

She gazed past him at the walls. Someone had stripped off the Victorian wallpaper of their bedroom and painted the room moss green, with white trim. Apparently, that someone had been her. Not so bad, then. At least the colour went well with their furniture.

Meanwhile, Frank continued to fuss and sputter. "The kids won't be home from camp until next weekend. I told you we didn't have to rush like this."

"What's the date today, Frank?" she cut in sweetly.

"The eighteenth. Why?"

Marcie started to shrug, then thought better of it. "I just sort of lost track."

"That's it," snapped her husband. "I'm calling the doctor."

Sighing, she made no protest. Doctor Brewster would only tell her she needed rest and hand her a prescription for tranquilizers, anyway. *Of course. God forbid the old geezer should actually take a female patient seriously.* He wasn't the reason she hadn't told Frank about her memory lapses. No. It was just that she knew how her husband would deal with this unravelling edge on his tidy life. He would call in a specialist to hem it back up again. And Marcie didn't need a psychiatrist.

She wasn't insane. She wasn't. It was just a little amnesia. A day lost here and there, nothing serious. At first, she'd been upset to the point of hysteria. But she recovered her balance almost immediately now, was hardly even inconvenienced by the sporadic gaps in her memory. No. Frank must never ever think that his wife was coming unhinged. *Why? Because he might do you a favour and cut you loose?* She'd lost a whole week this time, but she would deal with it. It wouldn't be a problem.

As he turned toward the door, she noticed a smear of green on his cheek. "You've got paint on your face."

"So do you, Rembrandt," he tossed back at her, scowling. Then he disappeared.

Marcie went to the mirror and saw a long vertical stroke of white paint crossing cheekbone and temple. She scrubbed her skin with soap, but the paint had dried there and wouldn't come off. It had to have happened much earlier in the week, she realized, while she was exploring the shady grottoes in the interior of the island. The air inside them had felt moist and heavy, laden with the pungent smell of freshly-turned earth. In the dim light, she had had to make her way slowly to avoid bumping into sharp edges or tripping over stones and roots sticking out of the floor. And, for the first time in this hitherto perfect dream world, she had felt uncertain of her safety.

Wearing her composure with pride and care, Marcie pulled on slacks and a cool mesh tee-shirt, recalling three other times in the past couple of months that she had awakened to find the previous days a blank in her memory.

In June, there had been the vegetable garden. The beans, squash and corn were all thriving, along with some other plants that she still couldn't identify. Marcie hoped they wouldn't turn out to be flowers. Frank was just beginning to appreciate the economic wisdom of growing vegetables. He'd even said it aloud a couple of times, after she'd prompted him.

Early in July, Marcie had opened her closet door and found a whole new wardrobe hanging there. All the tags had been cut off. Frank's face first blanched, then darkened when she said she couldn't tell him where the clothes had come from, nor even how she'd paid for them. And it didn't help matters that her entire former wardrobe had disappeared. In the end, Frank had let the matter drop. But he hadn't been happy about it.

Toward the end of July, his angry mood had finally begun to lift, and Marcie had dared to expect that things would soon be back to normal. But then, to her horror and consternation, she apparently made and kept a lunch date with an old boyfriend. At least, that was what she surmised from Angela's sly phone call and the message accompanying the dozen roses that were delivered to her door the following day. Of the date itself she remembered nothing. And Frank had been absolutely livid, before he'd calmed down and become...

Marcie frowned.

He'd become watchful. Frank had never paid her such close attention. And Angela had never cheered so loudly. And Marcie had never felt so adrift and vulnerable in her life.

And now it was mid-August and Marcie had lost an entire week. Doing what? With the children away at camp and Frank at work all day, the way had certainly been clear. It didn't take that long to paint a bedroom. What had she done?

She'd redecorated the entire downstairs was what she'd done, in shades of peach and green. Marcie strolled through the living and dining rooms, the kitchen, the powder room, the den, admiring every freshly painted wall, smiling with unqualified relief at a decor she couldn't remember choosing or assembling, but which had obviously taken her the full week to complete. Frank might not be overly fond of the colour scheme, but at least it gave him no further reason to distrust her.

And now he's living in your *house, instead of the other way around. Welcome home, honey.*

While descending the stairs, Marcie had noticed that the large oil painting was missing from its usual place on the stairwell wall. Thank goodness!

Frank's Aunt Hilda had given them Harlot's Revenge, an obscenity on canvas that looked like the aftermath of a raw hamburger fight, as a wedding gift. For the first few years of their marriage, Marcie had managed to bury it in the basement. Then, on the day they had moved into this house, Frank had proudly hung the Harlot where anyone going up or down the stairs would be forced to see it. Marcie didn't remember plastering over the hole he'd made. It was so high up and so awkwardly placed that she didn't even want to imagine how she had managed it. The important thing right now, however, was that the hole was gone. The wall was pristine once more, and the Harlot would never darken Marcie's stairwell again.

Really? Because you have a history of caving on matters like this, sweetie.

"That was Doc Brewster," said Frank, hanging up the phone in the kitchen. "He says it sounds as though you're suffering from a temporary reaction to the paint fumes. He wants you to rest and get lots of fresh air and call him back in a few days if the symptoms persist." He paused and studied her with worried eyes. "How do you feel?"

"I feel fine," she said with a shrug.

"Sure?"

"Sure."

"Because I wouldn't want you to be under the weather when Aunt Hilda comes to visit next week."

Marcie blinked hard at her husband. "What did you say?

Aunt Hilda's coming?" she echoed faintly.

"The twenty-third. She called me at the office yesterday afternoon. Figures she can spare us ten or twelve days this time."

Marcie's right temple was throbbing with tension under its stripe of white paint. If Hilda figured she could spare a week and a half, they would probably not get rid of her for a month. A whole month of nagging and criticism and getting dragged to every tea room and Bingo game in town. The woman insisted on being entertained. Frank wouldn't do it—he had to work. All that back-to-school shopping (Mrs. Ruttenbach's list was *extremely* specific) would just have to wait.

Marcie glanced imploringly at Frank. But he was grinning like a fool at the thought of Aunt Hilda's visit.

Of course he is! He adores that old bat. Maybe we can hire someone to blow up her bus before it arrives. Come on—it'll be fun. Frank can afford it. And then she'll never bother us again.

Hilda would expect to see the Harlot prominently displayed when she arrived. Marcie stared at the empty wall in the stairwell, her heart sinking slowly into her stomach. Rebellion was tempting at that moment, but she'd already rocked the Hayward family boat enough for one summer. With a sigh, she went to fetch the stepladder from the garage. When she returned, Frank was emerging from the basement, hammer in hand, and the Harlot was leaning against the wall of the landing.

"Do you need a hand with that, honey?" Frank's grin was looking decidedly smug now.

"No, thanks, I'm just fi—*yii*!"

One step short of the landing, Marcie went down and the ladder flew up. It turned in the air and descended sideways, its feet punching two large holes in the painting just as Marcie's head struck the edge of the landing with a sharp *crack*. All at once, the world was spinning away and she was...

...back on that tropical island.

No, she amended an instant later, this wasn't her island. It was a different place, a sunless strip of rock-strewn beach overshadowed by sheer cliff walls at one end and besieged by sheets of cold, salty spray. Shivering in the relentless chill, she backed away from the water, then turned and ran toward the forest, driven by an angry wind that roared in her ears and whipped her hair around her head. Just inside the tree line she halted, her heart pounding madly. The forest had changed. Its caves and shadows, once intriguing and mysterious, now seemed alive with menace. Feral eyes flickered in the undergrowth. Marcie visualized with dread-filled clarity the fangs and claws that probably went with them.

This wasn't a dream anymore. It was a nightmare, one she needed to escape. She wanted to wake up. She had to wake up, *now!*

❧

Marcie Hayward opened her eyes and found herself lying on her back in a tiny room that was not part of her house. In the dim light, she saw the outlines of a table and chair, a toilet bowl and basin, and the foot of a small, hard cot, all uniformly striped by shadows. She glanced automatically toward the source of the illumination—a fluorescent light fixture in the hallway, beyond a wall of floor-to-ceiling iron bars.

Fighting for breath, Marcie thrust herself to a sitting position. Her fingers clutched the side of the thin mattress, the cold metal frame of the cot. She was wearing a shapeless institutional garment made of coarse fabric. The wall behind her was cinder block, the floor beneath her feet solid cement.

This couldn't be real. What would it take to wake her all the way up?

The ragged sound of her own breathing filled her ears as she rushed to the bars, grasped them tightly, and shook them until the aching in her arms forced her to stop.

Nothing had changed. The bars continued down both sides of the hall, straight columns of metal marching in an unbroken line for as far as she could see.

Marcie backed away slowly, toward the table, and discovered that it was a desk. She opened the drawers, one by one. They were all empty. Empty, blank, bare, just like the walls and the floor of this prison cell.

She was in prison. People didn't go to prison for digging gardens, or buying clothes, or painting walls. Or even having a fling with an old boyfriend. So what had she done this time?

She'll never bother us again.

Numbly, Marcie shook her head. This was cra—

No, she mustn't let herself even think it. She wasn't losing her mind. She wasn't. She'd just lost some time, like all the other times. No problem. Frank would look after the children, and she would deal with this, as she'd done before, with a minimum of fuss. After all, she'd cancelled the belly-dancing lessons, and the moving van, and the airline reservation. And she'd hired a seamstress to make the girls' costumes.

Maybe we can hire someone to blow up the old bat's bus. Frank can afford it. It'll be fun.

No.

Angela was right. Marcie wasn't crazy.

She was just in a terrible, *terrible* rut.

This was my first professional sale in the genre, to H.P. Lovecraft's Magazine of Horror *(April, 2004). The story was inspired by an episode of* The Twilight Zone *in which a group of men discover that they've been playing poker once a week with Satan. As he explains in the episode, running Hell is stressful, and even the devil needs to unwind from time to time. Seeing that threw my writerly imagination into high gear. After all, if Lucifer can relax with a card game and a few beers, what other mortal-type things might he decide to do?*

Business is Business

Originally published in:
H.P. Lovecraft's Magazine of Horror, April 2004

The sirens had been swelling and fading on the margins of my awareness for about an hour, but it wasn't until I glanced toward the window and actually saw a hook and ladder truck wailing past that I realized there had to be a fire close by. A big one. It was a slow day in the store. I had just decided to go outside to investigate when *he* walked through the door.

He was medium-tall, with swarthy skin and dark, slicked-back hair. In his grey three-piece suit he looked like a professional, like a stockbroker or a junior law partner. I began mentally matching him up with a PC, maybe a white box with a gig or four of memory, an eighty-gig hard drive, internal CD-ROM and some of the latest multimedia software. And a fax modem, of course, and the thirty-dollar *Websurfer's Handbook*…

Then his gaze met mine over the top of a software display and I felt my blood turn to ice, even before the faint aroma of sulphur reached my nose. Those eyes! They were black pits in his face, as cold as the end of time and just as devoid of humanity. Not so much evil as inexorable, those eyes. As I stared helplessly at them, they reached right into the core of me and began fingering my soul like a shopper picking out grapefruit at the supermarket. That was when I realized I was in deep trouble.

Even an agnostic like me knows that Death is indifferent to souls and Angels are—well, *angelic*, not cold and black and brooding.

It took me a moment to find my voice. "Y-You're not—I mean—are you really—?" I finally managed to stammer.

"You recognize me. Excellent," he said, in a voice that rumbled like distant thunder. "Now we can skip the stupid parlour tricks and get down to business."

I would have preferred a few parlour tricks. "So soon?" I whimpered past what felt like a steel band tightening around my throat. "I'm only 55, and I've never even had a serious illness."

Satan heaved an exasperated sigh. "Not my business—*your* business," he snapped. "I've been looking for a computer system. You're the fourth place I've tried this morning." He began counting off on long, hairy fingers. "Computer Heaven refused to sell to me. The manager of Big Bytes not only turned away my business, he very rudely waved a crucifix in my face. And some snot-nosed salesman at ROMaRAMa tried to make a joke at my expense. He told me they were having a special on Apples." Another siren whizzed past my front door and we both turned toward the sound. "As you can hear," Satan continued, "they are all now having... er... fire sales."

I was aghast. "You torched them!" I blurted out, then nearly fainted with panic when he turned those eyes on me again.

But Satan just shrugged philosophically. "Regrettable force of habit," he sighed. Then he smiled, a cold black smile to match his eyes. "But there's no need for you to worry, my friend. I can sense that you're a much better businessman than they were. I am in the market for a computer system—state of the art and top of the line. Cost is no object."

Cost is no object. They were the words I'd dreamed of hearing ever since opening up Computer Safari, against my therapist's advice, eight months earlier. I took a deep, steadying breath and told myself that business was business. So what if the customer was evil incarnate and had powers beyond human imagining? He wanted something that I could sell him and he was willing to pay heavy money for it. It was like landing a government   contract,   only   without   the   paperwork.

Distractedly, I realized that I couldn't smell the sulphur anymore.

"What are your requirements?" I asked, in what I hoped was a businesslike voice.

"I have about a billion records, no more than 2K each."

"It sounds to me as though you ought to be looking at something bigger than a personal computer," I began hopefully. Then he pointed those eyes at me again and my heart nearly stopped.

"No, it mustn't draw too much power. You see," he said, leaning so close that I could feel the heat of Hades radiating right through his clothes, "I don't have official permission to do this. I'm going to have to smuggle this system past the upstairs people, so it has to be small."

"You couldn't disguise it as someone's… er…?"

"Instrument of eternal torment?" he supplied. "Sure, in a decade or so when I get a senior analyst whose idea of hell is writing sort programs in Assembler language. But I can't wait that long. Small," he repeated, and I could feel the hair slowly rising at the nape of my neck.

Satan knew something about computers. I would have to watch my step.

"Well, you're going to need large volume disk drives and rewritable DVD backups for that much storage, probably a server unit with a couple of workstations. Depending on the model you select, the server can even be built into a desk." Cautiously, I swung into the sales pitch I'd been delivering to the bathroom mirror for the past six months, just in case Mister Goodbyte walked into my store.

Satan nodded thoughtfully. "A desk. I like that."

Encouraged, I smiled and went on, "There are several companies that make these, or something similar. IBM, for example, have—"

"IBM?" he cut in.

"Infernal Business Machines." The instant the words were out of my mouth, I went clammy all over. That's what overconfidence does to you, even in small doses—you begin gloating about the sale and forget about the customer. I should have known better than to kid around with the Prince of Darkness. Now I would pay for it.

For a long second, he just stared at me. Then, at last, he

smiled his cold, black smile.

"That's a good one," he said. "I'll have to share it with my minions."

Suppressing the urge to mop my brow, I struggled to put my act back together. "Do you already have a computer?" I asked hesitantly.

"No. If I did, running Hades wouldn't be such a bureaucratic nightmare. The paperwork involved in processing all those hundreds of millions of damned souls… well, it's just hellish. I think I suffer as much as they do, from sheer aggravation."

I was confused. "But—But how can you have paperwork?" I wondered. "Don't you just throw them all into the fiery pit?"

Satan looked pained. "If only it were that simple. Listen, the pit worked fine a century ago, when being eternally consumed by flames was the worst possible thing people could imagine happening to them and only Satan could cause it to happen. But then you mortals discovered how to unleash those powers on yourselves. Hellfire lost its impact as an eternal punishment. So we had to come up with something much more evil and terrifying. It wasn't easy." Satan shook his head in disgust. "Operating a place like Hell for a race as sophisticated as yours became an incredibly complicated business. I've got nearly 800 million souls on individual programs, designed to take advantage of each one's most potent fears. The costs are enormous. And keeping track of everything is—Well, it's a torment. My minions have been complaining about burnout. They've begun making mistakes. And with any mistake, there's the terrible risk that one of those damned beggars will actually enjoy himself."

In spite of myself, I had to sympathize with his problems. Hell was a business like any other, I told myself. In fact, it was better in some ways than the company that had terminated me those two miserable years ago, knowing that I was too old and too qualified for the current job market. A minion had perfect job security. How could one be fired?

"We've had so many mix-ups lately that it's like a damned resort down there," Satan went on. "I hear they're even planning a New Year's Eve party. But once I've got everything on the computer it'll be different." He leaned closer and added ominously, "Won't it?" His eyes began to glow.

I thought about reminding him that the minions who would be transferring his files onto the disk drive were the same ones who were currently making all those infernal errors. For about one second I thought about it. Then I remembered the sirens that had been screaming up and down the street that morning and decided to let Satan find out about human error—or rather, minion error—by himself.

"There'll be a transition period while the data is being loaded," I pointed out.

"My minions work fast. They know how unpleasant I can be if they slack off."

"Computers can't stand too much heat," I warned him.

"We're mostly air-conditioned now. I'll have a room made ready, as far away from the pit as possible. Is there anything else?" he demanded.

"You're air-conditioned?" I echoed incredulously.

Satan shrugged. "We had this platoon of climate control experts just sitting around and suffering, and the minions formed a union to demand better working conditions... You know."

I did know. I had gone head-to-head with labour reps in the past, and had come away from each encounter feeling compromised and inadequate. Shrugging off the uncomfortable memories, I cleared my throat and went on briskly, "What about software? You're going to need a memory manager, diagnostic and antivirus utilities, a Database, maybe a Spreadsheet. Word processing, of course. There's a display over there."

Satan paused to consider this. "Once a record is inserted, it's permanent and immutable for all eternity," he finally said. "But I guess it would be helpful to have some inventory control and..." He chuckled to himself. "...accounts receivable. I also want copies of any games that'll play on the system." He scowled briefly at me. "For the minions," he snapped. "Thanks to their union, they now have time for such foolishness."

I wanted to smile at the irony of that moment, but decided against it. The customer was obviously impatient. He might be tired, too, after shopping around all morning. Burning down those other three stores might have taken a lot out of him.

"I nearly forgot." Satan snapped his fingers, and I half-expected a puff of smoke to float up to the ceiling. "Internet access."

Big mistake. I already knew what would happen when the information highway detoured through Hell. I'd seen it over and over. The web was addictive. When the minions tired of playing games, they would lurk around chat rooms or surf porn sites, running up one hell of an IP tab.

Should I warn the Prince of Darkness?

Nah. He already knew they were screw-ups. That was why they were on his payroll to start with.

"There are plenty of choices these days. Dial-up, cable, wireless..." I slid several brochures across the countertop toward him. My hand hardly shook at all. "And you'll need a good firewall—"

"A firewall? I have several of those. They're very effective."

"No, it's to protect your system from viruses."

He chuckled. "Nothing gets sick in Hades unless I ordain it."

I opened my mouth to correct him, but thought better of it. What if he was right, and his system was immune? Besides, anyone who dared to hack or infect Satan's LAN would certainly end up in Hell where they belonged, and who could object to that?

"Okay, last thing: I need a small printer, letter-quality so I can pass it off as a typewriter."

"I've got two or three you might like," I replied, pointing automatically at the floor model display. Satan strolled over and inspected it for a couple of minutes and came back looking genuinely pleased.

"I'll take the little inkjet at the end," he said, "and a case of extra toner cartridges. How soon can you have the rest of the system ready to ship?"

I was floored. The sale was closing and I'd barely brought the spec sheets out from under the counter. "But we haven't even started to discuss operating systems—" I stammered.

"I think I can depend on someone with your business experience to know what I need. State of the art, top of the line. Lifetime warranty. Put it all together."

Wonderful. Put it all together and pray—*really* pray—that it works. I thought with dismay about my paltry line of credit, about the chain of orders that would have to be placed, about the lies I'd have to tell if anyone inquired about the end-user—lifetime warranty? Satan was immortal, for Godsakes!—and that was assuming they'd even agree to ship me the stuff.

"It could take as long as two weeks," I told him.

For an endless moment those glowing black eyes appraised my face. I could feel my jaw begin to twitch as it dawned on me what this sale was probably going to cost me personally. If I followed through, I was damned for doing business with the devil. If I didn't, he would put me out of business. Either way, I was cooked.

"You have two weeks," he said. "Have everything delivered here and I'll send some minions to pick it up. And don't make them miss any of their coffee breaks, or there'll be hell to pay."

As he turned to leave, I called out in a strangled voice, "Wait—we haven't discussed the money."

He stood motionless, his rigid back to me, while my breath turned to dust in my throat.

"The money?" he echoed quietly. "I've just eliminated three of your biggest competitors. Your business is going to quadruple in the next six months. You're going to be set for life because of me, and now you ask me for money?"

I swallowed hard. "It's how we do business up here," I apologized. "It's a large order and this is a very small store. I'm going to have to buy some of your gear C.O.D."

"All right, then, mortal," he sighed. "What you really need is an extended line of credit. Correct?"

"That would work," I said carefully, "depending on where I got it." The thought of being stiffed by Satan was giving me a permanent facial tic. I wanted the money up front so he couldn't refuse to pay later. But I really didn't know yet how much the system was going to cost.

Satan turned slowly then, and nodded knowingly at me. "You *are* a careful businessman, aren't you?" He reached into his inside jacket pocket and withdrew a small card, which he placed deliberately on the glass countertop beside him. "Show this card to the manager of Grandiose Trust and Finance. I have an account there. He'll transfer funds from my account to yours without asking embarrassing questions. Consider it payment in full for the merchandise." Then he added, as an afterthought, "And in case you're thinking of... oh... instituting a special price increase...? As one businessman to another, I'd advise against it."

As he turned on his heel, some lunatic impulse made me call out, "There's just one more thing. I need a promise from you."

Satan spun around, clearly intrigued. "A promise from the Devil? What sort of promise?"

"Am I... um... tying myself to you by selling you this computer system?" I stammered. My imagination had caught in a loop over what the "upstairs people", as he called them, would think of this deal. I mean, business was business, but those minions had to come from somewhere. If profiting from Satan guaranteed me future membership in the union, then, air conditioning or no air conditioning, I'd give him the damned gear at cost.

"You mean, have you made a pact with the Devil? Of course not," he snapped. "Pacts are recorded, and our business transaction is completely off the record."

"In that case, I want your promise that when it's my time to... go, I won't end up... down there."

He stared at me wearily with those charcoal eyes and replied, "Poor creature of clay, I have no control over the way you lead the rest of your short, miserable life. If it pleases them upstairs, then that will be your eternal home when you die." Satan turned once again to leave the store, pausing only to remark over his shoulder, "Unless, of course, my system crashes."

In retrospect, I should have let him burn the place down. For that, I'm insured.

Maldemaur and Gershred are an "odd couple" of alien vampires. They began as supporting players in one of my novels, but the chemistry between them was so vibrant and endearing that they quickly became two of my favourite characters to write about. This is the first short story featuring them. I seriously doubt whether it will be the last.

Maury and Shred Go Ballistic

Professor Stuart Gershred sighed with contentment as the taxicab carried him between the stout, square pillars marking the entrance to Upper Canada University. He was returning from a months-long guest lecture tour to schools on three continents. It felt good to be home.

Gazing out the window of the cab, Gershred saw yellow-shirted student ambassadors leading groups of prospective registrants and their parents on orientation tours of the campus. The university's president was ex-military and believed in dressing up for inspection. Now that the snow was gone, swaths of carefully groomed lawn swept away on both sides of the road, drawing the visitor's eye to the exteriors of an array of spit-and-polished halls of learning.

The students in each faculty had put their own stamp on the occasion as well. So, the entrance to the Mathematics building was decorated to resemble the keypad of a huge scientific calculator. An entire outer wall of the Fine Arts building had been converted into a giant page of sheet music. And in front of the Chemistry building sat a—

No! It's impossible!

"Stop the cab!" he ordered, fumbling three bills out of his wallet and dropping them onto the front seat as he scrambled out of the vehicle.

He couldn't have. He wouldn't dare.

Moments later, gripping his briefcase with rapidly numbing

fingers, Gershred stood staring at a transparent laboratory flask at least eight feet high that had been planted squarely in the middle of the Chemistry building lawn. The mouth of the flask looked stoppered, and the vessel appeared to be filled with a swirling cloud of multi-coloured particles suspended in a milky solution. This "statue" had been roped off, with signs prominently posted all around it:

WARNING!
DO NOT TOUCH!!
This ice sculpture is maintained
at an extremely cold temperature
using liquid nitrogen.
Human flesh will freeze on contact.

Extremely cold was an understatement. Inside the roped-off area, the ground was completely frosted over. Even outside the ropes, Gershred could feel the air biting him right through his jacket and doing its best to rob his cheeks and forehead of sensation.

Cursing under his breath, he raced into the building. His long legs took the steps two at a time, up to the second floor. Maury's office was in a far corner, flanked by classrooms. Gershred paused just long enough to scan the appointment schedule on the wall. Then he burst through the door and exclaimed to the lone person in the room, "Please, tell me you had nothing to do with that *thing* outside!"

Doctor Malcolm de Maur looked up from the email on his computer screen and settled back in his chair with a reproachful expression on his lean, bearded face. "Welcome back, Stuart," he said with exaggerated civility. "I missed you too. How was your trip?"

Gershred batted away the question. "We had a deal, Maury. When we signed on here, we both agreed—no showing off our talents. No public displays. So what happened?"

"Nothing that I intended, believe me. It was supposed to exist for just a couple of days, until the judging of the ice sculptures at WinterFest. The Chemistry department had no entry, and a delegation of students waited until the last minute to ask me—" He shrugged. "It seemed harmless enough at the time."

"Harmless? That's not what those signs are saying down there."

"We had to do something to protect the public after what happened on judging day." Prompted by Gershred's razor-eyed stare, Maury continued, "Despite being emphatically warned by a student, one of the judges insisted on touching the flask. Fortunately, she was wearing gloves, so she got to keep most of her fingers."

"She's not thinking of suing—?"

"Not anymore. The poor soul died in her sleep shortly after the mishap. It was a shame. Such a young and vibrant woman. And such polluted life essence! It made me sick to my stomach for a day and a half."

Gershred's jaw dropped. "You drank her—! I thought we'd agreed!"

"We agreed not to hunt where we lived or worked, and I didn't. She was a local politician with no direct connection to the university," came the patient explanation.

Gershred shook his head in disbelief. "And that thing is still standing. How can anyone not realize it's a fraud? And just how cold *is* light, anyway?"

"Ah, therein lies the rub," sighed Maury. "By itself, coherent or not, light has no temperature. But this was supposed to be an ice sculpture, and ice is cold. Hence, the liquid nitrogen inside the flask. So far, so good. As we both know, solid light is normally a perfect insulator. However, when natural daylight encounters a barrier, its infrared energy is transferred, becoming heat. And when said barrier is a transparent enclosure, such as my flask made of solid light—"

"—there's a greenhouse effect. The temperature of the air inside rises rapidly."

"Not just the air. My flask has a curved surface. It's behaving like a lens, channelling heat to the nitrogen, which in turn imprints its own temperature on the substance of the flask. The last time I checked, it sat at minus two hundred degrees Celsius. It can rise another four degrees before the nitrogen comes to a full boil, so we've got time to figure this out."

"All right, so it's going to boil," Gershred repeated. "What's to figure out? Uncork the flask and release the pressure."

"It's not that simple."

Of course, it wasn't. With Maury, things never were.

Gershred sank wearily into a chair, feeling every moment of his more than 4200 years. "This is my coming home party, isn't it? Most people would decorate a room with streamers and prepare a bowl of punch laced with vodka, but not you. Where others would give gifts, you present dilemmas, the thornier the better. Is that why you're a chemist? Because you love dropping little bombs in people's laps?"

Silence. As it stretched between them, a horrible suspicion took root in Gershred's mind. All by itself, his head began to shake.

"It *is* a bomb, isn't it?" he said slowly. "Because it's been sitting on the front lawn of this building since WinterFest in February."

"You see the problem?"

Unfortunately, the answer was yes. At this point, enough pressure had built up inside the flask to guarantee that whatever they did—or didn't do—there was going to be an explosion. And that, Gershred thought with disgust, was why he hated science.

"Why did you leave it outside, then?" he scolded. "For that matter, once it had served its purpose, why didn't you simply get rid of it?"

"I tried to throw a tarp over it once the judging was done, but Dean Unger interfered. During the competition, for fun, I'd made it appear that multi-coloured fumes were pouring out of the mouth of the flask. As a result, the Chemistry department's entry won a special prize for ingenuity. Unger wanted to gloat for as long as possible, and he'd figured out that this sculpture would remain intact for quite a while. So, since I'd created it on department time and using department materials, he took possession of it on behalf of the faculty. We had a rather loud and public disagreement about that. The next day he had a lawsuit drawn up. It's in his office safe, all ready to file if anything happens to the flask before it has melted on its own."

"So, when it explodes, as it inevitably will..."

"...it will be assumed that someone sabotaged it, and that beady-eyed mudserpent will find a way to make sure I take the blame. I suspect he's naturally poisonous," Maury added darkly, "like one of those South American frogs."

"Never mind the beady-eyed mudserpent," Gershred advised. "We need to focus on the situation at hand. Tell me, how powerful will the explosion be?"

"It depends on the timing. The days are getting longer and warmer, and the potential energy within the statue will increase accordingly."

"Give me an educated guess. If it were to blow up tomorrow...?"

Maury let out a long breath, then pursed his lips. "It's a photonic bomb, which means the worst part will be the flash as the light I've trapped around the nitrogen changes state. I estimate it will last for three to five seconds, and will rival the sun for brightness. Anyone staring at it with unprotected eyes will certainly be blinded."

"And the heat released by that change of state?"

"It should be tolerable, as long as there's some nitrogen still in liquid form."

"Shock wave?"

"Of course. The only thing there won't be is solid shrapnel." Regarding him narrowly, Maury tilted his head. "I know that look. You're formulating a plan."

Gershred ignored the prompt. "And how long do you figure we have until the flask blows up?"

"Provided the temperature of the nitrogen keeps rising at a constant rate, and given its initial volume, a month, maybe. Longer if you can draw off some of the heat as it builds," he added hopefully.

Gershred ignored that prompt as well. He had no idea how much of his own life essence it would take to pull heat from something so cold. Besides, they needed to get rid of the statue, not put it on life support.

"All right. You're a Nash'terel master, a light lord," he pointed out. "Does that mean you can control the direction of the flash wave? Send it all upward, for example?"

Maury frowned thoughtfully and stroked his beard with a thumb and forefinger. Gershred could practically hear the wheels turning inside his head. "It's doable," he said at last. "I can reinforce the sides of the flask, making the mouth the weakest part. I'd have to feed on essence every third or fourth day. What exactly do you have in mind?"

"The spring ball is coming up next month, and unless I'm

mistaken, it's the Arts faculty's turn to organize it."

"Yes, it's on the Victoria Day weekend. And I repeat, what do you have in mind?"

"It's just an inkling right now. I'll let you know once I've worked out the details," Gershred promised. And he wheeled and ran out of the office before Maury could say another word.

He'd lied. It was more than an inkling. He simply didn't want to waste any time discussing it. Or rather, defending it like a thesis, while Maury tore it apart, picked holes in each bleeding fragment, and then reassembled it in a grotesque version of itself.

Sometimes he was convinced that de Maur was the poster child for the Arts versus Sciences rivalry on campus.

Gershred could understand why Maury was such a curmudgeon at times. They'd fled the genocide on RinYeng together, stepping through the rift some sixteen hundred Earth years earlier, and had found themselves on a world where beings like them were reviled and killed on sight. (Fortunately, the Nash'terel were shapeshifters who could assume human form and blend in. Otherwise, none of them would have survived this long.)

For someone who'd taken a lot of abuse on two different planets, it was natural to want to keep people at arm's length. However, exiles from RinYeng—and the Nash'terel in particular—needed to be circumspect in their treatment of others. After all, the First Ones, those earliest arrivals who had risen to positions of power and influence among the humans, hadn't achieved their high status by deliberately pissing off everyone they met.

Of course, Gershred mused with a grin, humans like Dean Unger seemed to *invite* ill treatment, in which case it would be rude *not* to piss them off.

On his way out of the building, he paused again to survey the flask.

It was going to explode in a blindingly intense flash of light. If he played his cards right, he could arrange for Unger to be standing at ground zero.

What a happy thought!

❧

A couple of fruitful phone calls later, Gershred was on his way to the Student Union office in the basement of the Arts building, where a meeting of the spring ball committee was already in progress.

He let himself quietly into the room and saw half a dozen undergrads deep in discussion. Four females and two males had dragged a bunch of old, mismatched chairs into a rough circle atop a well-used piece of woven carpet. Gershred smiled inwardly. Young humans, he had discovered, were very resourceful scavengers.

Who better to help him carry out his plan?

"Professor Gershred? Is there something we can do for you, sir?" said the young man chairing the meeting.

"Actually, Brian, I believe there's something I can do for *you*," he replied, stepping into the middle of the room. "How would you like a dynamite headliner for the stage show at this year's spring ball?"

"Can you be a little more specific, sir?"

"Torran Majestico," said Gershred.

The room went dead quiet for a moment as the meaning of that name sank in. Then Brian blurted, "The illusionist? The one who made a jumbo jet disappear? Oh, man! You can book him for us?"

"Wait a minute," cut in a girl wearing a pale blue hijab. "Don't get me wrong, I love the idea, but we're on a budget, people. Can we afford this guy?"

"I doubt it," Gershred replied. "But he happens to owe me a huge favour. Shall I call it in?"

From the expression on his face, Brian had already made up his mind. "I move we have Professor Gershred book Torran Majestico for the spring ball."

"I second!" another voice called out, and six hands immediately went up.

"Carried!" declared Brian triumphantly.

"Not to look a gift horse in the mouth, Professor," piped up a third student, "but—"

"—but why am I doing this? Glad you asked. Majestico is an illusionist who makes things disappear, the larger and heavier the better. Can you think of a large and heavy object on campus that needs to disappear?"

A smile spread slowly across the third student's face. "You

mean like that philistine ice statue down the street?"

"But it would just be an illusion," hijab-girl reminded them. "He doesn't make things go away. He just makes them *seem* to for a while, and then they reappear."

Gershred beamed at each hopeful young face in turn. "Well," he pointed out, "there's a first time for everything, isn't there?"

One week later, the master illusionist arrived on the campus, without fanfare, *sans* retinue, and wearing the shape of a stylish woman in her mid-fifties. She spent half an hour taking measurements around the flask and making notes. Then she handed Gershred two pieces of paper, got into a cab, and left, blowing him a kiss out the window as he stood waving goodbye.

While her taxi was passing between the pillars at the entrance to the campus, Dean Unger stormed into Maury's office, brandishing a poster he'd evidently ripped off a bulletin board somewhere.

"What are you trying to pull, de Maur?" he demanded.

Gazing wide-eyed into the dean's flushed face, Maury managed somehow not to smile. "Me? Not a thing. Why?"

"You're telling me this wasn't your idea?" Unger snapped the offending page open just inches away from Maury's nose, forcing him to lean back to read it.

"I had nothing to do with that. The Arts students are in charge of organizing the ball this year."

"Yes, and they're bragging all over the campus about making our flask disappear."

Maury's eyes wanted desperately to roll in their sockets. "Dean Unger, have you ever seen a Torran Majestico performance?"

"Nobody is laying a finger on that flask!"

"I should hope not. They'd be flash frozen," Maury agreed. "You do understand that he's an illusionist, not a sorcerer? He can't actually make things disappear."

"Damn right, he can't! And neither can you! That statue is the property of the Faculty of Science!" Unger pounded his fist on the desk for emphasis, making Maury's monitor bounce and nearly toppling the stack of journals beside it onto the floor. Then he stalked back through the doorway, clutching the crumpled poster in his other hand.

Within hours, there was a campus cop posted in front of the Chemistry building, with orders to keep an eye on the flask at all times. Shortly after starting his shift, he was wearing winter gloves and a parka, and a video of him stamping his feet to keep warm had gone viral, with the caption: Our boys in blue are turning blue.

~

Early on the day of the spring ball, a red and white panel truck pulled up in front of the Chemistry building and disgorged three men and two women, all wearing hard hats and steel-toed boots. The guard on flask duty unzipped his polar suit and made a radio call.

Gershred had been watching from the foyer of the Fine Arts building across the street, expecting the crew's arrival. As he began crossing the road, one of the men broke from the group and strode out to meet him halfway. "Are you the faculty member in charge?" he asked.

"I am," Gershred replied, handing him a clipboard. "Everything you need is there, per Torran's instructions. I've also provided a copy of the university's liability coverage for special events, and the president's personal authorization for the project. He's a big fan. And here comes someone who's *not* a fan," he added, noticing Unger quick-marching toward them. "Don't mind him. He's just the Dean of Science, coming to tell you that you have no right to be here."

The foreman grinned. "Torran warned us to bring our cold weather gear. I'm beginning to understand what he meant."

"What do you men think you're doing?" Unger bristled.

The two female crew members took umbrage at that. "We're not men!" they chorused.

"Fine! What do you *people* think you're doing?"

"We're setting up for Torran Majestico's illusion this evening," replied the foreman. "Here's our permission." And with a wink at Gershred, he shoved the president's letter under the dean's nose.

Unger stiffened as though a stench had risen from the paper.

"You're not allowed to touch that statue with anything. You hear me?" he shrilled.

"We have no intention of touching it, sir. Our job is simply to erect scaffolding around it and install the shroud."

"The shroud?" Unger peered suspiciously at him.

"It's just a screen that will briefly conceal it from view during the show, that's all."

"And the statue remains in plain sight up until that moment?" the dean persisted. "And there's no one hiding inside the shroud?"

The foreman cast a disbelieving look at the rest of his crew.

"You're welcome to watch us work, sir. It shouldn't take that long to hook everything together."

"Thank you, I think I will," Unger declared stiffly. Evidently feeling the cold, he hunched his shoulders and crossed his arms over his chest.

Gershred leaned close and murmured into the foreman's ear, "Do me a favour, will you? Work like you're getting paid time-and-a-half."

Barely repressing a smile, he replied, "My pleasure."

Torran Majestico made his grand entrance at seven o'clock sharp that evening, an hour before dusk. Clad in a dark green velvet jumpsuit decorated with silver sequins, he occupied the back seat of a flame-red convertible with the top down. Hundreds of cheering fans were waiting to greet him, all dressed in formal attire. Apparently, the illusionist had already worked magic: for the first time in five years, the spring ball had sold out.

With the president's blessing, a "standing room only" area had been barricaded off in front of the Chemistry building, where a foot-high platform trimmed with blue and gold bunting sat between the audience and the flask. The campus police were present as well, geared up for crowd control.

All eyes were on the illusionist as his car pulled up to the curb. The president of the university greeted him as he stepped out onto the sidewalk, then accompanied him onstage to make the formal introduction. Very few were watching the flask, and no one was paying attention to the open window on the third floor of the building, where Maury and Gershred stood observing the scene below.

"Are we all ready?" Maury asked.

Gershred nodded without turning away from the window. "I'm not sure I want to know how they did it, but my accomplices managed to scrounge up enough of those protective goggles to go around."

A pause, then, "I'm curious. How did you meet Torran Majestico?"

"It was a few centuries ago, during my mercenary soldier phase. I was between jobs and happened to wander into a village where they were preparing to burn a witch at the stake. Our eyes met just as the fire was lit. I saw immediately that she was one of us. So, I spent some essence and cooled the flames, giving her a chance to escape. The villagers were terrified. I stuck around long enough to point out to them that trying to burn a real witch was futile, since all it did was make her angry, and that burning someone who wasn't a witch was outright murder."

"Did you get through to them?"

"Oh, yes. After that they never again used fire against a witch. They switched to drowning them instead. Anyway, a couple of days later this fellow came up to me in a tavern, told me I'd recently saved his life, and offered to buy me an ale. We've been friends ever since."

"Ssh! It's beginning."

"—always asking me, 'Where did the jumbo jet go, Torran? Where was it between the instant it disappeared and the moment it reappeared?' Well, I'll tell you good folks a secret. I sent it into another dimension in time-space, a place made entirely of light. Tonight I'm going to open a portal into that dimension, and you're going to see some of that light. We're going to leave the top of the shroud open to let it come into our world. But I warn you, this is a very intense light, as bright as the sun. If you look right at it, it will blind you. So, I'm asking you all to put on the special goggles that you received along with your ticket for the spring ball. And I'd like the uniformed officers standing around the outside of the audience to check, please, and make sure that everyone is wearing these goggles, including themselves. I wouldn't want any one of you to lose your eyesight."

With that, Majestico materialized a pair of the same goggles out of his shock of dark hair and put them on. Amid murmurs and a lot of nervous giggling, the crowd followed suit.

"Before we proceed, I would like to call your esteemed Dean of Science, Doctor Norman Unger, up here," said the illusionist, extending a welcoming hand.

"Those goggles suit him," Maury remarked dryly. "Now he *looks* like a poisonous frog."

"I understand that you have personally stood guard over this statue all day, to prevent anyone from tampering with it," Majestico was saying.

"Ooh, nice touch," muttered Gershred.

"We're going to raise the shroud now, and I'd like you to walk all the way around it, to confirm for everyone watching that it contains no mechanisms or hidden pockets, no helpers concealed in its folds, and that it's nothing but a simple cloth screen."

Gershred cackled and began singing to himself: "Who ya gonna sue, who ya gonna sue, who ya gonna sue when your nightmare comes true?"

"Hey!" Maury smacked him on the arm. "Stay focused. Your cue is coming up."

As soon as the dean had returned to the audience, Gershred placed himself in front of the open window and began projecting heat to destabilize the light at the mouth of the flask.

"Is it working? I can't te—"

All at once there was a huge *crack*, as though the world itself were splitting open, and he was on the floor, with his ears ringing and Maury lying on top of him. As they disentangled themselves and sat up, Gershred noticed a cloud of grey smoke drifting past the window frame.

"Was that the shock wave?" he said, groggily shaking his head.

"Only partly, you moron," Maury grated. "I had to get you away from the light. Among other things, you forgot to pick up goggles for *us*!"

Outside, the audience had gone from oohing and aahing to exclaiming and applauding. Gershred hauled himself back onto his feet and looked down from the window. Where the statue had stood, a circle of dead grass now marked the middle of a large area of frost-covered ground. Of the flask itself, nothing remained. Every one of its imprisoned photons and nitrogen atoms had made a break for it, into the air.

The shroud had fallen, draping itself loosely around the base of the scaffolding. Gershred couldn't help noticing that both the fabric and the frame bore splashes of black.

"I think you may have underestimated the amount of heat in that explosion," he remarked evenly.

Standing beside him, Maury surveyed the clear evidence of charring and murmured, "Oops."

"As you may know," Majestico was saying, "it's my custom to return each object I disappear back to its original place. However, this evening's performance is part of a larger event, and so I'm going to make an exception. In exactly one hour, I'm going to bring back the statue in the ballroom of the Gladstone Hotel. Meet you there!"

The audience cheered wildly. Dean Unger, meanwhile, stood swaying in place, slack-jawed and empty-eyed, like an Edvard Munch painting come to life.

"That looks almost as good on him as the goggles did," Maury commented.

Gershred grinned wickedly. "If you think he's in shock now, wait until he sees what comes back from that other dimension."

True to his promise, the illusionist bounded onstage again at 8:30 sharp and announced, "I have to warn you that some of the objects I've sent through the other dimension have not returned exactly as they were before going in."

The audience uh-ohed.

"They've come back *better*!"

The audience whooped and clapped. Standing with his back to the wall, Gershred glanced at the corner to his left where Unger had chosen to lurk. The dean's complexion was visibly pale.

"He knows," Maury murmured. He shrugged, uncomfortable in the dark suit Gershred had loaned him for this occasion. "Can you give me a hint, at least?"

"Nope. Wait for it."

A framework and shroud had been set up on a wheeled platform that two assistants in glittery costumes now rolled into the ballroom. The shroud lay in folds around the base of the frame, and the illusionist once more invited a member of the audience to confirm that there were no trap doors or hidden mechanisms present.

Then one of the assistants pulled on a rope, raising the shroud to the top of the frame. Torran Majestico invoked the beings of light that dwelt in the other dimension, asking them to surrender back to him the object he had earlier asked them to conceal. When he had finished speaking, he signalled to the assistant to let go of the rope. The shroud collapsed again, revealing something considerably smaller than the original statue. Nonetheless, it drew gasps of surprise and delight from the audience.

Maury gasped too. "Is that white chocolate?"

"Probably. And spun sugar." Gershred chuckled with satisfaction. "Brilliant, isn't it? Torran was once a confectioner. The sweet table now has an edible centrepiece. It won't last the night."

They heard a *thud* from the corner.

"Dean Unger's down for the count," Maury remarked. "When he comes to, he'll be screaming for our resignations, you know."

"Screaming for yours, petitioning for mine. No matter. The academic life was getting a little boring anyway."

"And the litigious little weasel will put Torran Majestico's name on that lawsuit and haul his ass into court."

"No, he won't. One of the documents Torran had me obtain was a guarantee of indemnification against legal action, signed by the president of the university. Unger can try, but it's not gonna fly."

"After we've resigned, I think we should celebrate our new-found freedom by having Dean Unger for dinner. What do you think?" asked Maury.

Gershred didn't reply. He was watching Torran harvest life essence from an adoring crowd and fondly remembering his own time onstage as one of The Lord Chamberlain's Men.

Oh, what fools these mortals be!

I tend to write organically, responding to whatever sparks my imagination. Sometimes it's an opening sentence or an image. In this case, it was the title of a planned anthology: The Dame Was Trouble. As I was reading about the call for submissions, Margot Halvorsen sprang to life in my mind, bringing this story with her. It practically wrote itself. Unfortunately, the anthology fell through. However, Margot has stuck around, and I would love for you to meet her.

Doubling Back

Benny's text was short and to the point: *they're coming run* I tried to call him back, but his phone was turned off.

That kid never could get a message right the first time. Which of the many "they"s in my life was coming for me now? The feds? The local cops? The research lab that had swallowed my father and tried to put me on the menu as well? Some rival crime lord wanting to send a message to Gus "Mr. Big" Bigelow? It couldn't be Bigelow himself—our arrangement was far too advantageous for him.

Besides, even though they used different last names, Benny was Gus's son, loyal to his family until his final breath. If Mr. Big wanted me taken out, the kid wouldn't have bothered to warn me about it.

Not that this cryptic text qualified as much of a warning. Were "they" on their way to the downtown bar where I was currently nursing a ginger ale and waiting for a potential client to show up for a meeting? Or were "they" about to storm my office over Papparelli's Pizza Parlour on Yonge Street, where I'd left Benny holding the fort?

At Gus's request, I'd been teaching the kid "private eye stuff". Trying to, anyway. Nine cases out of ten, investigating is tedious detail work, nothing like what they show you in the movies. Then that tenth case comes along, making you wish you had a stunt double and a director to yell "Cut!" Once

Benny had realized we weren't going to be having shootouts and car chases every other day, all he wanted to do was sit around the office, talking tough on social media and filling his face out of my petty cash. Until today. Today he'd earned his keep.

Benny wasn't the sharpest knife in the drawer. Still, I liked him. I hoped the reason his phone was off was that he was on his way to somewhere safe and didn't want to be traced. He was a big strong kid, a star athlete fresh out of high school, but he didn't have my special talent for avoiding trouble.

I checked my watch. It was 2:32 p.m. Half an hour earlier I'd been driving around the neighbourhood in my twelve-year-old blue Chevy, looking for a legal parking spot. There was still time for me to double back. The client was twenty minutes late. In fact, if someone was after me, there was a good chance he wouldn't show at all, that this meeting was just a ploy to draw me into the open.

Thirty seconds more and I would be out of here, I decided. I started counting. When I got to twenty-three, a man slid onto the stool beside mine. Late forties or early fifties, medium height and build, a full head of neatly trimmed salt-and-pepper hair. His royal blue sports coat fell open, and I caught a glimpse of a pistol tucked into a holster at his waist. He was right handed. I jotted a mental note. Then he turned and gave me a brief, thin-lipped smile.

"Margot Halvorsen?"

"That depends," I replied, staring straight ahead at our reflections in the mirror behind the bar. I was wearing my "plain Jane" persona, to ward off pick-up lines. He was looking at me the way an aging cat would look at a mouse. "Who are *you* supposed to be?"

"I'm your date. Sergeant Wells." He flashed a badge and ID past my eyes, so fast that all I saw was a blur. Real cop? I didn't think so.

Apparently, "they" had arrived.

I spun my stool a quarter-turn. "And what can I do for one of Toronto's finest?" I asked, batting my eyelashes at him.

He clamped his large hand on my elbow. "You can come with me. Now."

Reflexively I doubled back, my consciousness entering my former self just in time to brake at a stop sign two blocks away. I now knew that the meeting I was hurrying to make was a trap.

But that was all I knew, and it wasn't enough. I still didn't know who "they" were, or whether they'd set other traps as insurance.

In any case, the second part of Benny's message had been quite clear: *run*. Fortunately, I had my go-bag in the trunk of the car and plenty of gas in the tank. Instead of turning the corner and parking on the side street, I chose to cruise through the intersection, headed toward the traffic light at Avenue Road.

Meanwhile, my mind was in overdrive. I'd really thought that those days of hiding out and looking over my shoulder were in the past. Gus had my back now. Everything was supposed to be good. So why was this happening to me? What had changed?

All at once it struck me that this might not be about me at all. Maybe Fake Cop just needed to keep me away from the office so someone else could move on Benny.

A man in Gus Bigelow's position had enemies to spare. He'd made it clear that as long as I was training his son I was also responsible for protecting him. It was gallant of Benny to try to protect me instead. (I'm short and girly-looking, and have often been mistaken for a damsel in distress.) But Mr. Big would not be impressed to learn that I'd been high-tailing it out of town in his kid's hour of need.

In about twenty minutes, Benny would be texting me his warning. As it happened, that was also how long it would take me to get to him from my current location. Swearing under my breath, I turned at the light and headed north, back to the office.

⁓

My father had always said that messing with time was both the best and the worst idea he'd ever come up with. His time machine had worked, but not in the way you would expect. It allowed people to send their consciousness into the past, with all their memories intact, into their own former body. They could relive events and, if they wanted to, remake earlier decisions, altering their personal timeline.

Dad had used the machine a lot at first, not to change the present for anyone else but rather to correct his own past errors. And, as he later found out, while he'd been tweaking his current reality, the machine had been doing the same thing to his genetic makeup.

That most of the scientific community refused to take his theories about time travel seriously had actually turned out to be a blessing. Dad had known from the start how dangerous his invention could be in the wrong hands. He'd kept its existence a secret for years. Then someone tried to break into the storage locker where he'd been hiding the machine, forcing him to do something about it.

He could have used it to go back in time and change his mind about building it in the first place, but that would have undone all the improvements he'd made to his life, including meeting and marrying my mother. So, he opted to destroy the machine, burn all his notes, and keep his fingers crossed instead.

He also kept the changes that had been made to his genome, and he passed them along to me. For obvious reasons I was home-schooled, at least until I'd learned to control my special talent. By my late teens I'd given it a name: doubling back. It made a great safety net. If I found myself in dangerous or unpleasant circumstances, I could go back and change the decision that had put me there—most of the time.

As with anything that sounds that good, there was and is a catch. I can't double back more than thirty minutes at once, and I need to wait at least an hour after doubling back before doing it again. If I don't let the new timeline settle properly, it can loop back on itself, creating echoes and multiple realities and a hell of a lot of confusion.

That was why I was cursing as I turned the car around to go check up on Benny. If this was a mistake, if he was already somewhere else and "they" were waiting for me in the office, then I would have to deal with the situation the old-fashioned way. Fortunately, I had more in my defensive arsenal than just the time travel gene. Besides my wits and a well-honed survival instinct, I had two small-calibre handguns, one in the glove box of my car and the other one locked in a desk drawer in my office. I was trained to use them but couldn't remember the last time I'd needed to fire either weapon. With luck, things would remain that way.

As I approached the entrance to the private parking lot behind Papparelli's, I noticed a dark green GMC Savana. It had tinted windows and was sitting on the wrong side of the road, as though poised to roll forward and block any vehicle attempting to exit the lot. I drove past the entrance without slowing down, mentally noting the van's licence plate number. Then I hung a couple of quick right turns and pulled over on the side road just north of the pizza joint, facing Yonge Street. I sent a quick text to my contact at Motor Vehicle Licences and Registrations. There was no point in checking the time of a decision I wouldn't be able to unmake, but I did it automatically: 2:29 p.m.

So, the parking lot was under surveillance. "They" were either lying in wait for someone who was arriving—me—or preparing to grab someone who was leaving—Benny. There were probably eyes on the front and back doors of the building as well. I was ready to take "them" on, but this only made sense if Benny was still in the office, needing to be rescued.

I tried calling him again. The line was busy. Great. A split second after I'd disconnected, his text came through: *they know run.*

All I could do was shake my head. This message was even more cryptic than his first one had been. Then I reminded myself that as far as the timeline was concerned, this *was* his first text. Fake Cop had arrived at the bar, realized that I'd blown off the meeting, and—alerted the rest of "them" to watch for me here? That didn't track. The timing was wrong. So was the time. The clock on the dashboard now read 2:26 p.m.

Consciously relaxing my neck and shoulders, I glanced in the side view mirror—and froze. A man was striding toward my car, coming up on it from behind. I recognized the sports coat. It was Fake Cop. Too late to duck down—he'd seen me. My next impulse was to turn the key in the ignition and get the hell away from there. Bad idea. There was wall-to-wall traffic blocking the way onto Yonge Street, and not enough road width on this side street to let me pull a fast U-turn.

A second later "Sergeant Wells" leaned over and tapped on my driver's side window a couple of times with the barrel of his snub-nosed revolver. I cast a longing look at the glove box, realized how slim my chances were of beating the bullet from his gun, and decided to go with plan D.

Lowering the window, I demanded in my most indignant voice, "Who are you really, and why are you waving that damned weapon in my face?"

He gave me a familiar reptilian smile. "Hello, Margot. I'm an old friend of your father's. I have something important to tell you, and I need you to listen carefully to what I have to say."

"Where's Benny?"

"Wherever you left him, I imagine."

"He was in the office. What have you done with him?"

"Not a thing. I haven't even gone inside the building."

"But how did he—?" A sudden chill went through me, raising gooseflesh on my arms. "Just a second." Fake Cop waited patiently outside the car as I pulled up the texting history on my phone. It showed that no messages had been sent or received in the past two hours.

This was impossible. Swallowing hard, I tucked the phone into the pocket of my jacket.

"As I said, I'm an old friend of your father's, and we have a lot to discuss, you and I."

"We'll do it in my office," I told him. This was another decision I wouldn't be able to unmake. I hoped it wouldn't turn out to be a mistake. However, if it did, at least I would be able to defend myself. "After I've seen with my own eyes that Benny is all right."

He nodded. "Agreed, but on one condition: you first let me remove the handgun currently sitting in your desk drawer."

There was only one way he could know about that gun. "You've been in my office before."

"Yes. Unfortunately, the last time I tried to speak to you there, things ended badly. So I rewound. I'm hoping this iteration will go much better."

❧

Sitting in the back seat of the green van with Fake Cop beside me, I called the office number. Benny picked up. "Halvorsen Investigations. No job too small or dirty," he carolled, giving me a sudden urge to smack the back of his head. "How can we help you?"

"You can start by ditching that 'small and dirty' bit," I told him tartly. "We're not a housecleaning service. Any messages?"

"Nah, it's been quiet. How did your meeting go with the

new client?"

I glanced at Fake Cop to my right. He'd crossed his arms over his chest, probably so I couldn't see that his gun was pointed at my rib cage. "He was a no-show. Listen, there's nothing happening right now and it's almost three o'clock. Why don't you go to the gym and work off that deluxe panzerotti you had for lunch?"

Mentally I crossed my fingers, hoping he hadn't forgotten our prearranged duress signal.

"Really? You're assigning me a workout?" he replied, sounding pleasantly surprised.

My heart sank. I'd have to make the message clearer.

"I am. Then you should visit your grandfather and see how he's doing. Maybe there's an errand he needs you to run. I think he'd appreciate the favour. Okay?"

"My grandfather? But he's been dead for—"

I doubled back.

❧

"We'll do it in my office," I told him. I was feeling mildly nauseated. This was the timeline, letting me know I'd been a bad girl.

"I don't think so," said Fake Cop with a sigh. He opened the driver's side door. "Get out slowly and keep your hands where I can see them," he instructed me, waving his pistol for emphasis.

I eased myself onto my feet on the pavement. "You're going to march me at gunpoint down Yonge Street again?"

"Of course not. We're getting into my van."

He gestured to my left. I turned and saw the Savana parked just a few metres away. As we walked toward it, I reminded him, "What about Benny?"

"What about him?"

"I need to know that he's safely away from here. Let me call him and tell him to go—"

"—to the gym? That's not going to happen, Margot. However, I will let you send him a text of my own composing, giving him the rest of the afternoon off. Then we really have to talk. No more rewinding. Deal?"

Reluctantly, I replied, "Deal."

Five minutes later, Fake Cop and I sat in the van—parked where I'd first seen it but on the right side of the street this time—watching Benny leave the building. He strolled to his silver grey Lexus without a care in the world, wearing shabby-chic designer jeans and a Tragically Hip T-shirt, and bopping to the beat of the music that his earbuds were blaring into his brain. I couldn't help worrying about him. Besides the fact that he would probably be deaf by the age of thirty, the kid appeared utterly oblivious to his surroundings. This was dangerous for anyone, on foot or behind the wheel, but especially so for the only son of Gus Bigelow. Fortunately, he wasn't on Fake Cop's radar. Not today, at any rate. Not unless someone changed their mind.

Briefly wondering which iteration we were in now, I resisted the impulse to check the time.

"Satisfied?" said Fake Cop.

I nodded. "Okay. You can put away your gun. You want me to listen? I'm listening."

He showed me his hands. They were empty. "How much do you know about your father's work?"

I gave him the uninformative version. "I know that he was a scientist and an inventor. For twenty years, while I was growing up, he taught at a technical institute. Then he got an offer he couldn't refuse from a big research laboratory somewhere in New England. Five years later he died."

Fake Cop smiled. "Come on, Margot. We both know that's not the whole story. Did you ever see the time travel machine? Did he keep any drawings of it?"

Now things were making sense. Fake Cop was a time traveller, like me. I needed to find out how much he knew. So I said, with what I hoped would sound like amused disbelief, "Really? You're telling me my father built a working time travel machine?"

"No, I'm telling you he didn't build it. He did the research and designed the device, but I was the one who constructed it. We were partners—equal partners, I thought. We passed that gadget back and forth for years. We gave ourselves charmed lives. We won the lottery, on purpose. Separately, we avoided car accidents, crime scenes, and at least one major plane crash. Then, one day, your father changed his mind about sharing the machine. He locked it up in a storage unit and told me never to come near it again."

"You're lying."

"Am I? This all happened before you were born, so how would you know? Because your father told you? Did he also tell you why he destroyed it?"

"Yes. It threatened the integrity of the time-space continuum."

"True, but that's not the real reason. We should have destroyed it the moment we realized that it should never have been built in the first place. And yet, he hung onto it, waiting until that precise point in time to get rid of it. Did he ever tell you why?"

When the revelation struck me, it felt as though I'd been hit by a city bus. "That was you, wasn't it? The person who tried to break into the storage unit."

"Yes, it was me. And I was careful to give your father the impression that he'd caught me before I was able to get inside. In fact, he arrived too late. I'd already broken in and used the machine one last time, knowing that he would destroy it immediately if he believed I'd been unsuccessful."

I frowned. "Used it to do what?"

"To change my mind once more about having an affair with your mother. You aren't the first iteration of Margot Halvorsen, my dear. You're the fifth."

All at once the bus was crushing me under its figurative wheels. I couldn't breathe. Fake Cop was still talking. I could hear his voice wallpapering my mind. But I knew that if I spent one more second in that van, I was going to die. I doubled back.

❧

Other than the Chevy, the side street was empty. I sat behind the wheel for a good minute, forcing my food to stay down and my lungs to accept air while I gathered my thoughts. There was no way Fake Cop could be my father—that was a given. So he had to have told me that story to throw me off balance. Since he'd apparently given up chasing me, he'd probably decided to bait a hook and reel me in instead. He was a time traveller, able to rewind, as he put it, and head me off each time I doubled back to get away. I had no idea how many times we'd already done this dance, but it was a safe bet that by now he knew everything about my talent, including its limitations.

The most important thing I'd learned from Gus Bigelow was that playing by the rules only made sense if everyone else was playing by the same rules as you were. Fake Cop wasn't. Clearly, it was time I broke a few myself.

I turned the key in the ignition, checked for traffic, and made a three-point turn. Then I retraced my drive around the block, stopping as soon as I saw the green van sitting on the side street. What I wanted was inside that vehicle. With luck, it would be unoccupied.

Parking the Chevy out of sight of the van, I reached into my glove box and slipped a bit of insurance into my jacket pocket. I mentally plotted a path that would keep me concealed from both possible vantage points: the interior of the Savana and the window of my office. Then I darted across the road and sneaked around the corner, ducking behind a series of bushes, a lamppost, and a mailbox. Finally, I took a deep breath, leaped out of hiding, and flattened myself against the passenger side of the van.

I could see my reflection in the side view mirror. That meant anyone inside the vehicle could see me too. I held my breath, waiting for some reaction. Seconds passed. Nothing. Evidently, Fake Cop was elsewhere.

The van's doors were locked, but breaking into a car was Private Eye Stuff 101. In a matter of seconds, I was rifling through the Savana's various compartments, looking for the vehicle registration slip that would give me its owner's real name and address.

My phone dinged. A text message had arrived: *Not feeling well. Come back to office.*

So that was where he was. Good to know.

I ignored the text and kept searching.

Inside the plastic folder containing the user's manual, I struck pay dirt. The van was registered in Ontario to a Jean-Pierre Dupuis. Cute. Dupuis was Wells in French. I called up Corinne, my contact at Motor Vehicle Licences and Registration, and asked her to send me a copy of the head shot from Jean-Pierre's driver's licence.

While I was waiting for her email, another text message

arrived: *Just threw up. Need your help.*

"Sorry, I'm not biting," I informed the screen. *You have mail,* it informed me back.

I opened my inbox.

The face in the picture Corinne had sent me matched the one Fake Cop was wearing. Excellent.

I doubled back. The clock on the Chevy's dashboard read 1:56 p.m. I counted slowly to ten. Then, against all better judgment, I doubled back a second time.

❧

At 1:26 p.m., I'd been at my desk, considering ways to drum up some business for the agency. But that had been then. Now, I was sitting at my desk, feeling my stomach heave and wondering whether I could reach the toilet down the hall before my lunch made an encore appearance.

Nope, it was too far. I reached under the desk, grabbed the metal waste basket, and upchucked into that instead. When I'd straightened again in my chair, Benny broke the seal on a fresh bottle of water and put it in front of me. Then he busied himself with the plastic bag that lined the inside of the waste basket, pausing only to ask with genuine concern, "Are you okay?"

"Oh, yeah, just peachy," I told him, and took a swig from the bottle to clear my mouth. I would be fine, once the timeline had had a chance to settle. In the meanwhile, I was expecting an important call on the office land line and couldn't leave my desk. "Bring me a couple of extra plastic bags, would you? And the air freshener."

"You're sure you're okay? Hey, maybe you're pregnant," he said with a grin.

Before I could respond with something appropriately sarcastic, the phone rang. I picked up the handset and gestured to Benny to be quiet. Then I opened the connection.

"Halvorsen Investigations. How can we help you?" I began.

"I have a rather delicate matter that needs to be resolved," said Fake Cop's voice at the other end of the line. The tone and wording were exactly as I remembered. As I was opening my mouth to reply, he continued, "I have an urgent message to deliver to a young lady that I've come to care about, but I'm afraid she doesn't trust me."

This was different from before. I paused to regroup. "Maybe there's a good reason for that."

"Oh, I know there is, but it's not the one you think."

I swallowed a sigh. Fake Cop had rewound again. Evidently, the only effective way to deal with him was going to be head on. "And which iteration are we in now? Aren't you getting tired of this?"

"It depends. Are you ready to listen?"

"To what? You mean there's more?"

"Much more. Ms. Halvorsen, I'm quite serious when I tell you your life depends on hearing me out."

"And it has to be face to face, not over the phone?"

"Yes. You'll just have to trust me. I know you've found out my name and address. Don't say them aloud, to anyone. Tell Benny that we're meeting at the bar. You know which one. Then come to my home, alone. I promise you won't regret it."

I was already regretting it. My stomach was winding up to pitch another inning and I needed to get off the phone fast. So I replied, "All right. I can be there in half an hour."

"It's a twenty minute drive if you leave immediately. I'll be expecting you."

I didn't argue with him. I just broke the connection and reached for the waste basket. When the retching had stopped and I was able to sit up straight again, Benny came to stand in front of my desk, his eyes wide as traffic lights.

"What was *that* all about?" he demanded.

"Just someone who refuses to come into the office. He wants me to meet him." I took a long swallow of water, thought for a moment, then scribbled Dupuis's home address on a memo pad. "Here's where I'll be. If you haven't heard from me after forty minutes, call Gus and give him this information."

"Sounds dangerous. You're not going there all by yourself, are you?"

"It's sweet of you to worry about me, but I'll be fine. Really."

"But what if he holds a gun on you and forces you to make the call? We should have a distress signal. Hey! You could tell me to go to the gym."

Right. Because that had worked *so* well before.

"Okay, here's the signal," I decided. "I'll pick a fight with you and tell you to go to hell."

He gave me a little-boy pout. "That's a dumb signal."

Actually, I thought it was brilliant. When Benny heard it, he would either know that I was in trouble and call Gus, or get pissed off at me and call Gus. It was a win-win.

❧

The address on Dupuis's license belonged to a ranch-style brick bungalow in an older part of North York. Whether the house actually belonged to Dupuis was another matter altogether, but it looked tidy and had what the real estate agents refer to as "curb appeal". Manicured lawn, sculpted shrubbery, decorative planters on the front porch. Very pretty. I checked the time on the dashboard clock as I pulled up and parked at the curb. It was 2:02 p.m., exactly thirty minutes since I'd ended his phone call.

For a moment I debated with myself whether to get out of the car and ring the doorbell. Then Dupuis settled the issue by suddenly appearing beside the passenger-side door.

"Unlock the door and let me in," he commanded, showing me his stern cop face. "We can't stay here."

I stepped out onto the road and stared a challenge at him across the roof of the Chevy. "Why not?"

"Because Bigelow knows you're here. In a few short minutes this car will be full of bullet holes and so will we," he spat. "There's no time to explain. Unlock the damned door so we can go somewhere safe and I can finally tell you what I've been trying to tell you from the start."

"Wait a second. You're saying I died?"

"Yes! A couple of times already. So did your assistant. Colucci's men tortured him for information about you, then left him for dead. Let's go, Margot!"

That explained the cryptic warnings. They'd been the last words of a dying man.

"Is Benny dead now?" I persisted.

Dupuis groaned impatiently. "I don't know. Probably. Margot, please! We have to leave. If they see your car here, there will be a bloodbath. And if you die and I rewind, you'll have no memory of any of this."

There was a writhing in my stomach that had nothing to do with the timeline, but at least things were starting to make sense. The first two times, Benny had warned me to run. This time, he'd evidently spent his last moments contacting Gus. And Gus had done what any grieving crime boss father would do after finding his son's murdered body: he'd ordered a hit on the person he held responsible for the death. In this case, it was the psychic who should have seen it coming and found a way to prevent it. Me.

Dupuis must have read my thoughts from my expression. "Don't rewind, Margot. It's useless. You can change your own mind, but you can't change Colucci's."

It wasn't Colucci's mind I cared about.

A black car was speeding toward us.

I doubled back.

❧

The cold water felt good on my face. It cleared my head too. As I reached for a towel, I knew what I had to do, and what Gus needed to hear.

Benny was still pouting when I came back from the washroom. "I've changed my mind," I told him.

He brightened instantly. "You're changing the signal?"

"I'm blowing off the meeting. I've finally figured out who this guy is." I sat down at my desk and speed-dialed Gus's private number on my cell phone.

"Margot! What can I do for my favourite girl?" boomed his hearty voice.

"Actually, it's something I can do for you," I told him. "One of your competitors has taken a page from your playbook and hired someone with the same gift as mine."

There was a pause. Then, in a much quieter and more ominous voice Gus asked, "Can you tell me who it is?"

"The competitor? It's Colucci. And his psychic goes under the name Jean-Pierre Dupuis. Dupuis called me just now, wanting to meet. I said yes, out of curiosity, but then I got a vision of guns being fired and changed my mind."

"Where is he expecting you to meet him?"

"Would you believe at his home address?"

Gus chuckled. "Of course. With cameras rolling, no doubt,

so Colucci can blackmail you into giving me bogus predictions. You made the right call, both times," he said. "Thanks for the tip, sweetheart. I'll take it from here." His last words echoed in my brain, long seconds after the connection was broken.

It's funny how people refer to it as "cold feet", as though that's the only part of you that goes icy when you realize you've made a huge mistake. I'd set out to change Gus's mind about ordering the hit. Instead, it appeared I'd just given him a different target. Bigelow could be subtle and indirect. He wasn't about to start a war by sending one of his men to knock off one of Colucci's. But regardless of who pulled the trigger, if Dupuis died before he could rewind himself out of danger, I would be an accessory to murder. It was a line that I'd sworn I would never cross.

Mentally kicking myself, I thought about doubling back. Then a burp burst in my mouth, leaving an unspeakable taste behind and reminding me of the vengeance that the timeline would wreak on me if I didn't give it a chance to settle down. That left only one thing I could do, preferably without any witnesses.

Benny heard the empty water bottle hit the recycling bucket and hurried to bring me a full one. "This is the last of them," he informed me as he placed it on my desk. "And forgive me for saying this, but you really look like crap, Margot."

Perfect.

"Yeah. I feel like it too. How about going to the drugstore and getting me some anti-nausea medicine?" I reached into the petty cash box and pulled out a twenty dollar bill. "Talk to the pharmacist and see what's available. Let them know that I'm definitely not pregnant. And stop at a grocery store on your way back, please, to pick up a case of bottled water and some salty snacks."

He headed for the door, grinning as though I'd just doubled his salary. The moment he was gone, I accessed the incoming calls list for the business line and found Dupuis's number. Praying that it wouldn't turn out to belong to a pay phone, I punched up the number on my cell. He picked up on the second ring.

"Margot, are you out of your mind?" he scolded after I'd identified myself. "What the hell are you doing contacting me like this?"

"Saving your life, I hope. I just told Bigelow about you and Colucci and our meeting at your house this afternoon. It got me back in Gus's good graces, but I think he's gunning for you now. You should probably find somewhere safe to be."

A pause, then, "Why the change of mind?"

"Don't you mean change of heart?"

"You just served me up to Bigelow on a platter, with good reason. Now you're warning me about him, also for a good reason. That's a change of mind. I'm curious to know what prompted it."

It was a good question. Dupuis had ripped into my life like a tornado, turning everything upside down, including my memories of the past. The only other person I'd ever met who was capable of doing that to me was my father. That made them both special, and I'd already learned the hard way that you don't throw away something special, no matter how painful or difficult it may be to hang onto.

Aloud, I said, "We're the only two people like us on this planet. For years, I thought I was the only one. I guess I don't want to go back to feeling that way again. Now, get your ass out of danger and call me as soon as you're safe so we can talk, Jean-Pierre Dupuis!"

"Yes, ma'am." I heard a smile in his voice as he broke the connection.

For ten long minutes I waited, watching the clock and hoping the phone would ring before Benny returned from his errands. When it did, I pounced.

"You're safe?"

"We all are: you, me, and Benny. I spoke to Colucci and straightened things out, for now. And you shouldn't feel guilty about handing me to Bigelow. It just means we're even, since I'm indirectly responsible for you being in Colucci's crosshairs."

I sat up straight in my chair. "*You* put Colucci onto me? I hope it was for a good reason," I said stiffly.

"It was the same one as yours: self-preservation. Colucci suspected that I was the one giving Bigelow advance warning about Colucci's raids on his shipments and warehouses. I made up a story about a secret government project and convinced him that there were other precognitives like me out there, and that one of them had to be on Bigelow's payroll."

"Who found me?"

"Colucci did. At first, I thought the 'psychic' he'd decided to take out was your father. That wouldn't have bothered me so much. But when I realized it was you, I—had a change of mind."

Hearing those words made my skin crawl. He'd evidently seen my corpse. "And Colucci doesn't suspect the truth about us?"

"Thankfully, no. That secret is safe. But let's face it Margot, we're living in a shooting gallery. We've been working for rival interests, neither of whom would think twice about killing us to tilt or balance the playing field. All it took for Colucci to order a hit on me was a phone call from Bigelow, claiming to have me in his pocket. Thanks to your warning, I survived to talk my way out of it—this time. The next phone call could be from Colucci to Bigelow.

"Like it or not, we need each other. Our special talent literally gives each of us the ability to bring the other one back to life. And you know as well as I do that if one of us dies, the other won't be far behind."

He was right. We needed a way to guarantee we would both survive. I could think of only one, and it was both the best and the worst idea I'd ever come up with.

I took a deep breath, then said, "We have to keep Bigelow and Colucci in balance. That means pooling information about their activities and deciding how much of it to share with each of them. Are you up for that, Dupuis?"

He let out a low whistle. "It's a dangerous game you're proposing, Margot. If they ever catch on to what we're doing, we're both dead, you realize."

"Hey, been there, done that," I told him breezily as Benny burst through the office door, loaded down with snacks. "And if we don't like it, we can always change our minds."

Dupuis laughed.

I glanced at the clock on the wall. It read 2:24 p.m.

Just under an hour had passed on the timeline. Longest damned hour of my life.

This story was written for (and rejected by) an anthology about superheroes before being published by Daily Science Fiction *in August, 2016. It was conceived to answer the question, 'Where do supervillains come from?' And although I was writing in general terms, not thinking of anyone in particular at the time, it appears my answer was spot on…*

Mightier than the Sword

Originally published in:
Daily Science Fiction, August 2016

Ultraman enters the room slowly, pausing in the doorway for effect. He has purposely kept us waiting for ten minutes. A smile tugs briefly at the corners of his mouth as he steps ponderously over to the dark green chair at the centre of all the lights and cameras. This is the final interview. All the safe and simple questions have been asked and answered. It's time for the tough ones. That's why the network hired me. Our viewers want to know.

The chair is especially designed to accommodate his bulk and support his weight. Hyperdeveloped muscles are evident even beneath the fabric of his suit coat. They bunch and shift beneath his skin with every movement he makes. Together with his granitic features and the brow ridge that canopies his eyes, they turn him into a caricature of physical strength.

The other ten are living caricatures as well, of keen sensory perception, flexibility, sensitivity and intellect. But there were twelve to start with, a dozen embryos in the first generation of the experiment; and eyes were averted each time I brought the subject up in the earlier sessions. Talk to Ultraman, I was told.

"I'd like to ask you a couple of questions about your brother—"

"The Infamous One?" he cuts in. The stony face is scowling.

I school my own features and keep my voice steady. "I was

going to use his given name."

"I'm amazed anyone even remembers it. Let me save you some time," he says, and there's a hard edge of impatience in his voice. "Everyone who interviews us is curious about the twelfth embryo. We answer their questions, then they edit out all mention of The Infamous One before publishing the article or releasing the video to the media. You didn't really think you were the first, did you?"

In fact, I already know I'm not. What I don't know is how someone whose evil misdeeds are a matter of public record could come to be so taboo that not even other investigative reporters will discuss his origins with me in private.

When I tell Ultraman this, he utters a laugh that rumbles inside him like an earthquake. "So you've come to the source. All right, I'll tell you the story. But don't say you weren't warned, any of you."

I am suddenly aware of the technicians holding their breaths all around us in the darkness, and I wonder whether I should ask them to leave the room. Then it's too late. Ultraman has begun to speak.

"When those scientists figured out how to activate the dark genetic matter in human chromosomes, they weren't sure what their tweaking would produce. They had an idea, of course—a human fetus goes through all the stages of evolution in the womb—so they were prepared for just about every eventuality. What they never counted on was a null result."

"The twelfth embryo."

He nods. "The Infamous One emerged from the crèche looking perfectly normal, but then so did most of us. As we grew older, our special abilities began to manifest themselves. By our fifth birthday, it was obvious that eleven of us were enhanced humans and one was a failed experiment... or so we all thought. Unfortunately, despite our superhuman powers we were still human children, reacting to the presence of someone who clearly didn't belong in the group."

He stares at me as he says this. Memories surface, and it takes all my self-control to remain still in my chair.

"You bullied him."

"We super-bullied him," he corrects me in a voice tinged with regret. "We tormented him at every opportunity, abused him in every way we could think of. And we felt we were entitled to, because in our little world we were the normal ones and he was different. If they'd realized what was happening, the adults would have put a stop to it; but we were all convincing liars, and our victim never snitched. By the time the scientists were ready to concede defeat and let him be adopted into a regular human family, the emotional and psychological harm we'd caused..."

He sighs, and I am certain he can see the scars of my past etched on my face. I remind myself that this interview is not about me.

"But you said... so he did have a special ability."

"His nervous system was attuned to the rhythm and harmony of the spoken word. There was no way anyone could have detected such a gift when he was young, and he naturally assumed that everyone was as sensitive to the music of language as he was, so he had no reason to tell anyone about it. Unfortunately, it amplified the effect of any verbal abuse he suffered. I'm sure you can imagine what it felt like to be reminded on a daily basis by everyone he knew that he was a failure and a disappointment, that he didn't belong—and to believe it. And then to realize that he did have an enhancement after all, that he was superior to all the normal humans around him...!"

"I'm sorry, you've lost me. If he thought everyone was just like him, then how—?"

"When he was adopted, The Infamous One was already damaged, and damaged kids are magnets for bullies. Naturally they came after him at school. At first he tried to fight, and that didn't work. So he talked. And he found that if they let him talk to them before they started throwing punches, the bullies always ended up walking away. It didn't take him long to figure out what was happening... and what he might have been spared earlier on if he'd used his words on us. A hard kernel of anger was planted inside him then. It took root immediately and began to grow. He'd been made to feel like an outsider by his crèche-mates, then dumped into the normal world where he really was different from everyone else."

Things are coming clear for me now.

"Different but superior this time," I murmur, and Ultraman nods.

"Words began as his shield. As he grew older they became

his tools, and he quickly learned how to wield them expertly to get ahead in the normal world. He became a trial lawyer. Never lost a case. Then he moved into politics, making speeches that gripped the masses, swaying their moods and opinions. Bending individuals to his will. They said he had charisma. They thought he could do no wrong. Nobody saw the anger gnawing at his core. Not until he'd risen to the leadership of a party, and then of a government. Not until he'd started a war that cost three million people their lives." Ultraman sighs heavily. "It took all of us to bring him down— a combined effort by eleven superhumans. Superheroes, they call us. We stepped up and saved the world. Everyone thought we did it because we're the good guys, and fighting evil is what good guys do. In fact, all that happened was that we drove our brother insane, stood by while he killed three million people to prove he was our equal, and then ganged up and murdered him. That's a lot of blood to have on your hands."

Words have always been my trusty tools, at times my only friends, but at this moment they fail me. I want to reassure him that he can't blame himself for the bad deeds of another, but the memories are too strident, and I know I would be lying.

He gazes thoughtfully into my face, and I am strangely relieved to see his eyes bright with unshed tears. "So there is your answer. Now you must decide what to do with it. Air it or bury it. Either way, none of us will blame you." And without another word he rises to his feet and walks out of the room.

The interview is over.

Every science fiction author has a cautionary tale to tell about a first contact gone sideways. This is mine. It was inspired by all the stories I've read or seen about Earth being invaded by aliens for purposes of exploitation, and it answers a question: what if the tables were turned and we were those aliens invading another world?

The Best Defence

Lieutenant Benjamin Loew sat on the hard wooden chair in the prisoner's dock, ramrod-straight, stony-faced, and counting. Eleven witnesses called so far by the prosecution. Five objections raised that day by Loew's appointed advocate, Captain Alvarez. Three of them sustained. A total of fourteen snaps and 33 fragments of the seven murder scenes introduced into evidence. (The investigative arm of Earth's space-going military was nothing if not thorough.)

It was the tenth day of the tribunal. The prosecution was summing up, and Loew was counting each deliberate breath he took as the prosecuting officer's voice bounced and skittered off the walls inside his mind.

A woman in the gallery briefly met his curious gaze, then shuddered visibly before turning away again. Loew wondered how she would have reacted to the sight of him four weeks earlier, before he'd been made presentable for his tribunal. Or seven months before that—no, he corrected himself, infraspace played tricks with time, so from her perspective it would have been five years ago when the *Croatia* had swung back to Marcusia to pick up his eight-man team.

By then it had been reduced to one—Benjamin Loew, caked with blood and filth and howling in mindless terror.

The crew had been forced to corner and subdue him, as they would any wild, wounded creature. Then they saw the gruesome bundle waiting to be onloaded with the rest of the freight on the pad, and they slammed him full of tranks and pitched him into the brig.

He spent the entire return trip shut away in a cell, wrestling with horrific memories and drug-distorted dreams, and painfully, block by block, erecting a keep inside his mind to imprison them. By the time the *Croatia* reached Luna, Benjamin Loew had won back control of his thoughts… and was driven by a single purpose, evidently the only reason he was still alive: to deliver a message from the aliens to Daniel Trevetti, if *he* was still alive.

The *Croatia* docked at Dianaport on Luna. A security detail whisked Loew away to a military shuttle, which transferred him quickly and quietly to the holding facility at Earthbase Delta. There, he was processed by a forensics team and provisionally charged with seven counts of murder before being allowed to shower and shave and put on a clean uniform.

"I need to see Trevetti," he called out for the dozenth time as the security field was activated around his new cell. "It's important. I have a message—"

"*Colonel* Trevetti has received your request. He says to tell you that he will try to fit you into his very busy schedule," came the brusque response. "But don't hold your breath."

So Trevetti was alive, and promoted in rank, and apparently still resentful over losing command of the second Marcusia mission to Loew, ten years earlier. The irony of this brought tears of frustration to Loew's eyes. Loew had never wanted that assignment. Trevetti had committed the original murder. He should have gone back there, so the aliens could deliver their message to him in person. Perhaps then, seven other men wouldn't have had to die.

No matter. Unless Trevetti had undergone a drastic personality change, satisfying his curiosity would always take top priority. He might not be visible at the debriefing but he would be present. Loew would deliver the message there.

When at last he was pronounced fit to be questioned, the lieutenant was escorted by a pair of armed guards to a cell in a different wing of the holding complex, where two other officers presided over an impressive array of blinking and purring hardware.

Loew stared directly into the pale eyes of one of them and growled, "Where's Trevetti?"

The officer squared his shoulders, then his jaw. Everything about him looked starched, Loew noted, including his straight blond hair. "I'm Major Corning, Lieutenant. This is Captain Robertson." The second man, seated behind a table, had a long, thin face divided by a double hyphen of dark moustache, which he now dipped in acknowledgement. "Would you sit down, please?"

A leather and steel armchair glided into place beside Loew. He didn't move. Trevetti had to be watching this. "Show yourself, Colonel!" Loew challenged the air in the room.

Corning scowled impatiently. "The colonel isn't on the base. Sit down, Lieutenant."

It was a sharp, direct order. Even before he realized he'd obeyed it, Loew was sitting. One of the security guards stepped forward. With practised motions, he anchored Loew's leg shackles to the base of the chair. Meanwhile, as Corning busied himself with a sensor, Robertson quietly repositioned the voice recorder. "All right, Lieutenant," he said on a signal from Corning, "just for the record, would you give us your name, rank and serial number, please?"

Just for the record, Loew complied.

"Okay. Now we want you to tell us in your own words what happened on Marcusia."

Loew shook his head. "I'll only talk to Trevetti."

Corning and Robertson exchanged a knowing look. "I'm sorry you feel that way, son," said Corning. "But you're still going to be debriefed." He pulled up a list of questions on his computer screen and read the first one aloud: "When exactly did the *Croatia* make planetfall on Marcusia?"

Loew opened his mouth to tell him he was wasting his time, but was stunned to hear himself reply, "Oh seven hundred hours ship's time, day 179."

Robertson's narrow face cracked something resembling a smile. "And when did you give the order to offload the command base gear?"

Loew fought the question. But the words tore free inside his head, forced their way through the walls, past his gritted teeth. And with them came the images, searing his mind like lightning—*Stanley in the gully with his throat slit while busy hands stripped off his shirt and pants and a hand with a knife waited to make the long incision… and blood, so much blood, lying in puddles everywhere he stepped…*

Loew gasped and shook off the nightmarish vision. A vomitous taste erupted at the back of his throat. The coffee had been especially bitter that morning, he recalled. They'd probably slipped a drug into it.

"State the purpose of your mission to Marcusia, Lieutenant," said Corning.

"To procure the skins and livers of as many Marcusians as we could kill."

The cracks in his walls were spreading. As Loew struggled desperately to shore up his fortress *he was standing in the gully, ankle-deep in red mud, feeling the raised emblem on the hilt of the knife brand the palm of his hand as he grasped a fistful of wiry black hair and forced Jeremiah's head back…*

"NO!" Loew shivered convulsively and scrubbed the palms of both hands on the fabric of his trousers.

"We've given you Veristatin. The harder you fight, the stronger it gets, son," Corning advised him.

Of course it did, Loew thought grimly. Veristatin had been Trevetti's creation, earning him one of the many doctorates hanging on his office wall. By now there were probably a few more. He collected and displayed them like hunting trophies.

Loew and Trevetti, thirty years apart in age, had both been picked to join the first scientific reconnaissance mission to Marcusia. Once there, the science team had gathered copious data on the Earth-like planet, and especially on the species that occurred in the greatest numbers—lemur-like creatures with large eyes and short tails.

Whether or not these creatures were intelligent, it was a first contact situation, and the mission commander had given the scientists explicit orders: they could observe the Marcusians and make notes. They could record images of the native flora and fauna for closer study. However, unless their own lives were in imminent danger, they mustn't harm or interfere with a single living animal or insect on the planet.

Trevetti made no secret of the fact that this was not his preferred way to examine specimens. Apparently, others on the team agreed with him. When Trevetti's vehicle veered into the brush, killing one of the smaller aliens, the official report described it as an unavoidable accident.

That wasn't the way it had looked to Loew. Evidently, the

Marcusians weren't buying it either. By the next morning, the curious and friendly little animals that had been swarming around the human encampment were gone, as was every other species of wildlife on the planet. The scientists searched for days, but all the living aliens had gone into hiding. The dead alien was the only one they could continue to study, and so that was what they did. The senior science officer performed the initial dissection, then parcelled out limbs and organs to various team members for further examination. Loew focused on his specialty, the alien's vascular system. And of course, each new revelation was immediately transmitted to the scientific community on Earth.

Trevetti wasn't stupid, Loew eventually decided. He had to have known there was more to the Marcusians than they let on. They should have been an easy meal for any of the indigenous carnivores on the planet, but the little creatures were never bothered by them, even when caught alone in the open. Any reasonable man would have followed orders and trodden lightly around them. But Trevetti's curiosity was a force beyond all reason, justifying anything done in the name of scientific discovery.

Earth's government seemed to share that philosophy. A state of the art laboratory and all the grant money they could wish for were waiting for the *Croatia*'s scientific team when they arrived home with their alien specimens. A month later, an enzyme found in an organ resembling the human liver was shown to be effective in dissolving cancerous growths in laboratory rats. Shortly after that, an interesting immunological property was discovered in the alien's subderma. All except Loew agreed that more samples from different subjects were needed in order to validate these findings; so, Trevetti hastened to draft a proposal for a second mission to Marcusia. He called it a procurement expedition, military-speak for a hunting trip.

Loew decided to approach the Ethics Council regarding Trevetti's conduct during the first mission. Their research had been tainted by a criminal act, he argued. It would be morally wrong to pursue it. The councillors hemmed and hawed. A couple of them nodded in solemn agreement. They muttered among themselves, then promised to send a message to the Expeditionary Funding Committee. Later, Loew learned that his petition to scrub the mission had been in vain. Not only was it greenlit, but Lieutenant Loew was assigned to command it. This was incomprehensible to him. He never did find out why he'd been chosen, but it was a direct order from a superior officer and had to be obeyed.

And now here he was, being painted as a heinous villain by a military lawyer with a flair for drama, and Trevetti, although undoubtedly present, was nowhere to be seen.

Loew stiffened involuntarily as the prosecuting officer aimed an accusing finger like a gun, directly at his forehead.

"They've practically got you in front of a firing squad," muttered Alvarez impatiently beside him. "Are you sure you won't testify—?"

Loew turned frosty eyes on his advocate. "Not until after I've spoken to Trevetti."

"I'm sorry. The colonel has instructed me…" His voice died as Loew deliberately returned his gaze frontwards. With a sigh, Alvarez turned around as well. "I'll see what I can do."

That night Loew sat on the edge of his cot, staring bleakly at the untouched dinner tray on the concrete floor of his cell. His appetite wasn't all that was waning. Slow-burning anger required energy, and Loew's had been diminishing with each passing day. Even the air seemed to be rarefying around him. It was becoming harder and harder to take a full breath.

Tomorrow, Alvarez would begin presenting the case for the defence. Unfortunately, there *was* no case for the defence— nothing he could document, at any rate. Suspicions didn't count in a tribunal. Loew could plead insanity, if he hadn't stepped off the *Croatia* so purposefully rational. He could even yield to Alvarez's urgings and speak in his own defence. But that would mean collapsing his walls, letting a flash-flood of bloody memories crash down on him.

A sudden violent shudder wracked the full length of his body. He had to hug his legs tightly with both arms to make it stop.

Lieutenant Loew did not welcome sleep that night.

The following morning, Alvarez met him outside the tribunal chamber doors. The advocate's shoulders appeared frozen in mid-shrug, and his eyes had the distracted look of someone trying to recall where he had last seen his security pass. The guards who had escorted the prisoner from his cell stood watchfully by, neither they nor Alvarez making a move to open the door. Loew gazed a question at him.

"Proceedings have been suspended," said Alvarez, tightening his grip on his briefcase. "There's important new evidence being presented and the tribunes have called a conference to consider whether to allow it." He glanced nervously at the still-closed door before continuing in a quieter voice, "Normally the defendant wouldn't be included in such a meeting, but your presence was specifically requested."

"Specifically requested?" Loew echoed thoughtfully. "By whom?"

Alvarez blew out a sigh. "By Colonel Trevetti. I have no idea what this is about. I guess we'll be finding out together. In the meanwhile, I'd advise you to be very controlled in there, very circumspect."

So Trevetti was finally going to show his face? Loew would have questioned further, but the door opened at that moment from the inside, and he had to follow Alvarez into the tribunal chamber.

This morning, the room was almost empty. The three tribunes who had been appointed to hear Loew's case were seated on their dais, looking as tradition-bound and difficult to move as the huge scrollworked oaken desk in front of them. The prosecutor and his assistant were already at their table, heads expectantly tilted toward the sound of Loew's and Alvarez's footsteps on the polished hardwood floor.

Loew took the place Alvarez indicated beside him at the defence table. Then he cast a routine glance across the room… and froze, choking on an unuttered oath.

The officer sitting beside the prosecutor was not his assistant. It was Daniel Trevetti.

"Lieutenant!"

Automatically, he snapped erect in his chair, seeing through a reddish haze that six pairs of eyes were now focused curiously on his face. Behind him, the two armed guards were moving, probably positioning themselves for a rapid takedown.

Controlled and circumspect, Alvarez had said. Loew sucked in a steadying breath and consciously relaxed his neck and shoulders.

The head tribune rapped his gavel sharply once, then again.

"Everyone is now present. Proceed, Colonel."

Slowly, Trevetti got to his feet. He wasn't aging well. His complexion was sallow, and he seemed to be staggering under the weight of his seventy years. He'd been soft and round the last time Loew had seen him. He was softer and rounder now. Evidently, Trevetti's position of authority was still the part of him that got the most exercise.

The colonel gazed once around the room, cleared his throat with a sound disturbingly like a death rattle, and began. "First, this tribunal should know that Lieutenant Loew and I have been in constant disagreement since the first day we met, which for him was about three years ago, and for me quite a bit longer. We argued in particular over the procurement mission to Marcusia. He told me it was morally reprehensible to exploit an alien species under any circumstances. I pointed out that humankind had a longstanding tradition of exploiting other species, and that it wasn't about to change any time soon. Our discussions became quite heated, to say the least. More than once, he called me a murderer. I hope the irony of his current situation hasn't escaped him."

Loew closed his eyes and focused on taking deep, calming breaths. First, deliver the message. Then he could rise to Trevetti's bait.

The head tribune leaned forward. "Colonel," he said, "I must ask you to get to the point."

"Of course. One of the possibilities that Lieutenant Loew raised during our discussions was that the Marcusians might be an intelligent race. Not having seen evidence at that point of anything but instinctual behaviour, I brushed aside his concerns, convinced that these creatures were simply wild animals that happened to live on an alien planet. I now believe I was wrong.

"Let the record show that the report I'm about to hand out was filed three years ago, while Lieutenant Loew was aboard the *Croatia*, returning to Luna."

Trevetti dropped a datapad in front of the prosecutor, then crossed to the defender's table and placed a second device in Alvarez's hands. Loew glanced over his advocate's shoulder, but had to look away. Alvarez was speed-reading, and Loew couldn't spare the concentration required to follow the text and graphics rapidly scrolling up the datapad's screen.

"These are the findings of an investigation into the crash of the *Saxony*, a survey vessel en route from Marcusia to Luna," Trevetti continued helpfully. "I've highlighted the data relevant to this case."

As he finished reading, Alvarez began to grin, then caught himself. He leaned toward Loew and explained in a taut whisper, "I think we may actually have caught a break. The *Saxony*'s orders had been to map Marcusia from low orbit. Halfway back to Luna, the captain declared an emergency and dropped them out of infraspace, directly onto a collision course with a large asteroid. There was barely time to release a location beacon before the ship was destroyed. All the information it had been gathering was lost."

"And this helps me how, exactly?"

"The recovered bridge readouts were all normal. There was no shipwide emergency. What's more, computer records indicated that the cartographic data had been corrupted and then deleted, long before the crash."

"It was sabotaged?"

"Evidently. But here's what's really interesting: there were seventeen humans in the crew, but organic matter from eighteen bodies was recovered, and one of them tested out as Marcusian. Somehow, they'd managed to pick up an alien stowaway."

...to ensure that the intel about its world could never be reported. Of course. Loew nodded and sat back, his lips pressed tightly together.

"So the question is," Trevetti resumed briskly, "what could have caused such a disastrous sequence of events? What made the captain overreact to a threat that apparently wasn't there? What could have induced the crew to destroy the information they'd been sent so far away specifically to gather? Our forensic scientists used Holmesian logic. They were able to eliminate everything outside the ship, the ship itself, and the crew, and were left with only one possible conclusion, improbable though it might seem: the Marcusian stowaway."

Silence hung heavily in the air for a moment. Then the prosecuting officer rose to his feet. Disdain sharpening his voice, he said, "Are you implying that the Marcusian somehow influenced the perceptions of the captain and crew? With all due respect, sir, that sounds a little farfetched to me."

"I know how it sounds, Captain. That was why I requested Lieutenant Loew's presence this morning. I believe he can confirm what I've just postulated, from his personal experience." Trevetti turned, commanding Loew's eyes with his own.

Alvarez pulled back, staring at him with anticipation as well.

"Can't you, Lieutenant?" Trevetti prompted.

Panic began creeping up the back of Loew's throat on small, clawed feet. Everyone was looking at him now. This wasn't fair. He'd already refused to testify. His walls weren't strong enough.

The prosecutor threw down his stylus and stepped out from behind his table. "Sirs, I must object! The prosecution is willing to concede that Lieutenant Loew may have been insane while committing the murders—"

"But he wasn't insane, Captain," Trevetti declared. "That's the whole point. He was confused, like the crew of the *Saxony*. Deluded by the Marcusian into thinking—" Trevetti whirled on Loew again, his expression morphing into a portrait of avuncular concern. "What *did* they convince you was happening, Lieutenant?" he coaxed.

Loew gritted his teeth and concentrated on the walls inside his mind.

"Answer the question, Lieutenant Loew!" ordered one of the tribunes.

"Nothing out of the ordinary." *That damned Veristatin! Did it ever wear off?* "I thought I was just waiting out the mission in my quarters, letting Levine handle things while I read, kept my personal log up to date…"

He swallowed hard. His walls were becoming spider-webbed with cracks. They wouldn't hold much longer.

"You had to sign off on the kill tally each day," Trevetti reminded him. "How many—?"

Loew felt as though his entire brain was springing leaks, dribbling bad-tasting words and phrases onto his tongue so he would have to spit them out. "Two hundred and twenty. It's on the record. I reported a total of two hundred and twenty kills."

"In fact, there were only seven," said Trevetti after a beat. "None of them were Marcusians." He paused again to let this fact sink in.

Loew couldn't speak. He was fully focused again on maintaining his walls.

"Sapient or not," Trevetti continued, "the Marcusians are apparently in possession of a powerful defence mechanism. They can induce a hypnotic state and make other beings do their bidding. Like making the crew of the *Saxony* destroy their own findings and then their own ship. Like making the procurement team on-world do to one another what they'd been planning to do to the Marcusians."

...skin peeling away from muscle, a blood-shining, fat-oozing slipcovering... Loew clenched his jaws, panic punching holes in his concentration.

"So you're saying Lieutenant Loew had no criminal intent, if and when he committed the crimes with which he has been charged," Alvarez cut in. "More importantly, if the Marcusians could induce mass hallucination—"

"Alien mind control? This is a serious allegation that you're making, Colonel," said the head tribune.

"You can call it whatever you like, sir. It's my conviction that they spun a dream around this man, while manipulating him like a puppet. He had no idea what he was doing."

Loew was so numb at that moment that he couldn't even be sure his heart was still beating. A crack widened to a crevice in his wall, and then another, and another. *The mud hadn't been red before they'd arrived there. His hand closed on the hilt of a knife, he didn't know whose, but it was slippery and sticky at the same time. Blood. He grimaced and bent to wipe it off in the grass.*

"If the tribunal accepts this postulation, sirs," said Alvarez, sliding rapidly out of his chair, "the defence pleads for a reduction and possible dismissal of the charges against Lieutenant Loew."

"On what grounds?" demanded the prosecuting officer.

With a quiet roar, Loew's walls folded in on themselves.

"...used him. He's no more guilty of murder than a knife or a pistol is."

Loew opened his eyes and blinked hard in disbelief. He was standing at the edge of the freight pad, which should have been covered with soft bundles waiting to be onloaded. There were just two, and only a single specimen barrel.

A smell was rising all around him, a hot, dark, visceral smell that he couldn't shut out, that made his imprisoned gut writhe and sucked bile up into his mouth. He looked down and saw the front of his uniform, a single huge bloodstain, drying black and stiff next to his crawling flesh. Then he stared at the neatly-trussed bundles of skins on the freight pad, and recognition struck and buried him like an avalanche, suffocating him in the horror of what he must have done.

"…a tragic misunderstanding, certainly, but perhaps we can salvage the situation, send a peace delegation…"

Loew lifted his eyes and saw Trevetti directly across the pad from him. And beside him, its needle-like fangs bared, its onyx eyes gleaming, crouched a metre-tall dark-furred animal that looked like a cross between a lemur and a baboon. There was intelligence in those eyes, and hatred on its face as it stared not at Loew but at Trevetti.

"You can't salvage anything!" Loew blurted out. "*You* did this! Before humans came to their world, the Marcusians used their powers for concealment only. But they're clever. Fast learners. And thanks to you, Trevetti, they've learned plenty. They've certainly learned how to deal with any other humans who show up there. So you can forget about making peaceful contact with them, now or ever. I was spared to bring humankind a message, and here it is: Stay the hell away from our world, or else!"

Arms spread in a gesture of appeasement, the colonel began walking toward him. Loew vaulted over the defence table, dimly aware of a chorus of startled cries, and before anyone could stop him he knocked Trevetti to the floor, straddled his ample torso, and grabbed him by the throat. Strong hands clamped onto Loew's arms and shoulders and an arm wrapped around his neck, pulling him back and away, just as one of the guards took aim with his service pistol and fired twice… into Trevetti's chest.

Time slowed to a crawl. The tribunes were on their feet, gazing in shock at the widening pool of blood around Trevetti's motionless body. The guard who had shot him stared at his weapon in confusion, as though seeing it for the very first time and wondering what it was for. Alvarez and the other guard let their hands drop to their sides and stood like slack-jawed robots awaiting instruction. And the prosecuting officer, kneeling on the floor beside Trevetti, looked up at Loew, aghast, before subsiding into a dazed trance.

The child-killer is dead now. This is what you wanted also, yes?

The voice Loew heard inside his head sounded like his own.

He gulped hard and tore his gaze away from Trevetti's final, astonished expression to find the Marcusian standing atop the prosecutor's table, its glittering dark eyes trained steadily on Loew's face as the realization struck him like a physical blow: the alien that Trevetti had deliberately run over, and that they'd then so callously dissected in the name of scientific research—it had been a juvenile.

All at once, the nightmare memories of the Marcusia mission were tumbling together, dissolving into an abstract blur in Loew's mind, like a dream at the moment of waking. Seconds later, the details were nebulous, elusive, leaving him with only a general impression of what had happened and a residual feeling of horror that clung to his thoughts like soot.

This is a promise. Only two have died, one of our kind, one of yours. We are on your world now. You will do whatever you must to prevent your kind from coming to our world. If you fail, then we will do what is necessary to keep you away. As long as you leave us in peace, we will not harm any of your kind. But know that we will be watching.

They were giving him too much credit.

I can't possibly control the actions or movements of every single human being in the galaxy, he thought.

The Marcusian's eyes remained steadily fastened on Loew's own.

No. But humans can learn. You did.

Alarms were sounding. Loew glanced toward the door and saw security rush into the tribunal chamber, weapons drawn. When he looked back at the prosecutor's table, the alien was gone.

Before the advent of large-scale industrial farming, food production was exclusively handled by families who passed down the fields they tilled, from one generation to the next. On Earth, farm folk have become a breed apart, with a special love for the land. How much more special might the relationship be on an alien world capable of loving them back?

Manua's Children

CHAPTER ONE

"The great ship from Mars journeyed through many Gates. It travelled for a very long time, more than fifty shipboard years, but at last it discovered this beautiful world we call…?"

"Manua!" chorused the children. Laurel Nyquist gazed indulgently into the faces of her nieces and nephews as they sat cross-legged on the carpet around her chair. They'd heard this story at least a hundred times, yet it never failed to excite them. Little Teddy, at three years of age the youngest of the group, was practically vibrating in place.

"Who can tell us where that name came from?"

"Me!" squealed Karin, her blonde braids bouncing. "Let me tell it this time. It's because they found the Hand, and Manua means 'hand' in an old human language."

Its full name was God's Handprint. At least, that was what the northern half of the land mass had resembled when seen from space—five long valleys separated by mountain ranges, all running roughly parallel to one another, as if a gigantic hand had come down and pressed them into existence. The captain had taken it as a sign, and had synchronized the ark's orbit with the middle of the broad prairie that resembled its palm.

"And the ship's captain spoke to the scientists," Laurel continued, "and they went down to the planet's surface and began taking measurements, to make sure the water was safe for drinking, and the soil was rich for planting, and the air was good for breathing—"

"And flying!" Teddy cut in proudly. "I can fly."

"Sweetheart, we've talked about this. You can jump very high, but that's not flying," she corrected him patiently. Laurel reached out a shadow hand, ready to stop him if he decided to demonstrate his talent for them. Mama Nyquist loved each and every one of her grandchildren, but she didn't look fondly on people who put marks on her shiny living room ceiling.

"And I can run," declared Sophia.

Yes, she could, much faster than anyone else in their family, Laurel reflected. Thank goodness for shadow hands. Three-year-old jumpers and five-year-old runners had to be the most challenging children to care for.

"—and when the measurers were satisfied that this was a welcoming place for humans, the captain notified the rest of the colonists. She programmed each of the habitat pods to carry its family to a different location in the Fingers or the Wrist or the Palm. Food-growing families like ours were sent to the Fingers. Each family was given the habitat pod to live in, and each valley received a share of the plant seeds and animal embryos that had been brought from Mars. Then the families in each Finger divided the land fairly among themselves and began to farm."

"And after the pods had all detached, the rest of the ship landed and was turned into a city," prompted nine-year-old Henrik. This was the part of the story that he liked best. It involved tools that could cut and shape metal, and large machines that generated electrical energy. Unlike his older brother Russell, Henrik had a fascination for things mechanical. Everyone in the Nyquist clan agreed that he would probably end up running one of the valley's fabricating sheds when he came of choosing age.

Laurel sensed a presence behind her and turned to see her father standing in the doorway. Peter Nyquist had years earlier turned over the berry fields and orchards to his three oldest sons, but he still dressed in coarse-woven shirts and bib overalls for working in the shed.

"Have you all completed your morning lessons?" he asked the children.

"Yes, Oppa," they chorused.

"Then you'd best wrap up this story," he advised, and under his thatch of gold and silver hair his dark blue eyes were smiling. "Nana says lunch will be on the table in just a couple of blinks."

"The end," piped up six-year-old Anders, already on his feet and ready to lead the charge to the wash-up room.

Laurel sighed melodramatically. "All right, go," she told them, and the future of farming in Central Valley promptly stampeded out the door.

"Stephen has offered to take them to the commons to play baseball after lunch," said Peter.

"No afternoon lessons? That will make Teddy and Sophia very happy," Laurel remarked. "And it will give Stephen a fresh-air break as well. He's been looking rather pale lately."

Only a year older than Laurel, Stephen was a climber, irresistibly drawn to heights and gifted with strength and nimbleness and instinctive sure-footedness. He had already explored every peak that put toes on Nyquist land. Stephen's farm job was harvesting the topmost branches of their apple trees. However, the Grannies and Goldens had all been picked, and until the Cortlands ripened, someone with Stephen's special talent would need something else to do. So, Peter had put his youngest son to work on a special project in the fabricating shed. He'd been at it for a while now.

"I crafted something for you," said Peter, placing a parcel in Laurel's lap. "It's a thank you for your help over the last few weeks."

Her hands swiftly unfolded the cloth wrapping, revealing a dark brown leather-bound book. With a soft gasp, she lifted it up and carefully turned it over. "Papa, it's beautiful! But where did you—?"

"I traded for some paper and cardboard at the market in the city. The leather and glue were already in the shed."

Laurel opened the book and leafed through the pages. They were blank. She turned quizzical eyes to her father's face.

It wore a gentle, faraway expression, as though looking at her sent his thoughts somewhere else. "You're so good at remembering, duckling," he told her. "One look at a page and you can recite every word, perfectly and without hesitation. A diagram flashes across the computer screen and you can reproduce it in every detail. I thought you might want to record some words and pictures for other people to remember for a change. When you think of something to write, there's a sack of pencils for you in the top right drawer of my desk."

❧

"Are you sure this is a good idea, Peter? Think about what the three of you are planning to do at this meeting."

"We're doing what's best for the community."

"But what if the others figure it out and disagree? What if they realize what *she* is?" The anxiety in her mother's voice carried out onto the front porch where Laurel sat, eyes closed, enjoying the tender touch of Manua's sunlight on her skin as she remembered *The Hobbit*. Mentally bookmarking the page, she blinked and looked around. It was mid-afternoon. Her brothers and sisters-in-law and their young'uns were all away, either working the berry fields or crafting trade goods in one of the fabricating sheds. The children were with Stephen on the commons. Her parents had probably forgotten she was there. For a moment she debated making her presence known. Then her curiosity got the better of her. Staying very still, her cheeks growing warm even as a cool breeze stirred the air, Laurel listened.

"They've no reason to realize it unless someone tells them. The girl is a reacher, Emma. That's the gift we've always advertised, a useful one for farm folk. And she won't be out of place there, if that's your concern. Other elders have brought young'uns to these meetings, so her accompanying me shouldn't raise any suspicions. Besides, Laurel will be of choosing age soon, and I'm sure she's feeling urges. How is she to choose well without knowing what her choices are? And how is anyone to choose *her* if they don't even know who she is?"

"It's not who she is that I worry about, it's who her family will be when the choosing is done, and how they'll react when they learn the truth about her. And if word should get back to the city—! Peter, she's a *rememberer*." This last word was pronounced in a furtive whisper.

"I know, but that doesn't change the facts." A stern edge had crept into her father's voice. "Laurel is fifteen years old now, almost an adult. When she was younger your fears were justified, so I let you keep her sheltered; but you can't isolate her from the community anymore. If she's truly to belong in this valley, to live the rest of her life in the Fingers, then there are things she needs to know and places she needs to become familiar with, beginning with the Sorensen house this afternoon. It's time she met the other Central Valley families, and past time they met her."

"But—!"

"Emma, enough! There will be no further discussion of this. I'm taking her to conclave with me."

Silence. Laurel could visualize her mother's mouth snapping shut and her lips pursing to hold back an angry remark she didn't dare speak aloud. After all, there was a *rememberer* in the family.

A moment later, Peter stepped out onto the porch. If he noticed Laurel's flushed complexion and downcast gaze he didn't comment on it. "We leave in half an hour," he told her. "You should dress up for this. Why don't you put on one of those frilly tops Margriet made for you? I like the green one—it matches your eyes."

Laurel nodded, not trusting her voice, as a stew of emotions bubbled inside her.

❧

Senior members of the ten Central Valley families assembled four times per year, meeting face-to-face to raise issues and discuss matters that were nobody else's business. Such things were never mentioned electronically. It was common knowledge that the high foreheads in the city had eyes and ears on all wireless infonet activity, making private messaging a sad contradiction of terms.

To link all the homesteads, a main road of sorts had been cleared along the wooded foothills of the western range, just wide enough to accommodate a draft animal pulling a wagon. Going nonstop from the tip end of Central Valley to the Palm, the journey took roughly three hours by wagon and just twenty minutes by car.

Each original habitat pod had come equipped with one of the small battery-powered vehicles. They looked like brightly-painted boxes on wheels and had apparently been a common sight in the Fingers and Palm when the colony was young. Electricity had been plentiful then. Now, energy was rationed, and car travel was reserved for special occasions. Farm folk relied primarily on horses to get them and their goods from one place to another, including on conclave days.

The Sorensen homestead sat roughly halfway down the Finger, so it made sense that the quarterly meetings should be held there. The Nyquists at the Palm end and the McQueens, closest to the tip, were responsible for stopping to pick up passengers at the farms along their way.

Greta Sorensen and her daughters-in-law made it a point of honour to have a generous meal waiting for the travellers when they arrived. By tacit agreement, each family therefore contributed something to help restock the depleted Sorensen larder. When Peter's wagon arrived, it was carrying two Nyquists and a bushel of Golden apples, two Barretts and a large sack of potatoes, one Leclerc and a thick, metre-long spiced sausage, two Zimmermans and three huge heads of red cabbage, and one Chen and a dozen and a half jumbo-sized chicken eggs. About five minutes later the McQueen wagon joined them in the yard, equally laden, and a moment after that, their hostess was rushing out of the house toward them.

Greta Sorensen was a plump, bustling woman with an exuberant laugh and a mass of curly orange hair barely restrained by the black and gold kerchief knotted at the nape of her neck. Laurel stared in fascination, for Greta was a hugger. Each of her guests was warmly greeted by name and then enveloped in an enthusiastic embrace before being shooed into the house to wash up for dinner. Mama Nyquist had never behaved like this. When it was Laurel's turn to be welcomed, Greta's effusive delight at meeting her left the girl groping for words.

Peter stepped up beside his daughter and quietly put his arm around her shoulder to escort her inside. "Not a word about that secondary talent of yours, now," he whispered into her ear. "Just keep your eyes and ears open, enjoy yourself if you can, and if you have any questions, ask me later and I promise I'll answer them."

Like every other dwelling in the Fingers, the Sorensen home had begun as an extendable titanium steel pod, containing fully-equipped kitchen and hygiene facilities and five spartanly furnished sleeping chambers. A hundred years and numerous Sorensens later, the pod had been stretched to its full capacity and had sprouted wings besides. Each boxy addition was made of wood and stone and had its own front door, giving grown children with offspring of their own a private living space within the family compound. The Nyquist homestead was similarly organized, with a spacious common kitchen and dining area.

Unlike Emma Nyquist, however, who took pride in the polished shine of her ceilings and accent walls, Greta Sorensen had apparently done her best to conceal every bit of metal inside the pod. Overhead, she'd done it with heavy cream-coloured fabric stretched over a series of wooden frames. In the living room, hooked and braided area rugs covered the floor in shades of green, burnt orange and soft gold. The colours seemed to flow up the walls as well, coming to rest in an array of painted pictures and woven hangings.

Laurel recognized one of the tapestries as her mother's work, and instantly her spirits rose. No matter how strange this place might feel, there was something familiar here, something Nyquist that the family who lived here had liked enough to want to own and display.

An intoxicating blend of aromas drew Laurel's attention and then her steps to the dining room, where the Central Valley family elders were filing in and taking their places. A sumptuous meal had been laid out down the middle of a long, bench-lined trestle table. Large oval platters were heaped high with slices of freshly cut tomato, zucchini, and green and yellow pepper. Serving dishes overflowed with steamed carrots and squash and chunks of baked sweet potato, all drizzled with honey. Square trays held a variety of hard and soft cheeses and thick slabs of roast beef. And ornately carved wooden bowls contained cloth-napkin-wrapped bundles of rolls, still warm from the oven and fragrant with rosemary. A tall glass of apple cider marked each place setting, and a block of butter sat at each end of the table, along with shakers of sea salt and jars of shredded herbs.

Laurel took a seat beside her father and found herself

looking across the table at a boy about her age, whose mop of thick dark hair kept falling down over his eyes. When he wasn't finger-combing it off his forehead and seeming to inhale every edible thing around him, he was smiling at her in a way that made her want to smile back. Maybe it was the mischief that glinted in his eyes, reminding her a little of Teddy.

"So, Nyquist, this is your youngest?" said the man sitting opposite her father. She recalled that someone had earlier addressed him as Reilly.

"Laurel is fifteen," Peter replied. "She's a reacher."

"What's her reach?" asked another man, pausing between mouthfuls of meat sandwich.

"We aren't sure what her limit is. But she can pick from the top of the tallest tree in our orchard, and I've seen her move things from a lot farther away than that on the ground."

"Impressive," said Reilly. Then he placed a proprietary hand on the shoulder of the boy who'd been flirting with Laurel and announced to the table, "This is Evan, my grandson, sixteen next month. He's a sender and receiver."

Peter was instantly attentive. "A telepath? What's his range?"

"He tells me he can connect with the other young'uns we heard about, that girl in Pointer Valley and the twins in Baby Finger. There's apparently also a boy at the tip of the Thumb with the same talent, sounds like he might be eight or nine years old. Shy about giving his name, that one is, and frightened that the voices in his head mean he's going crazy, but Evan's working the Reilly charm on him. He's a strong sender, is our Evan. I'll bet he can transmit from one end of the Hand to the other."

Twisting out of his grandfather's grip, Evan leaned across the table, prompting Laurel to lean in as well. "Don't you love it when they talk about you as though you were something they'd assembled in the fabricating shed?" he asked her with an impish grin.

He was being ironic, and a little disrespectful. Her first impulse was to tell him so, but strange things were happening to her insides, and she couldn't find her words. All she could do was grin back at him. It was, she decided, a disconcerting feeling, but not an unpleasant one. Meanwhile, her father sat watching her with laughter in his eyes as chuckles rippled up and down the table.

As platters and serving dishes emptied, the meat, cheese, and vegetables were replaced by broad, shallow bowls of fresh-picked fruit from the Sorensens' own orchards and vineyard—plump red grapes, purple plums, and succulent ripe peaches. Laurel bit into a peach and closed her eyes as its perfect sweetness exploded inside her mouth. This would be a memory worth revisiting.

At last the table was cleared. Greta took a seat beside her husband, and Nils Sorensen called the meeting to order.

"Last time, our main topic was energy," Sorensen reminded them. "Our last shipment of batteries from the Consortium was only sixty percent charged, and we were going to investigate alternative power sources."

"My sons have put some turbines together," said a leathery-looking man with voice to match. Laurel recognized him as Todd McQueen, the driver of the second wagon. "Once we've finished copying the specs from the city library, they're going to set up a hydroelectric plant to harness the waves at the base of the bluffs beside our property. Theoretically, it should generate enough to supply five families, maybe a couple more if we're all mindful of our energy consumption. I just wish the powers-that-be would either speed up the system or give each family databank access for longer than twenty minutes a day. Some days it takes us that long just to log in and locate the information that we need." There was muttered agreement all around the table.

"We've been looking into solar energy capture," Peter announced. "That's one of the systems being used in the city."

"Of course it is," muttered someone to Laurel's right.

Peter ignored the jibe. "I found a dealer there who would sell me used parts at a fraction of the market price, along with some specs he'd managed to download from the net. Long story short, we've built three large panels that we believe will provide basic needs for one farm each, once they're installed on our rooftops and integrated into our distribution boards."

"I hate to be a parade-pooper," said Rachel Zimmerman, the smugness in her voice and on her face saying quite the opposite, "but how are the powers-that-be, as Todd calls them, going to react when they find out about this alternative energy? Isn't interdependence one of the cornerstones of the colony? The city folk depend on our food and we depend on their technology, isn't that the way it works?"

Sorensen snapped to attention in his chair. "It works that way until it doesn't work," he growled. "Then we figure out a way that does."

"Besides," added Malcolm Chen mildly, "as long as we stay offline and synchronize our efforts, nobody outside the valley needs to know about this. Once we're able to switch over completely to other energy sources, we can keep using the batteries to run our cars."

"So what do you plan to do the next time we're overrun by that army of measurers from the Consortium?" she persisted. "Dismantle our secret technology and conceal it in one of the fabricating sheds until they decide to leave?"

Laurel heard her father fill his lungs and felt his large hand briefly squeeze hers under the table. "I'm sorry to disappoint you, Rachel, but they won't be coming back," he said.

For a single stunned moment no one spoke. Laurel had just enough time to register the dismay on Rachel Zimmerman's face and the wicked twinkle in Evan Reilly's eyes before Nils Sorensen's voice broke the silence. "And you know this how, exactly?" Already sitting stiff and erect, Sorensen lifted his chin and gazed narrowly down the table, directly at Peter Nyquist.

He shrugged and replied, "The last time I was at the city market, one of the scientists approached me. The long-term study they were conducting in the Fingers has apparently been concluded, and they're putting together an official report for the Consortium. But before they present their findings, this particular scientist wants the farmers to have a preview. I guess he's feeling guilty about all the trouble they've put us through."

Chen shook his head sadly. "How ignorant do they think we are?" Encouraged by an answering chorus of grumbling voices to either side of him, he continued, "For twenty years they've been descending on us without warning, commandeering our supplies without so much as a thank you. They've dragged their gear all over our land, trampled our crops, and treated our kin and our animals like laboratory rats. And they think that giving us a sneak peek at a report is going to smooth everything over?"

Peter said nothing, just shrugged again.

"You tell that *expert* from the city that we already know what's in his report," declared Reilly, his voice fairly dripping contempt, "because we're scientists too. We test soil and water samples at the start of each growing season, and we keep and compare statistics, and we *know* how things have been changing. We know that our sheep started out white and our cattle were originally brown and black and now it's the other way around. We know that our crops are growing larger and ripening faster than they were even five years ago. And we're aware of the special talents that have been emerging in our young'uns, different from one generation to the next.

"The city folk are mutating too. I've seen it on market days. So have you. Their noses are getting flatter and their foreheads are getting higher, and I swear, some of the adults are no taller than one of Evan's younger sisters."

Laurel glanced around and saw a double row of heads bobbing in solemn confirmation.

"There's been no measurable change in the air or the water or the soil, but anything or anyone that eats food grown in the Fingers has been affected," Reilly summed up. "Even Chen's bees, which have more than doubled in size during my lifetime. There, Nyquist, that's your report."

"So, you have no desire to attend a meeting with this scientist? No curiosity at all about what he wants to tell us?" said Peter, locking eyes with the man sitting across the table from him.

The Reilly jaw, already prominent, jutted belligerently forward. "None. I've had it up to *here* with those people." And he chopped the edge of one burly hand to his forehead to show exactly where *here* was.

"Is there anyone besides me at this conclave who would care to meet with the measurer to hear the results of the study?" Peter wondered loudly, directing his gaze at each face in turn around the table. A swell of muttering arose, growing louder by the second as each of them in turn looked somewhere else.

Then Chen laughed, silencing the chatter and drawing everyone's attention to his own disdainful expression as he faced Peter and said, "You want to waste your time, Nyquist?

Be our guest. The rest of us have more important things to attend to."

"That's right!" Reilly seconded, pounding the table with his fist. The conviction in his voice blew through the room like a powerful wind, scouring it of any lingering uncertainty.

"If you must satisfy your curiosity, Nyquist, then go and meet with this person," said Nils Sorensen. "But don't expect the rest of us to tag along."

"He always did have one foot in the city," murmured the snide voice again, somewhere to Laurel's right.

Peter's shoulders drooped a little. "Fine," he sighed. "I'll let you know if I learn anything new."

There was dejection in his voice, but something else entirely in his eyes. *Of course!* thought Laurel abruptly. This was what her father and the other two had been plotting to do all along. This was why her mother had been so anxious about it. The entire scene at Sorensen's table had been staged for the purpose of getting the Central Valley elders to send Peter Nyquist, alone, to the meeting in the city. Why, they had basically given him permission to keep secrets from them! (Actually, it was *more* secrets, she amended a moment later. The first was that he'd brought a rememberer with him to the conclave.) Malcolm Chen had to be one of his accomplices. Who was the other one? Reilly? Sorensen? If only she'd been able to identify the source of those heckling comments at the table!

❧

Manua's two small moons cast a pale glow over the valley, sketching the outlines of the jagged eastern peaks and lending a ghostly aura to the foliage in the Nyquists' orchard as Maisie, their white Percheron mare, picked her way along the rutted path home. Once the last of their passengers had disembarked from the wagon, Laurel moved up front to sit beside her father. The apple-scented air was warm and still, the silence disturbed only by the faint creaking of wheels and the rhythmic slapping of hooves on packed dirt. Laurel's searching gaze could just make out the yellow dot of light that marked the Nyquists' living room window, like a star sitting low on the horizon.

"You made quite an impression on young Evan Reilly," Peter remarked. "And Trent Barrett couldn't keep his eyes off you all evening. We heard the two of you laughing back there. Do you mind my asking what you talked about?"

"We talked about a lot of things," she replied primly, adding after a pause, "I didn't mention anything about being a rememberer, if that's what you're worried about." Another pause, then, "You said if I had any questions...?"

"Ask away."

"I overheard you tell Mama earlier that you were doing what was best for the community. How was playing that trick on the elders the best thing for the community?"

Startled, he fumbled the reins, nearly dropping them.

"Okay," he said, nodding and shaking his head at the same time. "Not the question I was expecting, but it's a good one nonetheless. You know that our colony is founded on four important principles: interdependence, equality, trust and priority. By far the most important one is trust. When that scientist came to find me at the market, he was very nervous. Their work in the Fingers was only part of the study. There was a bigger picture, including data from the Palm and the Wrist and the city. He felt the farming communities had a right to know all of it, but his superiors disagreed, even threatened to punish him if he spoke out of turn. So, he asked me to meet with him privately next market day and hear what he had to say, and I agreed.

"Now I had a problem. This is a very important meeting. If I take it without the knowledge of the other elders, I'm sneaking around behind their backs. Not a very trustworthy thing to do. And if the conclave understands how important it is and decides to ignore my advice and attend as a group, the scientist's superiors will probably find out about the meeting. Then they will either cancel it or switch out our scientist with someone more willing to toe their line."

"So, deceiving the elders tonight was the only way to ensure that they could learn the whole truth later on?"

"I'm afraid so. Sometimes round and about is the best path to a destination."

"You said he came to find you. Why you?"

"He knew he could trust me. I chose his sister."

"Oh." And then, as comprehension dawned, "Oh!"

"Don't sound so surprised," he chided her. "You've known for some time that your mother was born in the city."

Yes, she'd known. She'd just never thought of Emma Nyquist as having a family there. Not in the same way as sisters-in-law Margriet and Sara and Alexis did, whose birth families lived in the Finger valleys and got to visit back and forth on market days and on Choosing Day.

So, Laurel had an uncle who was a scientist in the city. Just thinking the words was enough to quicken her pulse. Maybe there were other aunts and uncles as well, and cousins her own age. Maybe if she just gave a little push to this door that had opened up a crack for her, she would find an entire treeful of relatives waiting to be discovered on the other side.

"Papa, will you take me to the city with you next market day?"

"Don't see how I have a choice," he said. "I'll need a rememberer at this meeting."

Not the answer she was expecting, but a good enough one nonetheless, she decided.

As Maisie continued her clip-clopping and the yellow dot of light grew steadily larger, Laurel mulled over the events of that evening. She remembered in painful detail every blushing, awkward silence, every stumbling, stammering word that had fallen out of her mouth each time Evan or Trent had looked at her. She recalled as well the way her heart had twisted in her chest when she saw how proud Mr. Reilly was of Evan's telepathic ability, and how diffident her father was about her own mental gift of reaching. The useful one for farm folk, he'd called it, and *not a word about that secondary talent of yours*.

The question had formed in her thoughts earlier that day, as she sat on the porch listening to her parents argue. There was probably no good time to ask it, but she'd been carrying it around for hours, and it seemed to grow heavier each time she remembered it. Now, as she and her father rolled through the night, the silence between them feeling like a third person on the front seat, the weight on her mind became unbearable.

"Papa," she blurted, "why is Mama ashamed of me?"

This time he stopped the wagon and turned to face her. His eyes were in shadow. Laurel felt rather than saw him staring at her in shock.

"Wherever did you get an idea like that?" he demanded.

"Did one of the elders say something to you?"

Laurel shook her head. "Mama said it. She's afraid of what other people will think if they find out that I'm a rememberer."

They were all alone between the orchard and the woods, a good kilometre away from any living soul except for their horse. Still, Peter Nyquist leaned close and lowered his voice, speaking as though each word was painful to pronounce. "Listen to me, duckling. Your mother has never been ashamed of you and never will be. But she is afraid. Not of what others will think, but of what they might say out loud, and of who might overhear them. Your ability to remember is a precious gift. Unfortunately, there are people in the city—people with power, with influence over others—who like to collect precious things. When your mother and I left the city and came back here to say our vows, those people were collecting rememberers. From what I hear and overhear, they still are. You're not a prize, duckling, you're a person. But if anyone in the Consortium ever found out about your talent…!"

He left the rest to her imagination. It worked. An icy shudder of fear scrambled down Laurel's back. And yet… there had been a shiver of something else underneath it.

She turned to face frontward again, carefully composing her features. The moonlight was soft and bled easily into shadow, obscuring the details of her expression. Still, her father knew her better than anyone else in the world, well enough to recognize her mood from as little as the tilt of her chin or the line of her cheek. "So you're saying that the city is a dangerous place for me."

"Or anyone like you, yes."

"But you're still going to take me to your meeting there next market day?"

"I'm sorry, duckling. I wish things were different, but like I said, I don't have much choice."

Laurel fell silent, unwilling to risk any further conversation. In a way, her father had been right about her earlier. She *had* been experiencing urges, just not the kind he'd been talking about. If Peter Nyquist even suspected how excited she was becoming about going on this perilous adventure, he might decide he had another choice after all.

~

"To the city? Peter, are you out of your mind?"

Laurel lay on top of her bedcover, fingering the soft woollen fabric and watching the shadows cast by her flickering lamp as they danced across the walls and ceiling of her sleeping chamber. Her parents were arguing about her again. Generally she just gritted her teeth and did her best to shut the angry voices out of her mind, hoping that Peter and Emma would somehow find a middle ground. Tonight was different, though. Tonight Laurel didn't want her father to settle for a compromise. She wanted him to win.

Laurel closed her eyes and remembered the first time she'd ever heard her parents fight. She had just turned nine years old, and everything about her had begun changing, becoming unpredictable, painful, and disquieting. Hearing her mother and father yell at each other on her account had been terrifying—especially the way Emma's voice went all shrill and hiccupy just before she burst into tears. For a long while, that recollection had been one of Laurel's waking nightmares, until she finally learned how to stop the replaying of a memory between *that it happened* and *how it felt*.

She had clear and vivid memories of that entire chaotic year, and of every day and every year since. The first shadow hand had appeared a week before her birthday, like an enemy leaping out of hiding to create havoc. (After that, it had emerged at random intervals for nearly an entire growing season, ambushing people around her, overturning furniture, and knocking things off shelves while she worked at learning to control it.)

Then had come the stomach-stabbing moment when she had opened her eyes after remembering a chapter of *Pride and Prejudice* for her mother, and had seen Emma backing away from her with an expression on her face that Laurel wished she could forget. That same night, the first of many such nights to follow, she had had the dream.

It attacked her sleep in fragments at first, dim and disjointed. She was being chased through a maze of narrow metal passageways, throwing herself around corners and bumping into the stair-ladders that hung down at intervals. A harsh white light glared off the walls, hurting her eyes. She didn't know who was chasing her, only that something horrific and agonizing would happen if she was caught. So she ran.

Every few nights this frantic race went on, lasting a little longer each time, with her pursuers' footsteps growing louder behind her and the sound of their heavy breathing fuelling her fear. Every few nights for a solid year, Laurel hurled herself awake, drenched with perspiration and gasping with panic. And then, one morning, she counted up the days and realized it had been a full week since the last time she'd had the dream. Another week went by, and then another, without a nightmare. It was gone... for a while.

On her fifteenth birthday it returned, much worse than before. The nameless, faceless pursuers had caught up to her, and she was launched into a second recurring ordeal. In this one she was motionless, strapped to a chair and unable to speak or move. Like the first dream, this one began as a barrage of disconnected images, driven by searing gusts of emotion. Each time it repeated, the images grew a little sharper, the rage and despair more wrenching. She was wearing a metal helmet that burned her skin, and her brain felt as though it was about to explode.

The dream always ended with a door crashing open and the sound of angry voices, and then a blanket of darkness falling over her. An instant later she awoke, muscles taut, with both hands clenched into fists at her sides and a scream climbing up her throat. And something else followed her into wakefulness and held her in its steely grip—the utter, unquestionable certainty that something even worse would happen if anyone else ever found out about these dreams. Each time she even considered telling her parents about them, a sick feeling broke over her like a giant wave, tumbling her stomach and draining the strength from her limbs.

"How can you even *think* of involving her in this? How many secret weapons do you *need?*"

Emma's furious words leaped through the metal wall, startling Laurel back to the present. She sighed and got out of bed. Clearly, the argument was far from over. There was no point in trying to sleep until it was done.

The leather-bound journal Peter had made for her was sitting in the middle of her desk. Thoughtfully, Laurel picked it up and turned it over in her hands, caressing its smooth spine with her fingertips. Her father had suggested that she use it for recording things for other people to remember. He'd been talking about stories. He knew how much she loved to read and tell them. What if the images and feelings in her dreams belonged to a story her brain was building? What if, by the simple act of writing them down, of building her story on paper instead, she could make the terrible dreams stop?

"Emma, she *will* be safe, I promise!"

Laurel opened the book to the first blank page and picked up a pencil, and she began to write:

The hallway is long and narrow and made of shiny metal, and it curves away into darkness. There is a hard white glare from the square lights overhead. It bounces off the walls and directly into my eyes as I run…

Chapter Two

"Why do you close your eyes when you tell us a story?" asked Sophia.

Laurel gave her niece a hug. The five-year-old had gotten her hands on a pair of scissors first thing that morning and had decided to change her hairstyle by snipping off one of her braids. After a solid hour of damage control in front of Nana's mirror, with a shadow hand holding the child in place as hair was trimmed and evened, Sophia was looking like one of the Gillespies' sheep after a shearing. Fortunately, the other children had opted to comfort rather than tease her, and Nyquist hair grew quickly. Sophia's mother, Sara, had managed to remain calm and not go into premature labour when proudly presented with the amputated blond rope tied with a red bow, so it was all good, so far.

"Closing my eyes helps me to concentrate on the words, so that I get them right."

"Maybe Teddy should close his eyes too, to help him listen better," sniped Russell, at ten years of age Markus and Alexis's oldest child. He was having a hard time. It was farmers' market day on the commons, and Russ was clearly unhappy about being left behind at Oppa and Nana's house with the little kids. He didn't *care* how many exciting stories Aunt Laurel would tell, or how many treats had been promised for lunch.

Laurel knew exactly how he felt. The farmers' market was a monthly gathering of all the families in the Fingers. Here, specialty produce and crafted goods could be traded, news and advice could be shared, and young'uns approaching their eighteenth birthday could socialize in preparation for Choosing Day.

She had never minded missing a market day before. Her brothers and sisters-in-law appreciated knowing that their youngest children were in safe and loving hands, and they always brought back gifts for her from the commons. But this month was different. Laurel had been to conclave, had had a glimpse of the world beyond the Nyquist orchards, and she wanted to see more. Specifically, she'd been hoping to see Evan Reilly and Trent Barrett again, and any other young'uns her age who might be there.

Sara had tried to help. She was heavy with her and Axel's fourth child and had planned to spend the day at home anyway, so she offered to take over the caregiving chores. Unfortunately, Mama Nyquist wouldn't hear of it. Emma was physically small, but she cast a large shadow. When her mind was this firmly made up, nobody dared to contradict her, not even Papa. Laurel's beseeching look at her father had gotten her only a warning shake of his head.

"Hey, story lady! You have a visitor."

Laurel spun around in her seat. Her brother Stephen was leaning into the living room with a big goofy grin on his face.

"A visitor?" she echoed, puzzled.

"Your prince has come to carry you away. Go on," he urged. "Sara and I can manage the little folk for a while."

A climber young'un and a breadmaker nearing the end of her third trimester, managing eight children including a jumper, a runner, and who knew what else waiting to emerge, and not a shadow hand between them?

Laurel opened her mouth to object, but before she could get a word out, Stephen had pulled her to her feet and was prodding her in the direction of the porch. In the front doorway, she halted, staring in disbelief.

There was a car sitting in the yard, and it wasn't the blue one that her father liked to tinker with. This one was a bright yellow four-seater with the convertible top folded down. It looked freshly cleaned and polished, not unlike the boy who stood beside it, wearing a grin even wider than her brother's.

"Evan?" she called to him from the porch.

"Care to go for a spin, Milady?" he said, making a sweeping bow as he opened the passenger-side door for her.

Laurel hesitated for a moment. She shouldn't do this. The children were her responsibility. Her mother had given her specific instructions. And hadn't her father stressed to her just a couple of days earlier how important it was to be trustworthy?

Then her brother's guitar started up behind her, and she heard the children giggling and clapping in time as he sang. A glance over her left shoulder revealed Sara, pausing for a smiling glance and a wave goodbye in the midst of making sandwiches. They both wanted her to go, to have fun. *They can manage for an hour or two,* thought Laurel.

With that, she skipped off the porch and across the yard and plopped herself into the front passenger seat of the Reilly electrocar, feeling light-headed with a mixture of relief and excitement. A beautiful sunny day had just opened up for her, rife with interesting possibilities. She was *so* ready to explore them!

"Whose car is this?" she asked Evan as he slid in beside her. He was fairly exuding mischief. If they were going to be in trouble for this, she wanted to know ahead of time.

"It's my da's. Don't worry, he doesn't mind me driving it. It's the horses he doesn't trust me with."

"You're a telepath. Maybe he's afraid you'll put ideas into their heads," she said, and he laughed and pressed the starter. A light flashed green beside the steering column. "How long have you been driving?" she asked him, as needles sprang to attention on a row of dials and gauges.

"Since ages ago," he replied distractedly, frowning at one indicator that still read zero. He finger-flicked the little window over the sluggish needle until it bounced vertical as well. "One of the first things my grandda taught me about this car…"

"…was how to wake up a needle?"

He turned and gave her a sly wink. "…was how handy it is for picking up girls."

Evan set the speed at eighty klicks, remarked, "You may want to hold onto something," and released the brake.

It was nothing like riding in a wagon. Laurel had experienced breezes before, but never a wind strong enough to push her back in her seat and make her own hair smack her in the face. Belatedly, she managed to capture all the long dark tresses and hold them at the nape of her neck as the little car raced up the road toward the Palm.

Evan was taking her to the farmers' market. With that realization came a roiling sensation in the pit of her stomach. Laurel willed it to stop, reminding herself sternly that this was what she needed. She would be visiting the city with her father in less than a week's time, and he'd warned her that the day might be unpleasant. The grand plaza where all the vendors' booths were set up would be crammed with people, all shouting at the tops of their lungs to be heard over the ambient noise of the crowd.

So far, her only experience with large groups of adults had been the one evening at the Sorensens' place. Each time she tried to reimagine the scene with thirty or forty strangers present instead of eighteen, her mind's eye went blank. Clearly, she couldn't just envision it—she had to be there, had to smell and feel and hear it. And if all those other people could regularly survive an entire day of milling around, packed together like sheep in a holding pen, then so could she. She was a Nyquist. Nyquists were strong, and she was not defenceless. If need be, shadow hands could push away as well as grasp and pull. She could do this.

Laurel pinned a brave expression on her face, tightened her grip on the thick skein of hair, and let the little yellow car carry her toward the huge open area on the north side of the Palm that the farm folk referred to as the commons.

The muffled roar of a sea of voices broke over them long before the farmers' market actually came in sight. Laurel had heard this sound before. Closing her eyes, she recalled a day trip with her father and Stephen to the Silver Cliffs at the Palm end of the Thumb.

She had just turned ten. A strong wind had been blowing in off the sea that day. The air felt cool and moist against her skin and left the taste of salt on her lips. The three Nyquists stood holding hands at the edge of the precipice, watching in awe as tall, white-capped waves dashed themselves against the big grey and purple rocks tumbled together down below. Over and over again, rearing up and smashing down, like the shadow hands of the sea trying to pull the stones back into the water and hissing with frustration at each failed attempt.

"Wake up, Milady. We're nearly there."

Laurel's eyes snapped open. At first, all she saw was the wagons, rising before her like a broad wall of wheels and weathered grey wood. Then, as Evan veered right, skirting the margins of the market grounds, she noticed the spacious paddock off to the east where the draft horses had been put out to graze for the day. Percherons and Clydesdales were large, powerful animals. Farm folk knew better than to force them close together in small enclosures.

Slowing at the last possible moment, Evan slipped the car between two wagons brimming with produce, and stopped. He waved to the hatless, stern-faced man who stood leaning against one of the wagons, munching on a Granny apple.

The man bobbed his head in acknowledgement. "My da," Evan explained, and Laurel couldn't help wondering whether he hadn't been exaggerating just a little about having permission to borrow the car.

As they walked past the wagon bed, she glanced over its side, noticing boxes of apples and melons, bushels of root and vine vegetables, and coarse-woven bags of grain. It also held several small and medium-sized sealed metal canisters, and two large wheels of cheese, one a deep russet colour and the other a pale orange. The Reillys were primarily dairy farmers, she recalled. They'd have brought the milk and cheese to trade. And since Laurel's father was the only grower of Granny apples in the Fingers, Mr. Reilly had clearly spoken with Peter Nyquist that day. Did her father know about Evan's plan to "liberate" her? Was that why he'd silently warned her not to protest her mother's decision that morning?

Sometimes round and about is the best path to a destination, said his remembered voice inside her head.

"This must be Laurel," said the man, wiping his right palm on his pants leg before reaching out to shake her hand. He wore a smile now, but there was a wariness about him as he looked her up and down. He was sizing her up. As a potential daughter-in-law? It was a little early for that. Wasn't it? "A pleasure to meet you, Ms. Nyquist. Evan holds you in the highest regard. Enjoy your day at the market." And with that, he strolled around the corner of the wagon and was gone, swallowed up by the restless sea of farm folk.

Evan nudged her gently with his elbow. "Twenty words in a row! He likes you."

"That wasn't the impression *I* got," she told him, eyeing the spot where Reilly senior had disappeared.

"That's just his way. Da doesn't talk much, and when he does it comes out sounding rehearsed and insincere. But he does mean what he says."

"Is he a telepath too?"

Evan shook his head. "What he is, is insanely intelligent. A genius with numbers, but uncomfortable around people. According to Grandda, when he was younger and guests came to visit, he would either turn into a stammering idiot or plant

himself in a corner of the room and pretend to be a piece of
furniture. Grandda was afraid his only son would never be
chosen by any of the girls in the Fingers, so he sent away to
the city for a special teacher who could help the boy develop
social skills. Imagine his surprise when a young girl arrived,
not much older than her student. And his chagrin when they
fell in love and ended up choosing each other as mates."

So Evan's mother was from the city too? Laurel might have
been sheltered growing up, but she was painfully aware of the
bias against city folk in the Fingers. Emma Nyquist had had to
work hard to earn her place as a Central Valley farmer's mate,
if only to ensure that her sons would have choosing
opportunities when they came of age. That was how a family
farm stayed in the family. Evan's father was an only son. So
was Evan, so far. His and Laurel's grandfathers would
certainly have commiserated about this.

"Come on," urged Evan, breaking into her thoughts. "There
are some friends I want you to meet on the other side of the
market."

He was pointing directly into the middle of the throng. Peter
Nyquist had pointed like that, extending his hand palm up
toward the sea when he told her and Stephen that there were
probably other land masses on Manua. Laurel felt as though
once again she was standing at the edge of a cliff, resisting the
treacherous tug of gravity as she stared thirty metres straight
down at a foaming stew of rocks and surging water.

She licked her lips and tasted salt.

I can do this.

Laurel moved forward, one step, two steps, then stopped,
suddenly finding it difficult to breathe. She wasn't at the top of
the cliff anymore. She was standing at the bottom, being
battered by the waves. There had to be two hundred people
here, shopping from the wagons on the perimeter of the
market or browsing the crafted goods displayed on parallel
rows of tables that stretched across its centre. Drenching the
air with an untuned symphony of voices.

The tables and wagon beds were protected from the sun by
cheerful red, orange, or green cloth canopies. There was also a
designated eating area, she knew, furnished with benches, but
at the moment all she could see was the crowd. Most of those
bodies were larger than her own, and they were in motion,

pushing and jostling and squeezing one another. Small children slalomed through the forest of legs at top speed, shrieking with laughter as they caromed off anything that stood still for five seconds. Something soft collided with her thigh. Something else bumped her left shoulder, pushing her sideways. Shadow hands emerged, ready to shove. She shook her head and forced them back inside.

No! I chose to be here. I need *to be here. I can do this,* she scolded herself.

Then, as though reading her mind (As though? He was a telepath, for goodness' sake!) Evan was beside her, holding her hand. "I thought I'd lost you for a moment. It's all right— crowds make us nervous too. Let's take the long way around."

Us?

As she let him urge her back through the broken wall of wagons, Laurel realized who the friends must be that he wanted her to meet.

The two young'uns strode eleven wagon lengths eastward to the corner of the market, then turned north and travelled the same distance again, over the stubborn living mat of scrubby grass that covered most of the commons. By now the sun was high in a cloudless sky, the air growing steadily warmer. So was Laurel. She was wishing she'd worn a lighter blouse, or at least thought to bring a hat with her.

A gentle breeze sprang up from the west. It felt good against her skin, but it was wafting some tantalizing aromas across her path as well. Each one was a siren song inviting her back inside the wagon-wall to sample some fruit, some cured ham, some savoury bread and cheese. Her stomach was growling. Laurel chose to ignore it. She continued to follow Evan around the end of the market.

Horses raised their great heads and whickered curiously at them as they passed the paddock, setting course for the tall grey peaks that flanked the entrance to Baby Finger Valley. A final turn westward and all Laurel could see ahead of her was mountains, range upon serrated range of them, stretching the full width of the horizon. Standing guard over the five valleys like rows of white-caped soldiers. Protecting the farm folk from the interfering curiosity of the outside world, and providing a playground for climbers like Stephen Nyquist. In fact, she reflected, there were probably enough mountains on

Manua to keep her brother happily exploring for the rest of his life.

"There they are," said Evan at last. Laurel looked where he was pointing. Near a hillock at the Palm end of Ring Finger Valley, three young'uns stood waiting in the shade of a huge basswood tree: a girl and two boys, one of them wearing a wide-brimmed hat.

"Evan Reilly...?" the girl called out. Tall and slender, with brown skin, she was bundled up in a sweater as though afraid of catching a chill, and hugging herself as though she had already caught one.

He waved at her and quickened his pace, pulling Laurel along with him, until they were all standing together under the heart-shaped leaves of the tree. "That's me. And this is Laurel Nyquist, the telekinetic I was sending to you about. You're Pilar Morales, right?" He pronounced her first name *Pee*-lar.

"I am. Please, call me Pill."

"Are you sure you want that for a nickname? It isn't very flattering," Evan observed.

"I agree. But it's better than what my brother calls me."

For a moment, Evan and Pill stared silently into each other's eyes as a series of paired expressions flashed across their faces: curiosity and resignation, amusement and disapproval, sympathy and martyr-like patience. Glancing rapidly back and forth between them, Laurel watched with wonder as a telepathic conversation took place in front of her.

"How long have you been telekinetic?" demanded the boy under the hat, startling her. He was fair-haired and blunt-featured, already beginning to show the muscled limbs and broad shoulders of a farmer. He was gruff-mannered too, and probably closer than she and Evan were to choosing age.

Telekinetic. Evan had called her that too, when he was introducing her. "I'm not sure what you—"

His expression pinched tight. "Telekinetic," he repeated impatiently. Then, speaking slowly, as though to a small child, he explained, "You move things with your mind, right?"

Laurel drew herself up to her full height and looked him straight in the eyes. "I'm a reacher, if that's what you mean," she informed him stiffly. *And I have a shadow hand that's just itching to give you a good hard shove.*

"Go easy, Nick," the other boy advised, clapping a brotherly arm around his shoulder. "After all, we're called senders and receivers by those who don't know the technical term. Don't mind my evil twin, Laurel. I'm Daniel Gorodin and this is Nikolai."

"You're from Baby Finger Valley," she recalled. "I'm glad to meet you."

Nick eyed her skeptically. "You're the first telekinetic— sorry, the first *reacher* to emerge in the Fingers. So how about a little demonstration? Show us what you can do."

Annoyed, Laurel extended a shadow hand and knocked the hat off his head. He ran after it on long legs, recapturing it easily.

"That's it? The *wind* could have done that," he protested as he strode back to the group.

Oh, really? she thought darkly. Then perhaps the next thing she sent flying ought to be the hat's owner. Before thought could become action, however, she felt a gentle tug on her arm and heard Evan murmur in her ear, "Turn around, Laurel."

They had an audience.

A man was standing there watching them with tears running down his cheeks. From the amount of grey on his head, Laurel guessed he was about her father's age. But he evidently had no one to keep his hair neatly trimmed, or his clothing clean and mended. And from the way his coarse-woven shirt and trousers bagged on his bony frame, he probably hadn't been eating properly either. In a community of farmers, for anyone to go hungry was unthinkable. Even a man living alone should have been able to put ample food on his table.

He was trembling all over, and beneath the skeletal tautness and pallor of his skin Laurel could see a network of blue veins around his eyes and across his furrowed forehead. There was clearly something wrong with him. She knew she ought to be afraid. But there was something else about him, about the expression on his face, that was familiar. She closed her eyes for a moment and remembered... her mother's reflection in the mirror. Laurel had seen that same mixture of relief and anguish on Emma Nyquist's finely-drawn features.

The man had been weeping. Searching their faces with red-rimmed eyes, he slowly reached out both his arms to them. "I'm here," he said simply.

This was no farmer, but he wasn't from the city either. At the corner of her eye, Laurel saw Nick take a determined step forward. *You're not going to drive him away,* she decided, and reached out a shadow hand to stop him.

With a cry of surprise, the telepath doubled up and sat down heavily on the ground.

"I think you've just had your demonstration, brother," Daniel told him.

"Is he sick?" wondered Pill aloud.

Before anyone could answer, the man uttered a sob that sounded as though it had been ripped from somewhere deep within him. He dropped his arms to his sides. "All those years." He spoke with an old person's voice, soft and thin and a little raspy. Sick or not, Laurel realized, this man was not a threat, not to her, not to anyone. "All those years that I thought I was crazy. That *they* thought I was crazy. I couldn't get the voices out of my head, you see. And none of them were talking to me, not one. I had all those people inside my brain, and they were *ignoring* me! For *years!*"

He made a bony fist and struck himself in the chest. Laurel half-expected it to sound hollow, like a drumbeat. "And then I heard your voices, and you were talking to each other like you were the only ones around. Like you were special and I didn't even exist. I was so mad!"

"That was you," said Pill with growing excitement. "You think-yelled at us. You wanted us to know that you were there."

"And you answered me. No one had ever answered me before." The man dropped his gaze to the ground. His chin wobbling, he continued, "I was afraid. Bess always told me it was all right to talk to my toys as long as none of them talked back. I was afraid you weren't real. But I wanted you to be real. So when you said you were meeting up here, I came…"

"…all the way from the tip of the Thumb," Daniel murmured.

"What's your name?" asked Evan.

The man threw back his shoulders and looked the young'un straight in the face. No words were exchanged, but Laurel could tell from Evan's expression that they were communicating.

"Everyone," said Evan to the rest of the group, "meet

Timothy Klein, the first telepath to emerge in the Fingers, thirty-eight years ago."

Nick stepped forward again, darting a wary glance at Laurel. Gently, as though afraid of breaking it, he took the man's hand. "Mister Klein, it's an honour to meet you. Welcome to our—" Mouth open, he stopped, perplexed, then turned and demanded, "Hey, Reilly, what are we?"

Evan thought for a second. "We have the oldest telepath and the oldest telekinetic in the Fingers. I'd say we're a conclave of mental talents."

"I disagree," said Daniel, "but conclave will do until we come up with something better."

Grinning, Nick returned his attention to Timothy Klein. "Welcome to our conclave, then, for lack of a better word."

Weeping once more and too weak to stand, Klein finally sank to the ground. The young'uns knelt around him in alarm.

"He needs medical attention," declared Pill.

Laurel shook her head. "Look at him. He's skin and bones. First, he needs food."

"If he walked here all the way from the tip of the Thumb, then he's been on the road for days," Daniel pointed out. "He needs to rest."

A sudden familiar voice cut through their discussion like a knife. "Actually, what he needs more than anything is to be reunited with his family," said Peter Nyquist.

How long had he been standing there? Laurel wondered.

"With respect, sir, it doesn't look as if he has a family," said Nick, now on his feet and drawn up to his full height.

Peter gazed benignly at him. "I can understand how you might have arrived at that conclusion. However, you don't know the whole story."

"I wouldn't mind hearing that story, sir," Daniel cut in.

"Neither would I," said Nick.

"And you will hear it," Peter told them, "right after you help me get him to the Kleins' wagon, second from the far end on this side of the market. I trust you both have permission to be here today?"

They nodded in unison.

He looked at Pill. "And you?"

"Yes," she replied uncertainly.

"Then you need to join your family as well. And Evan... if

it's your intention to have my daughter back home before her mother arrives there, I would suggest you begin heading toward the car right now. Our trading is done and I'm supposed to be fetching Maisie from the paddock."

"Papa, I—"

"Later, duckling," he told her. "We'll talk about this after dinner."

❧

Tension thickened the air over the Nyquist dinner table.

Since they'd both missed lunch and it took much longer to travel by horse and wagon than it did in a car, Evan had offered to treat Laurel to a snack before they left the market. Against her better judgment, she'd accepted. As a result, the adults and young'uns had returned from the commons in time to see the little yellow car that had zipped past them earlier make the turn back onto the main road and flee northward. Mama Nyquist had entered the house to find the children finishing up an early supper that looked more like breakfast— the only meal Stephen knew how to prepare—and struggling to keep their eyes open.

Their uncle had taken them to visit the ducks on the Chens' pond that afternoon, with a detour through the barrier woods, giving Sara a chance to rest up from the strain of preparing and supervising lunch. Naturally, they'd all needed baths when they got back to the house (something she insisted on overseeing herself) and antisepsis applied to the various cuts and scrapes they'd collected during their hike. By the time the last little one had been dried off and put into clean clothes, Sara was exhausted again. So, Uncle Stephen had offered to teach Henrik and Russ how to cook cereal and scrambled eggs.

Privately, Laurel thought they'd managed just fine without her. The look on her mother's face, however, told her Emma Nyquist did not share that opinion. Margriet and Alexis saw the storm brewing in their mother-in-law's eyes and rushed to the kitchen to throw a meal together for the adults and Sara's young'uns, Jens and Ilse. No need to fix dinner for Laurel and Stephen. It was a safe bet that neither of them would feel like eating once Mama Nyquist had finished giving them both a piece of her mind.

In record time, the dishes were washed, the adults had excused themselves and taken their offspring with them, and the elder Nyquists had the room—and their two youngest children—to themselves. For several long minutes the four of them sat silently at the table, nerves taut as bowstrings. Then Emma leaned back in her chair with a sigh and raised a hand to her forehead as though checking for fever.

To Laurel's surprise, her mother's first words when the hand came back down were directed at Peter Nyquist.

"Was this his doing, do you think?"

"I'm sure of it," he replied.

"So that's his secondary gift? He can charm people into doing irresponsible things?"

"No, but he can tip the scales if they're trying to decide between what they want and what they ought to want. That's why Sean brought him to conclave the other evening—"

"—where you introduced him to our daughter," Emma finished frostily.

Laurel and her brother stared at each other in confusion. She had braced herself for a stern lecture on not shirking an assigned responsibility. Strangely, however, it appeared that their father was the one who was in trouble.

Peter paused for a moment, visibly choosing his words. "Evan was there to ensure that the elders would choose the way we wanted, and Laurel was there to stop our valley folk from speculating as to why we were hiding her away," he explained. Rising impatience put an edge on his voice as he continued, "Yes, there was chemistry between the young'uns the moment they laid eyes on each other. And maybe I should have foreseen it. Laurel is a beautiful girl, after all, and no one at that meeting was blind, least of all Evan Reilly. Or maybe fate would have brought them together no matter what we did. In any case, it's happened, and there's no going back and unhappening it." He gave his mate a long, loving look. "Sort of like the first time I sat down at your parents' dinner table."

Laurel watched her mother's expression fight to remain angry, and lose.

"What an awkward evening that was," she recalled. "You were this upstart farm boy with basic schooling who'd had the cheek to apply to the advanced computer program my father taught at the Technikum—"

"—and I'd been accepted, confirming his low opinion of the admissions officer's intelligence. But then I was billeted with your family, which must have felt like a further insult. Oh, they hated me at first," he reminded her, his voice softening, "but your parents finally came around."

"Only after you'd proven you were worthy of me by scoring the second highest grade in the course," she pointed out.

"So what do you think, Mother Nyquist? Shall we give this boy a chance to prove himself worthy of our daughter?"

Her fine dark eyebrows drew together in a pained expression. "He has an undetectable talent that gets other people in trouble. There was no real harm done today, thank goodness. But what about the next time he decides to ply her with his 'Reilly charm'?"

"I can tell when he's doing it," cut in Laurel helpfully. "He gets a look in his eyes, a look of mischief. I saw it at the conclave meeting, and I saw it again this afternoon."

Peter leaned forward in his chair. "And what are you going to do the next time you see that look?" he prompted her.

"I'll tell him to turn off the charm and let me make up my own mind."

"And if he doesn't?" her mother wanted to know. "What if he refuses to wipe that look off his face?"

"Then I'll just have to reach out a shadow hand and wipe it off myself."

"That's my girl," declared Peter, laughing.

CHAPTER THREE

The sun had not yet risen when the Chens' wagon pulled up in the Nyquists' yard, guided by the light shining through the living room window. It was city market day. Swallowing a yawn, Laurel hugged her mother goodbye at the front door and clambered up onto the wagon bed. Her brothers Erik and Markus were busily loading crates of apples into the space Chen had reserved for them beside his bags of onions and jars of honey. The Nyquist men worked quickly and quietly, as though fearful of being caught. For just an instant Laurel was seized by the strangely familiar feeling that she was making an escape under cover of darkness.

Her story was building itself again, she decided. She would have to write in her journal tonight before going to sleep.

Gingerly stepping between bushels and baskets from at least two other farms, she made her way to the rear-facing passengers' bench behind the driver's seat and wrapped herself in the blanket she found there. The air was cool and still at this hour, a cocktail of aromas waiting to be stirred. In the Fingers, farmers specialized. It was their way of creating dependence on one another. From the earthy smell of fresh-picked root vegetables, the nutty tang of aged cheese, and the sweet fragrances of ripe plums and peaches, Laurel could tell exactly whose produce had been loaded onto the Chens' wagon that morning. She inhaled deeply, snuggled into the blanket, and closed her eyes. It would take them hours to arrive at the city market, and she was certain her father would want her fully awake at his… dangerous… private… meeting…

"Ready, duckling?" Peter Nyquist swung himself up and down beside her, pulling her back from the edge of sleep. He was clutching a sack Emma had filled with fruit and sandwiches to sustain them on their journey. But food wasn't what Laurel needed right now.

"Is she—?" Malcolm Chen's murmur drifted over her head.

"Yes. Young'uns need more rest than we old folks do," Peter replied softly.

Laurel felt herself being gathered into the crook of her father's arm. Safe at last (*Where had* that *come from?*), she relaxed against his chest and let herself doze.

Snatches of the adults' conversation periodically reached into her slumber and tickled the margins of her awareness.

"…Timothy Klein…?"

"…sending him away. That damned doctor from the city wanted to…"

"…our warm climate. Can't imagine how the boy would have survived if…"

"…glad we're finally doing something instead of…"

"…they won't, not if we're careful. The important thing…"

"…how does she figure in your plan to…?"

"…the longer I can keep her from knowing…"

"Laurel? Wake up, duckling. I think you'll want to see this."

Her eyes blinked open on what she took at first to be an orange sky. Then she realized that she was looking at the inside of a canopy shading the produce around her from the bright morning sun. The blanket had been moved to provide extra cover for a cluster of bushel baskets near the foot of the wagon bed. And the rising warmth under the canopy had intensified the perfume of apples and onions, plums and cheese that filled the air around her, making her mouth water and her stomach growl.

"Are we there, Papa?"

"We're a half-hour away. Time enough for you to have some breakfast. I saved you a sandwich and a couple of Granny apples. But first, turn around," he instructed her.

Laurel did as she was told, grasping the top of the driver's seat to pull herself up. Roberta Chen slid aside to give her a clear forward view.

Laurel's first look at the city nearly took her breath away. She must have told the children a thousand times how the ark ship had made planetfall, how it had then been cut and shaped into a permanent habitat for hundreds of people. Piecing together details from conversations with family members who had visited the city, Laurel had formed a mental picture of it and had shared that with her nieces and nephews as well. But it was the wrong picture, she now realized.

This wasn't a city. It was a castle, straight out of one of the old legends she sometimes remembered for the children, only this one was made of metal. At its centre, standing tall with its nose pointing at the sky, was the original ark ship. Its grey skin shone like silver, and Manua's sunlight splashed and sparkled on the roofs of the many turrets and towers that seemed to sprout from its sides. Surrounding this keep was a high, uneven wall, a stern and gloomy patchwork of stone and concrete. Clusters of small wooden buildings had sprung up at the base of the wall, as though the ark ship was trying to regrow the habitats it had lost a hundred years earlier. To someone who saw stories everywhere, it was a saddening thought.

Ships ought to fly, not be planted in the ground like a shrub and expected to flower.

A meat and lettuce sandwich appeared in front of Laurel's face. "Eat," her father urged her. "Things are going to become very strange once we're inside those gates, and I don't want you feeling faint from hunger."

Of the strangeness, she had no doubt. If Evan's grandfather was to be believed, the city folk were all transforming into hobbits with oversized heads. Or maybe they were becoming munchkins, like the ones in *The Wizard of Oz*. Was that what her uncle would look like, a munchkin from Emerald City? And would the farm folk look like giants by comparison?

Laurel turned and sat back down to eat. She could see other wagons, a whole caravan of them, formed up behind the one she was in. Their colourful canopies bobbed and swayed as draft horses negotiated the rutted trail worn by a century's worth of metal-clad wheels crossing the Palm.

Laurel had never visited the city market, but she knew this much about it: where the farmers were concerned, it was all business.

Each of the valleys was permitted to send up to three wagonloads of produce and fabricated goods to the city every two weeks. The drivers—two per wagon—were then suffered to spend the rest of the morning and part of the afternoon inside the city walls. To make sure everyone had a chance to shop and visit, the Central Valley conclave had drawn up a schedule, rotating the driving responsibilities among the ten families. Technically, Peter Nyquist shouldn't have been part of the exercise today. However, he did have a meeting to attend in the city, with the blessing of the elders… sort of.

"Is everyone clear on what has to happen in there?" said Peter, the unaccustomed tension in his voice drawing Laurel's focus.

"Don't worry," Malcolm Chen assured him, still facing forward. "We have our shopping lists, and you'll have your distraction."

Distraction?

Hurrying through the rest of her sandwich and one of the apples, Laurel stuffed the other one into her jacket pocket. Then she turned around again to stare at the city as they approached it. Men in bright blue uniforms were walking back and forth along the top of the wall, carrying things that didn't look like any tools she'd ever seen. At that moment, it occurred to her that getting inside the city was only the first part of their mission today. They had to get back out as well. Was that what the distraction was for, to ensure that they could make their escape once the meeting with her uncle was over?

The wagon was heading toward a large square opening cut into the north-facing side of the wall. Laurel inhaled sharply as the Chens' big Clydesdale walked through it with barely a hand of clearance.

Peter leaned over and muttered urgently into her ear, "Duckling, this is important. Don't react to anything that happens, and try to avoid making eye contact with anyone."

"What if someone asks me a question?" she whispered back.

"Let me answer it," replied her father. "You just keep your eyes and ears open and be a shy little girl from the Fingers. We mustn't do anything that will set us apart from the other farm folk. That means no reaching, or anything else that might be *memorable.*"

She understood. No reaching and no remembering. No speaking, no staring, no moving… that's a good little LMC. (*What was an LMC? Where had she heard that before?*)

They were in an enclosed area the size of a corn field, with a high ceiling and large yellow numbers painted at regular intervals along its grey metal walls. Chen halted the wagon in a space adjacent to one of those numbers. A moment later, a raised platform glided over and stopped beside them, carrying a short man with a large belly, a clipboard, and very little hair on his head. *A hobbit,* Laurel decided, *with most of his hair concealed by those brown leather boots on his feet.* He scowled when he saw how many passengers were in the wagon.

"Four in and four out?" he snapped. Chen nodded, and the man made a notation on his clipboard before turning his attention to their cargo. His lips moved as he tallied everything up. Finally, several notations later, he announced, "Two hundred and fifty," and handed Chen a cloth bag with a drawstring top before gliding away again.

"That should just about cover our energy allotment for the month," Peter remarked dryly.

"This is ridiculous," said Roberta Chen to her husband. "Our load is worth at least a hundred and fifty more than that." She sprang to her feet, ready to argue, but before she could utter a word Malcolm reached up and pulled her back onto the seat beside him.

"There's no point," he told her, facing down her angry stare. "It didn't work for the Gillespies last time and it won't work now."

Peter climbed down from the wagon, signalling to his daughter to follow.

"Wait a second," said Chen. He reached into the bag, counted out four leather discs, each stamped with the number 5, and placed them in Laurel's hands. "In case you see something you like at one of the vendors' stalls," he explained, then turned to her father and added, "It's her first time. She should have something nice to remember it by."

"Thanks, Malcolm," said Peter Nyquist. His mouth was smiling, but there was no laughter in his eyes.

❧

They were the first of the Fingers folk to step through the exit at the back of the receiving zone and into the city marketplace.

The grand plaza turned out to be a roughly rectangular area between the inner and outer city walls. Lined on two sides by supply sheds with open doors and large plastiplex windows, it also held rows of canopied tables, presumably displaying goods for sale. It was difficult to see through the crowd of city folk that swarmed noisily back and forth among them. These people appeared determined to fill up all the remaining space with their bodies, and to banish any silence with their voices.

Although they were loud, none of the voices sounded angry. They belonged to vendors trying to attract people to look at their wares, and buyers trying to negotiate a more attractive price. This scene was similar in many ways to the farmers' market on the commons, she decided. Except for the city dirt under her feet, of course. Anything that might once have grown here had long ago been trodden out of existence, and nothing had been put down to replace it. Only three steps from the doorway, her boots were already covered with a layer of dust.

Peter took her hand then, gave it a reassuring squeeze, and began leading her through the crowd. The farm folk were easily a head taller than anyone else at the market. Trying not to think of rocks and white-capped waves, Laurel concentrated instead on keeping up. Shadow hands surfaced, ready to push if necessary, despite Peter's earlier warning. To her relief, however, the mob parted smoothly to let the strangers pass, then closed ranks behind them. It was clearly not meant to be a welcoming gesture. The closer the visitors got to the middle of the plaza, the louder and more excited everyone else became, as though raising an alarm.

Laurel tightened her grip on her father's hand.

Peter leaned down and spoke softly into her ear, and the confidence in his voice was instantly calming. "Look around you, duckling. What doors do you see?"

"The main gates," she replied, pointing. The portals were just the other side of the plaza, made of metal and apparently quite heavy. They were also tightly closed and guarded by four men in uniform. "And the door we just came through." Laurel turned and searched it out, in the process noticing another door she hadn't seen before, this one cut directly into the metal skin of the castle's keep. It was closed as well, and standing beside it were two more men in uniform.

"And that one," she said. "And all the doors leading into the supply sheds."

He stood for a long moment grimly eyeing the crowd. Laurel followed his gaze across the plaza and realized what he was doing. He was locating the other farm folk. She remembered that they'd been given lists of items to buy. Apparently, this was part of a plan—*his* plan—and he wanted to make sure things were proceeding smoothly.

Finally, he relaxed. "Do you have any idea what you'd like to get with your twenty units?" The twinkle in his voice told her he already knew what the answer would be.

"Books, Papa. I want to get some books."

They made their way hand in hand through the crowd, past window after window displaying clothing and household items. As they walked, Laurel also caught glimpses of tables covered with brightly coloured scarves, belts, jewellery, fancy soaps, and lotions. At the end nearest the main gate were the sheds holding goods from the manufacturers in the Wrist: plumbing and electrical supplies, electronic components, and furniture, among other things. These had all been milled, stamped, carved, and moulded using the natural resources found south of the Palm. Somewhere in the middle of all this fabricated output, Peter assured her, was a place that held books.

It was a computer parts shed. The man in charge was tall for a city dweller, with a round face, brown skin and a head full of tightly curled black hair. His pleasant smile widened with delight when he saw them come inside.

"Peter Nyquist!" he exclaimed, coming out from behind his counter with his arms spread for a hug. "It's been too long, my friend. What can I do for you today?"

"My daughter Laurel has some units to spend and she would like to trade them for books."

"Well, she's come to the right place. We have the largest nonfiction collection in the city, outside of the central library."

"Don't you have any stories?" Laurel piped up.

He made a show of being startled by her request. Then, gesturing to her to be silent, the man reached down, pulled out a compupad, and thrust it across the counter toward her. "Select whatever you want from that list," he told her, "and it will load up a ROM card for you. Or two."

"Take your time choosing, duckling," said Peter, giving her a significant look. *As if she needed reminding!* "Read over the entire catalogue."

"You know," the man remarked in a lowered voice, "if it were anyone but you, I might be smelling a sting."

Peter tilted his head. "It's getting worse?" he murmured.

"Much. Vendors are being harassed and fined just for having more than one title at a time in their shops. Not for sale, mind you. For their own personal reading between customers."

"Where does it end?" Peter wondered, then added, "So, what are you charging for banned books these days, Andre?"

"For you, my friend, the same as I was forty years ago. When you finish reading them, reinitialize the cards. And if you get caught with them before that, you never heard of me."

Laurel left the shed with a head full of questions, an anxious stomach, five units left to spend, and nearly three hundred works of fiction in her inside jacket pocket.

❧

"It's time," said Peter Nyquist.

For at least an hour, they had strolled up and down the rows of what city folk apparently called "shops". They'd browsed the tables, pausing at each one to survey with feigned interest the variety of crafted goods on offer. They had spent Laurel's last chit on lunch, and had taken another hour to finish eating it: a flaky pastry filled with vegetables and ground meat, large enough to feed two, and two bottles of fruit-flavoured carbonated water to wash it down. Then they'd walked some more, ending up in front of a shop with a black lace curtain drawn across its window and the words "Jewellery Repair" painted on the inside of the pane.

Peter's body was rigidly expectant as he scanned the crowd, but not for farm folk this time. Following his gaze, Laurel saw the uniformed men at their posts. Some were chatting and laughing amongst themselves, and one or two were actually leaning against the metal skin of the inner wall, looking quite bored. None were counting up tall visitors or tracking their movements.

"In here," said Peter, and he pulled his daughter quickly into the jeweller's shop.

An old man sat at a table, cleaning small pieces of metal in a container of liquid. His arms were bone-thin, and he had just a couple of wisps of white hair at the crown of his head. As he glanced up, Laurel saw a momentary *click* of recognition in his eyes.

Peter pulled something out of his jacket pocket and placed the item on the table in front of him. It was a watch on a fob, she noted, not the one he usually wore. "My daughter needs a washing-up room. May we use yours?" he asked.

The other man's voice sounded thick and hoarse. "If you can find one back there, be my guest."

"And how long will it take you to clean my watch?"

"No more than an hour. Be prompt."

Nodding his thanks, Peter nudged Laurel toward the back of the shop, to an unmarked wooden door. Behind it was a room that might once have been for washing up but was now serving as storage space. Without hesitation, he ran his fingers along the top of the inner wall, found a recess, and tugged. The wall swung aside, revealing a metal door with rounded corners. He rotated the small yellow wheel in the middle of the door and pushed it open. A loop of rope on the inside of the wooden panel allowed him to pull it closed behind them as they stepped through the inner wall of the city, into a narrow service corridor.

Laurel looked around her, at a shiny metal wall that curved away into darkness, a ceiling studded with square, harsh white lights, and flights of metal stairs that dropped periodically from above. Abruptly the air seemed to thicken, and she was back in her nightmare, frozen in place, struggling to breathe.

"Papa," she told him in a horrified whisper, "I know this place."

He took her by the shoulders and turned her to face him. "How is that possible, duckling?" he demanded, concern hardening his voice. "You know you've never been here before."

"I have, in my dreams."

"No," he said, gazing deeply into her eyes. "This is not a dream, Laurel. This is here and now. We have a job to do and less than an hour to do it. I need you to stay calm and focused and trust me to keep you safe. Can you do that?"

I'm a Nyquist, she reminded herself sternly. *Nyquists are strong. And he's right—it was a terrifying dream, but just a dream, after all.*

"I trust you, Papa."

"Good. Let's keep moving. Your uncle is waiting for us."

❧

"Come in, quickly!"

Laurel felt her father's hand on the small of her back, urging her through the doorway and into the home of Doctor Roger Bertrand. Definitely not a hobbit, her uncle was the same height as she was, slenderly built and with the same fine features and full head of dark brown hair as Emma Nyquist. The longer Laurel looked at him, the stronger the Bertrand family resemblance seemed to grow. He leaned out into the corridor, glancing left and right to make sure nobody had seen his guests arrive, then quickly slapped the door closed behind them.

"So," he said with forced heartiness, "this is Laurel. And she's the image of her mother."

Laurel opened her mouth to say hello, then thought better of it. Her father had chosen not to respond to Bertrand's pleasantry. Clearly there was something going on here.

City habitats were small rooms, subdivided into even smaller ones. Laurel recalled her mother telling her that most of the apartments had originally been crew quarters. Living space inside the star ship would have been cramped during the voyage. Apparently, it still was, even though the colony had been on the ground for a hundred years. The Bertrand living room was half the size of Laurel's sleeping chamber and held seating for only three people.

Standing stiffly inside the entrance, Peter remarked, "It's awfully quiet in here. Where is everyone?"

Behind them, Bertrand had flattened himself against the door as if to block them from leaving. If so, it would have been a futile gesture. Peter was a full head taller and wore at least thirty kilos more muscle than his brother-in-law did, and could probably have picked the other man up like a doll. Choosing to remain motionless, he repeated instead, "Where are they, Roger?"

Bertrand's nervous hands began sculpting the air. "Marie is in the bedroom," he replied. "I'm sorry, Peter. I know this wasn't your plan, but she was terrified of leaving. I had to sedate her."

"She's unconscious?"

His expression became a portrait of misery. "I had no choice. She'll sleep for at least six hours. That should give you enough time to get her safely away from here."

"What about Annelise?"

Bertrand pushed himself away from the door and moved

past them into the living room, seeming to deflate a little with each step he took. "She's been arrested," he replied sadly. "She's not just a librarian anymore. She's a writer."

"Of nonfiction. She records and posts the minutes of the governing council's meetings. How does that get her arrested?"

"It doesn't. But reading and writing fiction does. She was cleaning out a storage space and came across our old family copy of *1984* by George Orwell, and… it inspired her to write a story of her own, about this colony. About the way it began, and the way things have changed over the years, and not for the better, thanks to the Consortium's interference."

"A fiction based on truth." Peter spat a syllable of disgust. "She's given herself no way out. If she claims it's fiction, they've got her for promulgating falsehoods. If she pleads that it's nonfiction, they'll charge her for spreading sedition. You chose a rebel, Roger."

Pulling himself erect, the other man locked eyes with him. "I chose a woman with a brilliant mind and a lot of courage, just as you did, and I'm not leaving the city without her."

Laurel had been silently looking back and forth, from father to uncle, stitching them together with her gaze until a wave of comprehension finally broke over her. The scientists' report was secondary. This was actually—had always been—a rescue mission.

"Fair enough," said Peter at last. "We go to plan C then. Did you get the information we discussed?"

"I did. I copied all the files on the same day that we spoke in the plaza. And you were right, by the way. Last week all the scientists involved in the study were summoned to a meeting with the Consortium. When I got back home, I discovered that someone had remotely accessed my computer and wiped all evidence of the project from my hard drive. I checked with my colleagues. Their records were gone as well. The Consortium has made a clean sweep. Not a single document is left to back up anything we reveal about that study… except this."

Bertrand reached into his pocket and pulled out a ROM card. "This is the culmination of fifty years' work by dozens of scientists. Every device in the city is linked to the infonet, so I can't restore my files or clone the card without the Consortium knowing about it. And… I've downloaded Annelise's story for you, along with the research that supports it. It's an account of how the Consortium has influenced the council to violate every one of the four guiding principles of the colony. Please, take this and copy it if you're able, and guard each copy with your life."

He handed the card to Peter Nyquist, who then turned and handed it to Laurel to add to the ones in her pocket. Meanwhile, a sheen of perspiration had appeared on Bertrand's forehead.

Peter stared into his face. "Does the Consortium suspect you?" he asked quietly.

"I don't think so. I've been waiting for the knock on my door for five days now. If they were going to arrest me they'd have already done it."

"And if they've been watching you, they still might, after our meeting today. If they learn that you copied Annelise's story, they'll charge you as an accessory to her crime. You can't help your mate if you're in custody yourself," Peter pointed out.

But Bertrand shook his head emphatically. "I can't leave her. I won't. Just—Just sit down and let me tell you what I know."

There were three pale green upholstered armchairs in the room, each facing the other two across a squat round table with a transparent top. Reluctantly, Peter sank down onto one of them, gesturing to Laurel to do the same.

Bertrand remained standing.

"The study wasn't supposed to be generational, not the way the Consortium proposed it, but in the end..." His hands were sculpting the air again. "Scientists spent the first ten years trying to make sense out of what was happening to the folk in the city. They spent another twenty years analyzing the miners and fabricators in the Wrist. Then the project was turned over to my group, and we spent the last twenty years trying to understand what had happened to you in the Fingers. We examined all the previous data, compared and tested everything we could think of, and came up empty. All we managed to conclude was that the farmers were right. Briefly put, the humans on this planet are mutating, and it's happening differently in each location.

"It's not just our physical appearances that are diverging. It's every system in our bodies, and even our population distribution. Birth rates are declining in the city, remaining stable in the Wrist, and rising in the Fingers. If these changes weren't occurring so rapidly, I'd say we were evolving to fit our respective environments. But this—It's as though our living DNA is being rewritten, by something we're unequipped to detect or measure.

"Special talents and abilities are emerging at a greater rate in the Fingers than anywhere else in the colony as well. Ten to fifteen percent of us in the city are enhanced, as opposed to forty percent in the Wrist and nearly one hundred percent of the farm folk. So you're taller, stronger, and healthier than we are, with all kinds of special gifts, and your numbers are increasing steadily. That's enough to make a lot of city dwellers nervous. Fear can make people do cruel and irrational things to one another. It can make them forget where they came from, and what's really important in life. That's why Annelise felt compelled to write her story."

Peter cast a glance in the direction of a door that Laurel realized must lead to Marie's sleeping chamber. "Tell me something I don't already know, Roger."

"All right. How about this? Five years ago, a little girl from the north tower was murdered by her own parents. Drugged, and then smothered as she slept. Not even nine years old. They said they had to do it because the child was a memory thief. She had just emerged as a rememberer, but she could remember things that she'd never experienced, things that had happened to other people."

"You're saying she was both a rememberer and a receiver? That's a dangerous combination," commented Peter.

"Dangerous for everyone. Her family did their best to keep her gifts a secret, but that's not easy when people live as close together as we do in the city. And when a child wakes up screaming from bad dreams night after night... well... One of the neighbours found out about her. That's when things became really ugly. Her parents figured they had only two choices: surrender her to the Consortium to suffer the slow death of being turned into a living memory chip, or kill her themselves in some humane way."

Living memory chip. LMC. Feeling suddenly sick to her stomach, Laurel couldn't help herself. "But they could have sent her away," she blurted. "Maybe to a farm family."

"There were already guards watching every exit from the

city at that point. And even if there hadn't been, adding a city child's gift to the Fingers would only have increased the existing tension," Bertrand told her. "Now the Consortium is forcing everyone to walk an even finer line. They began by clamping down on 'fantastical tales', reasoning that if everyone were only remembering things that had actually happened, it would be much easier to identify the next memory thief. So now fiction is locked up in an encrypted compartment of the library database and it's illegal to buy or sell 'untrue literature' within the city walls."

Remembering Andre's parting words, Laurel had a sudden urge to pat her jacket pocket.

"And as if that isn't bad enough," Bertrand continued, "the Consortium has decided not to wait for rememberers to emerge anymore. They're examining family trees, calculating the odds of a young'un developing the talent and using that as justification for putting the child under 'clinical observation'. That's Consortium-speak for arrest and confinement of a minor."

Peter leaned forward in his chair. "Does Marie show signs yet—?"

"Her talent emerged a couple of months ago. She's highly creative, with total auditory recall and perfect pitch. Sings music as though it's a language. I've managed to keep her beneath the Consortium's notice so far, but with our family history of giftedness, you know it's just a matter of time."

"I know," said Peter, grim-faced. "And speaking of time—"

"Wait. There's something else you need to hear. A vocal faction on the governing council has been pushing for a while now to leave Manua to the farmers and miners and move the city to another part of the planet. They've currently got more than one third of the Consortium supporting the idea, and have begun laying the groundwork for secession. Last year they set up hydroponic gardens and a meat lab in the inner city. It's taking a lot of energy to maintain them."

Peter's expression darkened. Laurel could see his jaw muscles working as he fought to keep his composure. "They're reducing their dependence on the Fingers and starving us for electrical power in order to do it," he said in a hard, flat voice. "When were they planning to let us know about this project of theirs? Or were they just going to up and leave one day, taking all their technology with them?"

Bertrand blew out a breath. "Judging by their reaction when I suggested giving the farmers advance notice of the report to the administrators, the answers are probably 'never' and 'yes'. You should leave now. Take good care of my daughter. When she wakes up, tell her I'm doing this because I love her, and I'd rather lose her this way than—Well, you'll know what to say," he concluded, wiping away tears.

The brothers-in-law exchanged a long, wordless hug. Then, in a terse voice, Peter gave Laurel her instructions: "You'll go back the way we came, duckling. Retrace every one of our steps. Retrieve my watch from the jeweller, then leave his shed and walk in the direction of the receiving docks…"

∿

She remembered every turn they'd made, every number scratched or painted on the overhead conduits, every rust halo around every rivet driven into the service corridor walls. Peter had emerged from the sleeping chamber with Marie in his arms, so thoroughly wrapped in a blanket that she might easily have been mistaken for a parcel. Laurel and her father had hurried along the empty corridor, parting ways when she had to go down one of the staircases. And now she was alone, trying to step lightly through a metal hallway in which every sound echoed loudly off the walls, and listening for the tattoo of pursuing footsteps…

…because she knew now that her dream hadn't been just a dream. It had been someone else's living nightmare. Like the little girl who had been killed five years earlier, Laurel had been reliving someone else's memories, someone who'd been captured, perhaps in this very same stretch of corridor, and had been taken to a laboratory somewhere in the city.

But Laurel was more than a rememberer, more even than a memory thief. She was also a smuggler, carrying outlawed books in one jacket pocket and a secret report in the other, and despite the promises he'd made, not even Peter Nyquist could keep her safe if she were discovered here.

This was what true danger felt like. It was a pounding in her chest, a swirling sensation in her stomach, a treacherous weakness in her knees.

It was, she decided, everything she'd hoped it would be.

The Chens would be watching the entrance to the jeweller's shop, her father had told her. There would be farm folks' eyes on her all the way across the plaza to the receiving area. But first Laurel had to find the metal door with the yellow wheel at its centre… there!

She raced toward the hatch, unsealed it with trembling hands, and stepped through it to the relative safety of the little back room in the jeweller's shop. For a moment she just stood there, waiting for her heartbeat and breathing to return to normal. Her stomach was still doing somersaults, but there was no remedy for that, not as long as she was within the city walls.

The old man looked up, one shaggy white eyebrow raised in surprise, as she emerged from the "washing-up room" alone. Without a word, he handed her the watch. Laurel felt his eyes follow her out the front door of his shop.

According to Peter, her return to the plaza was the signal for Chen to create a distraction.

They'd been gone for just under an hour. The market was still teeming with vendors and buyers. Consciously relaxing her shoulders, Laurel forced herself to stroll around the edge of the crowd. Each step moved her closer to the receiving area entrance and the two uniformed men standing guard at the door beside it.

One of them smiled at her, and she automatically smiled back. Instantly, a knot formed in her midsection, bringing her to a halt. If she got any closer he might think she was coming over to talk to him. With difficulty, she resisted the urge to pat her jacket pockets. The cards were safely tucked away. They hadn't fallen out in the corridor, and they weren't about to slip out now. And where was that distraction Chen had promised?

Abruptly, something flew past her right cheek. It grazed her hair, moving fast and buzzing loudly. A second later several more of them jetted past her into the middle of the plaza. Screams and angry shouts erupted behind her. Laurel spun and saw everyone running around, frantically waving their arms and tossing their heads.

A swarm of large bees had invaded the marketplace. City folk and farm folk alike were dodging and feinting and turning in circles, as though performing a complicated dance routine.

It made a fascinating spectacle. And Sean Reilly was right—away from the orchard, Chen's bees looked enormous.

Only half-feigning fear, she backed up against the wall between the two doors and waited, staying calm by focusing on her father's instructions. The moment had to be right, he had told her. When the guards were fully distracted, she was to reach out a shadow hand and rattle the handle on the door behind them to let him know.

It took a full-on bee attack on the guards to move them away from their posts, but eventually they were bobbing and swatting along with everyone else in the plaza. As Peter emerged through the door, Roberta Chen uttered a bloodcurdling shriek and made a dash for the receiving area, followed closely by the rest of the folk from the Fingers. Malcolm paused to let Peter and Laurel slip in ahead of him as the crowd of farm folk rushed toward their wagons.

By the time the dockmaster came over to take his departure head count, Marie had been safely concealed in the folds of the Chens' orange canopy. And as the Clydesdale pulled their wagon through the wide doors and away from the city, two Chens and two Nyquists breathed four sighs of relief.

❧

Chen waited until they were well on their way home before asking, "How did it go?"

"It confirmed our suspicions," said Peter. "I'll be making an interesting report at the next conclave."

"Will *she* be all right?" Roberta said, tilting her head toward the blanket-wrapped girl lying beside him on the wagon bed.

"I'm not sure," Peter replied. "I hope so. I hated having to leave her parents behind."

"So we're going back for them?" Chen said over his shoulder. "I'll let the bees know."

Nestled in the crook of her father's arm, Laurel had closed her eyes and given herself to the rocking motion of the wagon as the adults' conversation floated around her. But Chen's last remark made her sit bolt upright.

"You talk to your bees?" she exclaimed.

"Not really," he replied, laughing. "Not in words. But we have a mental connection. Bees are a lot more intelligent than anyone might suspect. And they're loyal. They'll help us out again if I ask them."

Laurel settled back thoughtfully against her father's chest, her curiosity burgeoning as his embrace gathered her closer. Bertrand had said that nearly one hundred percent of the farm folk were gifted. Clearly, bee whispering was Malcolm Chen's talent. So what was Peter Nyquist's?

"It won't be easy, you know," Chen was pointing out. "Each time you breach the city boundaries and steal one of its citizens, the members of the Consortium beef up its defences. After Emma, they put up that perimeter wall and restricted admission to the Technikum. After Colleen, they established their own central marketplace and set guards around it. After today, it wouldn't surprise me if they roofed over the grand plaza and put a locking gate at each end."

"If their intention is to keep farm folk away from the city, they're more likely to cut back on the frequency of our produce deliveries, from twice a month to once every month or two," said Peter. "Meanwhile, did you get everything on the list?"

"It took some creative bargaining, but we did," Roberta replied. "And we kept one of the chits to serve as a template. Are you sure they won't be able to tell the difference?"

"I'm positive. Counterfeit currency is the last thing they'll be expecting from a bunch of ignorant hayseeds from the Fingers. As long as we aren't greedy, no alarms should go off. But the next time the Central Valley farmers bring them twelve hundred units' worth of goods, that's how many units we'll be spending in their sheds."

"Papa?" Laurel cut in.

"What is it, duckling?"

She sat up straight beside him on the passengers' bench. "If everyone in the Fingers has a special talent, like Doctor Bertrand said—"

"You're wondering what mine is?"

"It's sneaking around the city," declared Roberta Chen over her shoulder.

"Laurel, you're old enough to know this now," said Malcolm, his solemn words laced with laughter. "Your father is a criminal mastermind."

Peter uttered an exasperated syllable. "Don't you listen to

them," he told her with mock severity. "The fact is, I'm a planner. That's why I'm so good with computers. My head is full of flow charts. I can tell just from looking at a problem what would be the best way to solve it."

Laurel darted a glance at Marie, still sound asleep in her blanket cocoon. "And do you know how to solve Annelise's problem?"

He paused for a moment, then replied, "I think I do. Unfortunately, it's going to take a lot of preparation, and I don't think she has much time."

"That's plan A. What about plan B?" she demanded, tears welling up and overflowing her eyes. "Or plan C? You mustn't give up on her, Papa. All she did was write a story."

Peter gathered her into his arms and hugged her tightly to his chest. "No one is giving up on anyone, duckling, but there are limits to the abilities of even a planner. All I can promise is that I'll do my best."

Chapter Four

Emma Nyquist came running out the front door with Axel and Erik on her heels as the Chens' wagon rolled to a halt in the yard.

"Is everyone all right?" she demanded, her eyes anxiously searching the faces of her chosen mate and their daughter. "Where are they, Peter? Where's Roger? Where's Annelise?"

"Annelise got herself arrested a few days ago, and Roger refuses to leave her," he told her. "We were only able to bring Marie back with us." As Axel helped Laurel down from the wagon, Peter passed the sleeping bundle that was Marie Bertrand down into Erik's arms.

"*This* time," said Emma, her lips a hyphen of determination. "This time, Marie. Next time, Roger and Annelise."

Laurel saw her father's mouth open and close, as though he'd been about to say something but decided against it. Then he and Malcolm Chen exchanged a freighted look.

Halfway to the door, Erik turned and called out, "What's wrong with this little girl, Dad?"

"Nothing," Peter replied. "Put her in the spare sleeping chamber. She'll wake up in a couple of hours." Noticing the stiffness of her father's movements as he climbed down from the wagon, Laurel realized how tired he must be. Roberta Chen was leaning back in her seat and yawning as well. This had been a long and stressful day for all of them, and it wasn't over yet.

"Looks like we've got company, Pop," said Axel. Everyone turned to look where he was pointing and saw a bright yellow car racing toward them. A moment later it lurched to a stop just behind the wagon, and a pair of Reillys tumbled out of it.

Peter walked over to Evan's grandfather and extended his hand to be shaken. "Your timing is perfect, Sean. We've got a problem, one that the three of us need to discuss privately right now."

"Not until you've eaten something," Emma cut in, in that voice that no one dared to question. "We've been waiting dinner until you arrived, and while you may not mind missing a meal, the rest of us are famished. Reillys and Chens, please be our guests at the table. There's plenty of food to go around."

In fact, there was enough for second helpings. The Chens hadn't just picked up apples that morning—they'd also dropped off the carcasses of three large chickens. Margriet had cleaned, stuffed, and roasted the birds, together with enough potatoes, squash and green beans to feed a small army. For dessert, Alexis had made several strawberry rhubarb pies, sweetened with honey.

When the meal was over, Sean Reilly leaned back in his chair and studied Peter's face across the corner of the table. "So, Nyquist," he said softly, "I gather your suspicions turned out to be correct."

Peter glanced furtively at Emma, who was on her feet and busily collecting empty plates. He nodded silently and gestured to the other man to wait until later.

Laurel looked into Evan's eyes as he sat across the table from her and saw not a trace of mischief. The thoughts and feelings churning her stomach at that moment were entirely her own. She was a memory thief, one careless word away from being claimed by the Consortium as a living memory chip. Even if she never went near the city again, she would always be in danger. Earlier, that idea would have excited her. Now it was a problem, one that not even Peter Nyquist might be able to solve.

Emma returned from the kitchen with a large bowl of fruit in her hands. Setting it in the middle of the table, she leaned down beside her mate and scolded quietly, "Look around. There's no one but conspirators and secret weapons in the room, so you may as well speak freely. Now tell us, what did you suspect?"

Reilly gave Peter a look that said, *Don't fight it.*

"Fine," said Peter abruptly. "We thought there might be a spy in our midst, someone feeding information to the Consortium about what was discussed at our conclaves. We were right. They knew about my secret meeting with one of the scientists, and that he was planning to show me the results of their study, but only after I'd mentioned it at conclave. I never identified Roger by name, so they didn't know which scientist to arrest. However, they took steps to prevent the information from being passed along."

Stunned, Emma sank slowly down beside him. "One of the elders warned them?" she said wonderingly.

"Not necessarily an elder," he replied. "After all, I share information with you and our three oldest, and I'm sure Sean discusses valley matters with Patrick and Colleen."

Reilly's face reddened. "Are you suggesting that my kids would—!"

"Not at all," Peter assured him. "All I'm saying is that if we're talking with family members, then other elders are probably doing the same. This informant could be literally any adult in Central Valley."

Laurel had been listening quietly. Now she just had to speak up. "At the conclave, there was someone making nasty comments about you, Papa."

"I heard him," Peter replied. "Sid Cameron can be a curmudgeon at times. He hates everything to do with the city, and disparages anyone who's associated with it, but he's pretty harmless."

"Unless those remarks are meant to deflect suspicion away from him and onto someone else," Roberta pointed out. "After all, you're the one who keeps going back and forth, Peter. That puts you in a perfect position to be relaying information to the Consortium."

Her observation silenced everyone at the table for a moment.

"What about Rachel Zimmerman?" Reilly piped up. "Did you see her reaction when you announced that the study had been completed?"

"This discussion is getting us nowhere," Peter told them. "If we tried hard enough, we could probably point a finger at everyone who was at the conclave table that night."

"All right, then. You're the planner. How do you propose we flush out the spy?" asked Malcolm Chen.

"I'm not sure we should just yet," said Peter thoughtfully. "This person could be useful if we wanted to deceive the Consortium with false information."

"It sounds as if you're planning our next rescue mission," Roberta remarked. Laurel tried to read the expression on her face—*approval? disapproval?*—but had to give up.

Peter shook his head. "Malcolm was right earlier. Any plans I make will have to take into account the Consortium's response to today's little adventure, and we don't know yet what that will be."

"So why wait?" Reilly was leaning forward now. "Seems to me now's the best time to hit them, while they're still reeling from the first punch."

"And under what pretext am I supposed to return to the city so soon? It took me months to orchestrate the Bertrand rescue without raising anyone's suspicions, and it was a near-total failure. If Laurel hadn't been with me, I probably would have had to leave Marie behind as well."

"I wouldn't call it a failure, Peter," Malcolm Chen pointed out quietly. "You did obtain a copy of the scientists' report to the Consortium, after all."

Reilly perked up at this. "And do you know what it says?"

"Not word for word," Peter replied. "I'll have to review it before the next conclave. But Roger summarized it for me.

"We've been right to be concerned about the energy situation," he continued. "Electrical power isn't being rationed because it's in short supply—it's being diverted to projects within the city to make the city folk less dependent on our produce. It appears that they're preparing to break away from the rest of the colony entirely."

Reilly made a rude sound with his lips. "And go where?"

"The original planetary surveys must still be in the library database," said Peter. "My guess is that they've already picked out another land mass and will shortly begin building boats to carry them there, along with as much of the city as will fit on board."

"Hmph! So much for interdependence, eh? Well, if they want to leave, I say let them. We'll probably all be better off that way," Reilly declared.

Laurel stole a glance at her mother. Emma's lips were pursed, holding back words she knew she would regret if she spoke them aloud. Peter had noticed her expression as well. "I disagree, Sean," he said stiffly. "This colony was built to stand on three legs, just like one of your milking stools. Remove one and the stool will fall over."

"And the amputated leg can't stand on its own either, to continue your analogy," Chen supplied. "The problem is, the city leg is too afraid of the farming leg and the industrial leg to listen to logic. So, how do we break through that fear and get the Consortium turned back around?"

"Or get rid of it altogether?" said Reilly. As shocked stares settled on his face, he snapped, "Come on! You know you're all thinking it. I just said it out loud."

Peter raised a hand to rub the back of his neck. "I don't know how to fix this. And to be honest, until Roger and Annelise are rescued, I'd rather not even think about it."

"Fair enough," said Reilly. "Are you at least curious to know what brought Evan and me over here this evening?"

"Besides showing that you cared whether we got back safely?"

Reilly let out a deep chuckle. "Of course, we care, Nyquist, but if that were the only reason, I'd have come alone. The young'un and I have been talking, and we've hatched an idea. It saves you from having to wait for an excuse to go to the city."

"We're not digging any tunnels, Sean," Chen warned him.

"Just hear me out," said Reilly. "Laurel is a reacher, right? And don't you have a climber in the family as well? And Evan is a telepath. They'd make a powerful team, Nyquist. I'll bet you anything they could get you inside the walls without having to go through the gate."

Scowling, Peter gave his head an emphatic shake. "Absolutely not! It's unconscionable to put young'uns in that kind of danger."

"I'll bet this was Evan's idea," Emma bristled. "Tell me, Sean, was there a look of mischief on his face while he was proposing it to you?"

When Reilly failed to answer, she shot him a look of exasperation. Meanwhile, Evan was working to suppress a smile.

Watching this scene, Laurel grew thoughtful. Apparently, no one was immune to Evan Reilly's charm, not even people who knew he had it. He'd even convinced Tim Klein to come out of hiding and join them at the market. And if he could influence the choices of people from a distance, that presented some very interesting possibilities.

"Are there telepaths in the city?" she asked abruptly.

"There must be," her father replied. "Roger told us that at least ten percent of the city population have some sort of special talent. What are you thinking, duckling?"

She gave a little shrug. "That if the Consortium has spies among the farm folk, then we should have a spy or two in the city. Evan can convince them that it's the right thing to do. And if it's all done telepathically, then no one has to go there, and no one will be in danger."

Peter's eyes widened. "That... actually... makes very good sense," he declared, adding, "as long as the Consortium has no telepath spies of its own among the city folk to give us away. Everyone there is on edge right now. I don't know how hard we can push without triggering an armed conflict, and I'm certainly not anxious to find out."

"I can be careful," Evan promised. "We all thought Tim Klein was a child until he showed up at the market. I can pretend to be someone else as well."

"You mustn't reveal any specific information until you're certain your contact can be trusted," Chen warned him.

"Or until you know they *can't* be trusted," Reilly added. "For when we want to send the Consortium misinformation."

After a pause, Peter said, "All right. But we can't let any of this be known at conclave. Is anyone here uncomfortable with that?"

A high-pitched shriek erupted from one of the sleeping chambers then, startling everyone in the room. This was followed by Stephen's voice calling loudly, "Emergency! Female presence required!"

Laurel could hear the *crash* of things being thrown against a wall, and Stephen's yelps of pain as some of them collided with parts of his body.

"Excuse me, please," said Emma, calmly getting to her feet. "I believe my niece is finally awake."

When the Chens and the Reillys had departed, it fell to Laurel and Stephen to clean up the kitchen and get things ready for breakfast the next day. Emma was fully occupied reassuring Marie. The little city girl had been living with enormous stress for the past several weeks, far more than any child should have had to endure. While still adjusting to her emerging gifts, she had recently watched her mother being dragged away to detention, and had just awakened, alone, in a strange place among people she didn't recognize. For reasons she didn't understand, her whole world had suddenly turned itself inside out. It would be a while before she calmed down enough to feel safe.

And Laurel was a memory thief. Perfect. She shuddered, not looking forward to the dreams she would probably be having that night.

By tacit agreement, she always washed the dishes and Stephen dried them and put them away in the cupboard. Now he paused with a stack of plates in his hands and asked, "Are you all right? I mean, I know it's been a very long day and all, but—"

"She'll be fine," said Peter, clapping a hand on his shoulder. "And you're right, it's been a long day for all of us. Why don't you go on to bed? I'll finish helping your sister."

"Okay, sure," he said, and handed over the plates and the dish towel. But the look he gave her as he left the room told her that he wasn't sure at all.

When Peter and Laurel were alone together in the kitchen, he set the plates on the counter, leaned down, and said softly into her ear, "You're not a memory thief, duckling."

She froze and stared at him, wide-eyed. "How did you know—?"

"I saw the look on your face when Roger was telling us about that poor girl in the city. You were wearing the same look when I came into the kitchen a moment ago."

"But I'm remembering things that never happened to me," she whispered tearfully.

"I know. It's what your mother has been afraid of, ever since the day your talent emerged. You were never in that corridor in the city—she was. She's a rememberer, just like you."

Laurel was shocked. Emma had always been an artist, a threadworker with an instinctual gift for matching and blending colours. Never once had she even mentioned having a secondary talent.

Dreading the answer but desperately needing to know, Laurel said, "She was captured, wasn't she?"

"Are you remembering that too, now?" His eyes filled with sympathy. "Yes, she was. And she was taken to a laboratory. Roger and I managed to find and rescue her before they could perform the memory wipe, but the trauma of being prepared for it was indelibly imprinted on her brain. When you were born with your mother's gift, a special mental connection must have formed or remained between you, making it possible for you to experience some of her memories."

"The bad ones. The nightmares," she said with a shudder. Then she glanced up at him, her mouth forming an O as comprehension dawned.

"The bad ones," he confirmed. "She generally keeps them locked away. But when she's asleep, if something is preying on her mind, sometimes they escape her control.

"We're not sure, but Roger believes that the remembering gift is gender-specific, like colour-blindness. And it doesn't emerge every time. For your first nine years, we kept our fingers crossed, hoping it would skip your generation. Then your secondary talent showed itself, and your mother's nightmares returned. And because she was having them, you started having them too."

"Papa," she said in a horrified whisper, "that little girl in the city who was having bad dreams...!"

"...was probably the daughter of a rememberer who lived in terror that they would both be identified and taken away to be experimented on," he said in a voice weighed down with sadness. "What they did was cruel, but they felt they had no other choice, because they didn't have family members in the Fingers who could swoop in and rescue them."

"Like Dr. Bertrand and Annelise do. We're going to rescue them, aren't we?"

"Yes, we are, duckling. We're going to find a way to bring Marie's parents here. But listen to me now. Your mother wants what is best for you, just as I do. We want you to be happy. But first and foremost, we want you to be safe. And that means you do not, for any reason or under any circumstances, go near the city again. Especially not if the suggestion comes from Evan Reilly. Is that understood?"

Laurel's mind was teeming with questions, but she had no words with which to ask them. All she could do was obediently nod her head.

That night, she didn't sleep at all. Her thoughts were chasing one another around inside her head, and she had to keep consciously relaxing her muscles. It didn't help that her parents' urgent voices filtered through the walls of her sleeping chamber for a good two hours after she'd gone to bed. It didn't matter whether they spoke her name. Every time they argued, Laurel knew it was about her.

Finally, she gave up even trying to rest. She opened her journal and began writing, and didn't stop until the sky lightened, bringing a new day.

~

The following week was busy, leaving her no time to dwell on unpleasant things.

Sara's water broke, and six hours later, with Ruth Gillespie's midwifely assistance, baby Willem was joyfully welcomed into the Nyquist clan. Jens, aged 14, was thrilled to have a little brother for a change. Two younger sisters were more than enough for anyone, he declared. Then, Markus let slip at the dinner table that he and Alexis were expecting their fourth child as well, and there was an instant celebration.

In the embrace of such a large, loving family, Marie was slowly coming out of her shell. Within days, the nine-year-old cousin from the city went from looking lost and fearful to simply looking sad. Stephen's gift of his guitar didn't stop her from wedging herself into corners and humming dreamily to herself. However, the melodies she played seemed to have a calming effect on the children, especially Karin and Anders, and that was something to be grateful for.

Meanwhile, the Cortland apples had ripened. As was customary in the Fingers, the valley families sent their oldest young'uns to help the Nyquist men bring in the harvest. Also customary was the bushel of fruit they would each earn as payment for their several days of work.

Trent Barrett and the Leclercs' youngest son, Avery, had come to assist with the picking. There would soon be others as well, Laurel knew, for harvest time was about more than simply gathering a crop. It was also an opportunity for near-choosing-age sons to become acquainted with prospective mates and make a favourable impression on potential future in-laws. There were at least half a dozen boys Laurel's age in Central Valley alone. As Dr. Bertrand had pointed out, farm families on Manua were large, and getting larger.

Now that people knew who Laurel was, Peter and Emma

could no longer leave her behind when they went to the monthly farmers' market on the commons. It would probably make Emma feel better if her only daughter remained in Central Valley. However, the choosing went both ways. Axel, Erik, and Markus had found their mates at events where all the Fingers families came together, and it wouldn't be right to deny Laurel the same breadth of opportunity.

Three days into the picking, Marie was in her sleeping chamber, strumming a sad melody while Laurel supervised the other children. They'd just finished a lunch of gooey cheese sandwiches, Golden apple wedges, and milk. Now they were taking turns in the washing-up room before settling down for their afternoon lessons, and Emma was at the sink, tending to their dirty dishes.

Startled by the sudden slamming of a door, Laurel spun around in time to see her father stride into the kitchen. He deposited his empty plate on the countertop and announced, "Reilly's just called an emergency conclave. It starts in less than an hour, at his place. We're going in the car. We should be home in time for dinner."

Emma paused, wet hands hovering over the soapy water. "And by *we* you mean…?"

"I'm taking Laurel with me. I've already spoken to Alexis. She's coming over to mind the children. Stephen can stay in the orchard for now, but if the discussion goes the way I think it will, he'll have quite a bit of preparation ahead of him."

"Peter," she began, concern furrowing her features, "what is this all about?"

"There's no time. I'll fill you in when we get back, I promise."

It was a ten minute drive north to the Reillys' property line. Laurel recognized Reilly land immediately by the waist-high rail fences that marked its boundaries, and by the broad hayfield that served as a buffer between the southern cow pasture and the Sorensens' vineyard. Manuan cows, it seemed, had a taste for grapes.

Dairy cattle on Manua were large white beasts, nearly as tall as Maisie, with sharp black horns on their heads and huge swollen udders hanging between their hind legs. Laurel counted fifteen animals in the south pasture, roughly half of Reilly's herd. Today they stood placidly chewing their cud, observing the world through heavy-lidded eyes while bees darted unremarked around their legs and little electric cars zipped along the road that bordered the field.

"Just think, Laurel," Stephen had teased her earlier that day. "If you and Evan choose each other, the Reilly farm will be all yours someday. Of course, by then you'll be a mother six times over, with a whole flock of grandchildren. Won't that be exciting?"

No, she thought, it wouldn't. In fact, the more she thought about it, the less certain she became that she even wanted to be a farmer's mate. She loved children, but she had no special affinity for animals and no real interest in growing food. Her father was always saying that farmers belonged to the land, not the other way around. If that was true, Laurel couldn't help feeling that her place was somewhere else. Somewhere where she could immerse herself in stories the way Marie immersed herself in music. Now, *that* would be exciting.

"You're awfully quiet, duckling," Peter remarked. "What are you thinking about?"

"Papa, do I have to be chosen?"

He chuckled. "Not unless you want to be. Choosing Day isn't just about one gender or the other picking a mate, like selecting something at a supply shed. You both have to be sure that you're right for each other. Eighteen is the youngest you can be to declare your intention to say vows. It's not the only age you can be. Now tell me, what brought this on?"

She gave a little shrug. "Just something Stephen said to me."

"I see. Well, next time he does that, tell him that when the time comes, you'll be making your own decisions, and thank him very much."

They passed two more fenced fields before arriving at the road to the Reilly homestead. As Peter made the turn, Laurel looked ahead and saw five other vehicles parked in the yard, each a different colour.

"Light green for Chen, red for Barrett, purple for McQueen," said Peter, "orange for Gillespie, and brown for Sorensen." He lined up their blue car with the Chens' vehicle and cut the power. "The others will be here soon. With luck,

Ben Zimmerman will leave Rachel at home this time." Then, catching himself, he turned and added in a stern voice, "And you never heard me say that."

"Say what, Papa?" she replied, keeping a straight face.

According to Laurel's parents, dairy farming had been a lost art on Earth and Mars for nearly two centuries when the habitat pods touched down on Manua. The families designated for dairy production had had to learn everything from reference texts in the library database. Evidently, they'd learned it well. The Reilly farm was a thriving concern, with a milking shed, an enormous refrigerated warehouse, and outbuildings dedicated to food processing and animal feed storage. Besides milk and cheeses, this farm produced enough cream, butter and yogourt to supply all of Central Valley.

However, things hadn't gone smoothly at the beginning. It had taken years to grow the first animal embryos into breedable heifers and then into milk-producing cows. During that time, the interdependence cornerstone of the colony became more than an abstract concept in the Fingers. The four dairy farming families barely managed to scrape by, kept afloat only by the patience and generosity of their neighbours. Eventually, that patience had paid off. But Laurel knew now about the scars left by unpleasant past experiences.

As she crossed the threshold of the Reilly home, she couldn't help wondering. Did not having enough in the past make people want to own a lot of things in the present? Did it make them ungenerous, or even stingy? Or would they just be overly careful about not wasting things?

Peter stepped up beside Laurel and placed his arm around her shoulder. "Relax, duckling. The emergency is ours, not yours," he whispered into her ear.

She nodded absently, her gaze attracted to the array of spherical objects suspended at various heights from the ceiling of the Reilly living room. They crowded the room, creating an obstacle course for anyone wishing to cross the habitat pod. They'd been painted to resemble planets. And one of them in particular appeared very familiar.

"Is that supposed to be Manua?" she wondered aloud.

"No, luv, it's Earth, the first home world of humans," said a warm voice to her right. Laurel turned and found a slender, white-haired woman watching her with eyes that teetered on the edge of mischief, just like Evan Reilly's. "And that's its moon," she said, stepping closer and pointing with a finger at the much smaller sphere hanging alongside the first one. "Luna, they called it. They also thought it made people crazy once a month and called them 'loony' as well. Strange, but not surprising. This is not my usual decor, by the way. It's Donna's science project." Pointing again, she continued. "That's Mars, the first human colony, which also happens to be our home world. Its moons have names too, in case you're interested. And Venus, and Mercury, closest to the sun. The asteroid belt was a challenge to fit inside the habitat, but we managed rather well, I thought. Unfortunately, Colleen didn't agree. She only gave it a B. Teachers," she said, lowering her voice and making a face.

"I heard that, Mother Reilly," came another woman's response from the kitchen.

Laughing, Peter said, "Thanks for the tour, Sybil. This young'un is my daughter, Laurel."

"Laurel," she echoed softly. "So, you're the girl who's stolen my grandson's heart." Then she turned toward the table where Sean and Evan were sitting with the other adults and declared, "I approve, darlin'!"

Now they were all laughing. Her cheeks burning, Laurel stared at the floor, wishing she could sink through it. As three more people walked through the door, drawing Sybil away, Peter spirited his daughter over to one of the unoccupied chairs where she could recompose herself.

A moment later, Colleen put a glass of milk in front of her. Evan's mother was short and sturdy, with pleasant features and a dimple in her chin. She was from the city, Laurel recalled, just like Emma Nyquist, but neither of them looked as terribly different from farm folk as Mr. Reilly had earlier described.

"Don't mind my mother-in-law," Colleen consoled her quietly. "It's just her way. She loves louder than most, and she won't be happy until every young'un in the valley is paired up."

Once each family was represented at the table, farm hospitality demanded that every guest get a generous slice of Sybil's famous custard pie and some milk to wash it down. Then the dishes were cleared away and Sean Reilly called the meeting to order.

"Some important information has come to light that can't wait for the next regular conclave," he announced. "Before I present it, though, we need to hear from Peter Nyquist about that discussion he had with the scientist in the city."

Gazing around the table, Peter began, "I've been doing a lot of reading since the last city market day, and a lot of thinking. I told you I would notify you if there was anything in the scientists' report that we didn't already know. It turns out there are a couple of things worth mentioning."

"Wait a minute. You said you read it," Nils Sorensen interrupted, frowning. "Does that mean you got your hands on an actual copy of the report?"

"It does. And anyone who doubts my word, or who believes I may be misinterpreting its contents, is welcome to read it for themselves."

Laurel stiffened in her chair. It wasn't like her father to issue a pre-emptive challenge like this. He was daring them to question his trustworthiness.

But the only voice that answered him was Malcolm Chen's, urging, "Please go on, Peter. We're listening."

"All right. First, those scientists have been focusing on small details, cluttering up the big picture with numbers and statistics that are actually preventing them from seeing the truth. The fact is, this planet has been playing favourites. All the evidence indicates that it loves farmers, tolerates miners, and dislikes the city folk. That has to be the reason that we're changing in such different ways."

"Are you suggesting that Manua is alive?" demanded Sean Reilly.

"In a way, yes," said Peter. "And I do have proof to back that up. The scientist that I met with was able to give me some additional research data from the library, information that the Consortium has been suppressing. He's also given me transcribed copies of the ark ship's logs, beginning with the first sighting of Manua from space and concluding several days after the ship landed. In her final log entry, the captain officially resigned her command and handed the vessel over to the colony's governing council."

Turning to his daughter, he continued, "Laurel, you've been telling our children the story of how the colony was founded. Tell it to us the same way."

Caught off guard, she stammered a bit. Then she closed her eyes, drew a steadying breath, and pretended that she was sitting in the big chair with nieces and nephews at her feet. "The ark ship left Mars and travelled through many Gates, searching for a world where humans could make a new home for themselves. The voyage was very long. It lasted fifty years. Then, the captain found this beautiful planet that we call Manua."

"So far, that matches the account in the ship's logs," Peter interjected. "Keep going, Laurel."

"And the captain showed Manua to the scientists, and they went down to the planet to take measurements. They checked to make sure the water was safe for drinking, and the soil rich for planting, and the air good to breathe."

"Actually, that's not quite true," said Peter. "According to the ship's logs, the scientists followed standard procedure. They went down in Personal Life Support suits and collected samples, which they brought back to the ship for analysis."

"What difference does that make?" demanded Sid Cameron. "She's telling a story to children, for God's sake! And the result was the same, wasn't it? The planet was declared fit for human habitation."

"That's the thing, Sid," Peter told him. "It wasn't. According to the records, every sample was loaded with alien bacteria, all extremely robust and some of it described as 'inimical to human life'. The air was breathable, but everything else was toxic. The problem was, the ship was in uncharted space and getting low on fuel. Somehow, they had to make this planet their home, because the odds of finding another that was even close to being habitable were heavily against them.

"So, they activated colonization protocols. The ship entered orbit, and everyone remained aboard her while the scientists worked to develop a vaccine that would protect humans from the bacteria on the surface. It took time. When the laboratory trials showed favourable results, all the crew and the colonists were inoculated. Then they were placed under observation and regularly tested to determine whether their immune systems were developing the necessary antibodies."

"Obviously, they did, since we're here," said Todd McQueen.

Peter shook his head sadly, and Laurel saw eyebrows rise and shoulders sag all around the table. "Twenty percent of the vaccinated colonists died of bacterial infection while aboard ship, and the clinical results from the survivors were inconsistent. However, they'd run out of time. After two years in orbit, the ship had just enough fuel for a controlled descent to the planet's surface. Meanwhile, the habitat pods could only be deployed from the air. So, whether or not the colonists were adequately prepared to survive in the alien environment, the captain had no choice but to program the pods and send them down."

"But they had the PLS suits," piped up Emil Leclerc.

"Just enough for the crew. Not enough to make a difference," Peter replied.

"You got all this from the ship's logs?" Reilly asked.

"And the shipboard scientific records, yes," Peter assured him. "We've been telling our children a fairy tale when in fact it was a horror story. The Consortium decided that it needed to be revised. So, they reset the clock. Those two years in orbit never happened. We saw Manua, it tested friendly to human life, and we settled here. Period."

"I still don't see your point, Nyquist," said Ken Barrett. "So what if the colony didn't begin the way we've been telling it? Is that really what's important here? However it came about, Manua is our home now, and life here is good. Maybe burying the truth wasn't such a terrible thing to do."

"And maybe it's going to come back and bite us one day, and we'll be sorry we ignored it," Sean Reilly informed him hotly. "You may enjoy being manipulated and lied to, Ken, but I for one do not."

The room went silent. For a long moment, all eyes focused on the two men glaring at each other. Then Chen cleared his throat, dragging their attention to the other end of the table. "Why don't we let Peter finish explaining?" he said mildly, and gestured to him to continue.

"My point is, because that earlier information was withheld from the scientists conducting the study, their baseline data is incorrect. It invalidates every comparison they have made between what we are now and what we supposedly were at the founding of the colony. A hundred years is not that long. It's just one human lifespan. When the study began, fifty years ago, the scientists were able to interview people who remembered coming down in the pods, and the transcripts of those conversations were included in their final report."

"Which the Consortium didn't want us to see," said Nils Sorensen.

"That's right. And here's why." Peter produced a folded piece of paper and opened it carefully. "This is an excerpt that jumped out at me while I was reading: 'The first thing we did was drill down to the water table and bring up a sample. The water was cold and clear, with a PH level of 6.8. It tasted a little strange, but it didn't make us sick, so we kept using it, and after a while we noticed that the taste had gone away.'

"When we arrived on Manua's surface a hundred years ago," he said, dropping the paper onto the table, "the fresh water was safe for us to drink. Nobody made that up. Two years earlier, it had tested toxic and would have poisoned us. Nobody made that up either. There's only one possible explanation for the discrepancy: the alien bacteria used to create the vaccine must have altered our DNA, making it compatible with the planetary environment. I'm guessing that the scientists weren't able to weaken the alien organism enough for our antibodies to eliminate the infection entirely. Instead, they managed to slow it down so that it could mutate us without killing us."

"That might explain the changes in us. It doesn't explain the changes to the water," McQueen pointed out. "The scientists would have been using the same testing equipment, looking for the same things both times. Whether or not we could tolerate drinking it, for samplings taken just two years apart, their readings should have been nearly identical."

"I know," said Peter. "The soil and water haven't changed appreciably during our lifetime, but they obviously underwent some drastic transformation during those two years that our ancestors spent aboard the ship. Meanwhile, everything else on this planet is in a state of flux, and the changes have been happening too quickly to be written off as a process of evolution."

"And do you have a theory to cover that as well?" Sorensen asked.

"I do, and you're not going to like it," said Peter.

"Here we go again," someone groaned, prompting a

scattering of tentative laughter.

"After reading the report, I looked up 'terraforming' in the reference database of the library," Peter told them. "I got an error message that said, 'The information you have requested is classified for Consortium use only.'"

"That's strange. It wasn't classified when I accessed it from my home computer in the city twenty years ago," Colleen said.

Laurel did some quick math. The scientists had been more than halfway through their study when the Consortium decided to put "terraforming" beyond the colonists' reach. Whatever that word meant, clearly it frightened them.

"You don't honestly believe the Consortium has been secretly terraforming this planet, do you?" demanded Barrett.

"No," said Peter. "I believe someone else has been doing it, someone who started the process before we arrived and doesn't know we're here. I'm afraid we may be trespassers, camping out on private property."

Everyone leaned backward at once, as though pushed by shadow hands.

"That's quite an accusation, Nyquist," Sid Cameron observed.

"It's only an accusation if we knew we were doing it. Otherwise, I'm just stating a possibility."

"But you suspect the Consortium had an inkling?" said Sean Reilly.

"Twenty years ago? More than an inkling."

"And that brings us to my reason for calling this emergency meeting," Reilly announced to the room. "Evan, tell the elders what you told me earlier today."

Evan got to his feet. For the first time since Laurel had met him, he looked nervous. "I've been sending and receiving with Timothy Klein. Everyone was curious to know where he'd been hiding for the past thirty-eight years, so I asked him straight out. He told me about a special place he'd found, inside a mountain in the eastern range of the Thumb.

"He thought of it as a habitat, because it had rooms, and the walls were made of metal, like our pods. He said he could communicate with the habitat, too. He just pictured in his mind whatever he needed, and what he'd imagined would appear. When he needed to sleep, the habitat could even turn off the voices inside his head."

"A telepathic habitat? That sounds familiar. Wasn't the Consortium experimenting with mind-linked technology for a while?" said Todd McQueen.

"They still are," Peter informed him stiffly. Laurel reached for his hand under the table. He gave it a reassuring squeeze and she relaxed. Nyquist family secrets would not be revealed at this meeting.

"But that's not the important thing," Reilly said. "Tell them the rest, Evan."

"Tim thought to me about the locations of several more of these habitats. He says there are three in the Fingers. One is in the eastern range of Central Valley, near the bluffs."

"I see two possibilities here," said Peter, raising his voice to be heard above the sudden swell of murmuring in the room. "First, the Consortium may have planted the pods around Manua so they could spy on us. Or second, what I believe is more likely, the mountains may have formed around those structures as part of the terraforming process. They could even be observation stations, programmed to transmit a signal to the planet's owners when the process is completed. Either way, I feel strongly that we need to verify Tim's story. If we can find the habitat in our own eastern range and determine whether its origin is human or alien, that will help us decide what to do next."

"What exactly are you proposing, Nyquist?" demanded Sorensen.

"An expedition," Peter replied, "to investigate the mountains east of Todd and Linda's farm."

"Led by your son Stephen, no doubt, who happens to be a climber," said Malcolm Chen, the corners of his mouth twitching. "And Laurel is a reacher. And we already know that Evan is a telepath like Tim Klein, and that he likes to take risks."

"Just as you know that I would never suggest sending three young'uns into danger on their own," Peter reminded him sternly. "You're right, though—their skills could prove quite useful for an excursion like this." Addressing the entire group, he continued, "Whether this conclave supports the idea or not, I intend to put a climbing party together. It will need to include a telepath, either Evan or one of the others in the Fingers, along with a couple of impartial witnesses who will attest to whatever we find in that part of the range. If any of you would like to volunteer...?"

Chen leaned forward, his expression serious now. "Are you sure about this, Peter? Absolutely certain?"

"About what I've told you, yes," he replied firmly. "About Tim's story, no. That's why I'm asking for witnesses, plural, and the more skeptical they are, the better."

"I'm a climber," said Todd McQueen. "I've been in and out of those mountains for years without coming across anything like what Evan just described. Count me in, Nyquist."

A long moment of silence later, Ken Barrett raised his hand. "I'm not a climber, but I have long-distance vision. I'll come along. Just don't expect me to leap from rock to rock like one of Gorodin's goats out in Baby Finger Valley," he grumbled.

Laurel nudged Evan gently and murmured, "Nick and Daniel's parents raise goats? Why?"

"For milk," he replied. "It's just as good as cow's milk, and goats are smaller, so they don't need as much land."

"If Evan goes with you, you're taking me as well," declared Sean Reilly, jutting out his jaw. "I may not have a useful talent to contribute to this adventure of yours, Nyquist, but he's my only son's only son."

"Understood," Peter replied. "And that completes our group."

CHAPTER FIVE

"You know, it's ironic," said Colleen between sips of fruity herbal tea. She was trying a new blend and had invited Chen and the Nyquists to stay behind after the meeting and sample it. "The Consortium decided to evacuate Mars on ark ships because aliens were threatening to wipe out all human life in our solar system and we needed to make sure our race survived. Now, here we are, doing more than surviving, but only because we're not human anymore."

"Those alien bacteria did us a favour, luv," said Sybil. "For all we know, Manua is still toxic to human life. Without the vaccine, we wouldn't be here, the animals wouldn't be here…"

"The cows got the vaccine?" Laurel said.

"Oh, yes!" Sybil told her. "As soon as they were born. Remember, Sean? What was the name of that veterinarian your granddad told us about? The one who went from farm to farm giving the new calves and lambs their shots."

"And the foals, and the kids, and the hatchlings," her mate added, setting his half-full cup back on the table. "Doctor Pelletier. He made a point of inoculating every animal on Manua for the first few years, to ensure we'd have healthy herds and flocks. Nice blend, by the way," he told Colleen, "but I'd prefer a little less fruit and a little more kick, if you catch my meaning."

She did, along with everyone else at the table. Sharing a look with her mother-in-law, Colleen drew herself up in her seat. "This is a tea tasting, Dad," she reminded him, not unkindly. "Tea adulterating is a separate event."

Meanwhile, Chen had emptied his cup and poured himself a second helping. "Roberta will love this flavour," he declared. "Be sure to bring some to the next farmers' market." Addressing Peter, he added, "So, what tipped you off, Nyquist? To the terraforming, I mean."

"The description of Manua in the measurers' reports. It was outwardly perfect, as though someone had made it to order, just for us. In the Goldilocks zone, with every type of terrain, soil for farming in five protected valleys, a variety of complex vegetation, the ample water table, the warm climate… and not a single species of fauna. No birds, no fish, no mammals or reptiles. Not even an insect. Put that together with the abnormally rapid rate of change and the aggressiveness of the bacteria in the water and the soil, and there was only one explanation that made sense. This was a world still under construction. And when we settled on it, we became absorbed in the process as well. You might even say we're being xenoformed."

"Fortunately, it hasn't been a painful process," Sybil commented. "How different from human do you think we are?"

Peter shrugged. "No idea. The research materials and historical records I was given are all written transcripts. There are probably some images or vids taken during the voyage that we could use for comparison, but I'm pretty sure the Consortium will have locked them up tight somewhere."

"Speaking of the Consortium," said Chen. "It occurs to me that by presenting your theory to the entire conclave, you've also alerted the spy in our midst."

"I know," Peter replied. "I'm actually counting on word getting back to the city. McQueen and Barrett aren't the only witnesses we'll be taking with us on our expedition. Evan is part of a network of telepaths, including one in the Wrist and several who live in the city. It will be a live telepathic broadcast to every part of Manua. I'd like to see the Consortium try to bury *that*.

"Meanwhile, if Tim Klein's story turns out to be true, it will support my contention that someone else got here ahead of us and began terraforming this world. And that the process is still ongoing, with us caught in the middle of it."

"The moment we make it public knowledge, we'll have a battle on our hands," Reilly warned. "The Consortium likes being in a position of power. That's why they treat people the way that they do, doling out technology and information, and controlling movement into and out of the city."

His last words struck a nerve. Earlier conversations surfacing in her mind, Laurel watched as Colleen stared at the tabletop, her cheeks flushing. The story was that Peter Nyquist had brought Evan's mother to the Fingers to be a teacher for Patrick Reilly. But Mr. Chen had said that after Colleen left the city, the governing council tightened its security measures. Apparently, she hadn't simply been sent for—she'd been rescued, just like Emma and Marie.

Marie remembered everything she heard. Laurel and Emma remembered everything they experienced. Was Colleen Reilly a rememberer too? Laurel dropped her own gaze to her lap, yearning to ask but not daring to.

"They only think they've got the power, Sean. Some of them are waking up to that fact. That's why they're so desperate to hang onto what they *do* control. But don't worry. I have no intention of starting a war," Peter assured him.

"Unless they refuse to hand over Roger and Annelise?" Chen suggested.

Peter paused, staring at him across the table. "Let's not get ahead of ourselves," he said at last. "What we do next will depend on what we find in the eastern range, near the bluffs. And we'll make that decision together."

∿

It didn't rain often on Manua, but when it did, it rained hard. Water came down in wind-driven sheets, sometimes for hours at a time. It drenched the soil and replenished the wells, quenching the thirst of the trees in the orchards and triggering an explosion of growth in the fields.

For three days after the emergency conclave, clouds gathered over the Fingers, eventually blanketing the sky. As they darkened, the air beneath them grew still and heavy. Then, as the Nyquists were finishing up their evening meal, they heard the deep rumble of thunder overhead, and the drumbeat-like sound of the first fat water drops on the roof of the habitat.

Laurel had felt something inside her wind itself up a little more tightly with each passing day. Climbing was second nature to her brother, but she'd never done it before. She guessed that mountain climbing was dangerous, perhaps even more dangerous than visiting the city. And she knew why her father wanted her on this expedition. She was a reacher, with shadow hands that could push and pull. She might be able to prevent injury by holding someone in place or slowing a fall. At least, that was what he was apparently hoping.

Laurel wasn't so sure. Shadow hands served quite well for holding a squirming five-year-old in place. But there was a huge difference between keeping a child safe inside a habitat and watching out for a group of adults and young'uns on a perilous outdoor adventure. They would be depending on her. What if her shadow hands weren't up to the challenge? What if someone got badly hurt and they had to turn back, and all of her father's planning ended up being for nothing, because she wasn't quick enough or strong enough to do what was needed?

The progressive glooming of the sky had been reflected in Laurel's journal entries as well, and in her dreams. It came as some consolation that these nightmares about struggling up mountainsides and tumbling into abysses were entirely her own. But it didn't make them any easier to bear.

Then the clouds cracked open, seeming to break Laurel's tension as well. She fell asleep to the pounding of the rain and awoke to a world that had been scoured and scrubbed bright as new. The air smelled crisp and clean, and everything glistened in the sun, from the distant apple trees to the weedy clumps of wiregrass that huddled beside the porch.

"Stephen tells me he's ready to go, but safety is important, and wet rocks can be slippery. I think it would be wise to wait for things to dry out a bit before we attempt a climb," said Peter at breakfast. "Whatever's there now will still be there tomorrow, I'm sure."

Laurel swallowed a sigh of disappointment. Her father was right. One more day probably wouldn't make a difference to the outcome of the expedition. But it was one more whole day for her to spend worrying about it.

Peter and Emma locked eyes for a moment. His eyebrows rose. She dipped her head slightly. He turned to Laurel and said, "I could use an extra pair of hands in the fabricating shed this morning, duckling. Would you like to learn something about maintaining a car?"

Her first impulse was to say yes, but duty compelled her to ask, "What about the children, Papa?"

"Margriet and I can take care of them for a couple of hours," said Emma. "It won't hurt them to have story time *after* lunch for a change. And if they finish their lessons early, Marie can play them some music. Go with your father, Laurel. We'll find a way to manage without you."

"She sounded sad," Laurel remarked as they walked across

the yard together, headed for the large building at the far end of the compound.

"You're getting close to choosing age, duckling. Your mother is realizing that it won't be long before we have to manage without you, period. Ilse just turned twelve, so she'll take over as teacher when you leave us. The lessons won't be a problem, since they're all on the computer, but I fear the children are going to miss your wonderful tales."

"Do I have to leave? Can't my mate come here to live instead?"

He stopped in mid-step and gave her a strange look. "You know that's not the way it's done in the Fingers. Menfolk belong to the land. Womenfolk travel."

"It may be the way it's done, but is it the only way it *can* be done?"

Unexpectedly, he chuckled. "You seem to have inherited my rebellious streak. When I was your age, I asked myself that same question."

"Is that why you went to the Technikum in the city?"

"Yes. I had a talent, and I wanted to do more with it than grow apples. And if I'd had even one brother instead of two sisters, and if I hadn't fallen in love with your mother, things might have gone very differently for me. And you and your brothers would not exist."

She frowned. "You came back because you had to, not because you wanted to."

"I came back for several reasons. Not the least of them was that I'd finally come to realize that being a farmer didn't mean I couldn't also be and do other things. And not just other things, but useful things. Enjoyable things. I'm a planner, and I love to work with my hands. That makes me a pretty good crafter and engineer. And thanks to those years at the Technikum, I know my way around a computer system as well."

"And you're a criminal mastermind, and you grow apples."

"And *Nyquists* grow apples," he corrected her with a smile in his voice. "And look at you, now: you're a reacher, and a teacher, and a captivating storyteller—"

"Because I remember everything I read." She hesitated, dreading the answer but needing to hear it. "Papa, am I going to have to keep this secret for the rest of my life?"

"I hope not, duckling, I really do. But until people are willing to open their minds…"

"Is Evan's mother a rememberer?" The question had just popped out. She clapped a hand to her mouth, too late.

"Possibly, but I doubt it," he told her, swinging open the square front and side doors of the shed. Daylight flooded the lower level of the building, rebounding off the polished surfaces of the Nyquists' blue car. "I knew about her from your Uncle Roger. She and Annelise were students together back in the city. The governing council was preparing to arrest her for speaking out against the Consortium. So, we arranged for her to get away before they could serve the warrant."

"Evan says his grandparents sent for her so she could teach his father. Was that a lie?"

"No." He took down a leather apron from a hook on the wall and slipped the bib on over his head. "When the Reillys heard what I was planning to do, they told me they had a job and a room for her, if she was interested. It turned out she was. No one was lying," he added, fastening the rest of the apron around his hips. "Evan told you what he'd always been told. It just wasn't the whole story."

She considered for a moment. "So it isn't a lie to hold back part of the truth?"

"It depends on what part is being withheld, and whether people really need to hear it. Sometimes it's a kindness not to reveal everything you know. Like the fact that you and your mother are rememberers. Is it a lie if I tell people that your talent is reaching and hers is threadworking?"

This required a bit more thought. Eventually, Laurel shook her head. "It doesn't feel like lying," she told him.

"Good answer," he said. "If it feels like lying, then it is. Here." She glanced up and saw something in his hand. "I made this one for you," he explained, opening it up to reveal a second apron, smaller than the one he was wearing.

She put it on. "Did the city people ever find out who was responsible for Colleen's escape?"

"Fortunately, no." He opened a drawer and extracted several strange looking devices wrapped in coils of insulated wiring. Then, pausing, he added, "Or maybe they were just relieved that she wouldn't be around to build opposition to their unspeakable experiment anymore, so they decided to let the matter drop."

"The living memory chips?" Laurel's vision suddenly clouded with tears. "Papa, if people knew about that and didn't say anything to stop it—!"

"It feels like lying?" Peter gazed deeply into her eyes. "It is. Sometimes I wonder whether saving her was the right thing to do. And now you have two secrets to keep, duckling: yours and mine."

An hour after dawn on the fifth day after the meeting, Peter Nyquist drove his blue car out of the shed. He paused in the yard while Stephen and Laurel got into the back seat. Then, he headed up the road to pick up Ken Barrett before speeding north to the McQueen farm. It was a quiet ride. A trunk filled with specially-crafted climbing gear had been strapped to the back of the vehicle, not for Stephen but for the others in the party who lacked his special gifts. The extra weight at one end made the car slower and harder to steer. As it wove in and out of the water that still puddled in deeply worn ruts on the path, Peter drove with his lips pressed tightly together and both white-knuckled hands gripping the wheel.

Evan and his grandfather were standing at the head of the McQueens' driveway, chatting with Todd McQueen and a heavy-set woman with a thick blond braid hanging down her back. As the Nyquist car slowly approached, she shook her head and went inside the habitat.

"I gather Linda McQueen doesn't approve of our little enterprise," Peter commented. "That's too bad." Turning to Stephen, he explained, "They were both climbers when Todd chose her. She doesn't explore much anymore, but Todd is still game, or he wouldn't have volunteered to come with us."

As soon as Peter had parked, McQueen stepped over and leaned his leathery face through the open window. "You may as well cut the power, Nyquist. The most direct route to the mountains is along the top of the bluffs. Unfortunately, it's cross-country over uneven ground. Too rough for a fully loaded car, unless you're fond of broken axles."

"And the less direct route?"

"That's even worse. Shale going up and scree going down,

and no flat stretches at all. And it adds an hour to the trip."

"All right, then," Peter replied, and turned off the engine.

Once Stephen had distributed the gear and taken inventory of the various talents at their disposal, the little group set out for the bluffs.

McQueen hadn't overstated the difficulty of the trek that lay ahead of them. All but him and Stephen were doing this for the very first time. Initially, they'd been like children on a pleasure hike: spread out, cheerfully chattering, and taking in the scenery. But it wasn't long before the weight of their packs, the heat of the sun, and the hard terrain began to take a toll. An hour later they were walking single file, too preoccupied with avoiding the partly buried rocks and hidden depressions in the ground to engage in idle chatter.

Sweating beneath the ten kilos of climbing gear slung over her back, Laurel was wishing she had shadow legs to go with her shadow hands. However, the two climbers were in their element right now. When their party finally reached the eastern range, they both stood with their hands on their hips, grinning with anticipation at what lay before them.

Laurel had to admit, it was an impressive sight. The row of jagged grey peaks towered over the land like ancient sentries. It was a challenge truly worthy of a climber. However, as the unease furling and unfurling in her stomach kept reminding her, she wasn't a climber. Even with Stephen's help, getting up the side of one of those mountains wasn't going to be easy.

Evan stood quietly for a moment, gazing at each of them in turn. Then he raised his arm and pointed to the peak immediately to their right. "Over there."

"That's the one? How do you know?" McQueen asked.

"I thought-sent a question, and it answered me."

"The mountain spoke to you?" he returned with evident skepticism.

Evan shook his head. "Something inside it did. It knows we're here now, and it's waiting for us."

That could be good or bad, Laurel reflected with a shiver. She shouldered her rope and harness again and set out with the rest of the group for the base of the mountain. It was farther away than it looked. Half an hour later she was perspiring and panting once more.

Trudging along at the back of the line, she risked an

occasional glance upward. From a distance and with the sun behind it, Evan's mountain gave the appearance of a dark, featureless wall. She doubted whether even a climber as talented as her brother could scale such a monolith safely. However, as they drew closer, the smooth rock face sprouted blemishes—nicks, crevices, and shallow ledges. They snagged the sunlight that slipped between the peaks, casting odd-shaped shadows that lengthened as the expedition party approached.

"We'll stop here and put on the harnesses," Stephen instructed. "There's a deep ledge about a quarter of the way up the slope. I'll go up first and make sure it can hold all of us. If it can, I'll secure a double line, and Laurel and I will help you climb onto it. If it can't, I'll find us an alternate route."

Meanwhile, Barrett was staring intently up the mountainside.

"What are you seeing, Ken?" Peter inquired.

"If I didn't know better," he replied slowly, "I'd call them tool marks, Nyquist. That ledge? It looks carved out of the rock."

"Then it appears we're in the right place."

Laurel's harness had been crafted from strips of double-stitched leather. It went around her upper body the way Maisie's bridle fitted her head, and it fastened the same way, with locking hooks and rings made of metal. If she lost her footing, a line attached to one of the rings was supposed to stop her from falling.

The longer she thought about this, the queasier her stomach felt. The straps were awfully narrow. Stephen had made these harnesses himself, and he was an excellent crafter, but what if he'd misjudged her weight? If she fell, she wasn't sure her shadow hands could save her either. They'd never been tested in a situation like this. Unfortunately, the only way to guarantee that she didn't slip while climbing was by remaining safely on the ground, and a farm girl with four older brothers could not afford to be a coward.

"Quite an adventure, isn't it?" came Evan's voice over her shoulder. "I can hardly wait to see what's inside that mountain."

Already knowing what she would find in Evan's eyes if she turned around, she kept her gaze fixed on Stephen instead.

Her brother had begun to climb, wearing two coils of heavy rope slung across his chest and a sack of tools clipped to his belt. Second nature was an understatement, she decided. Stephen scaled the rise in smooth, liquid motions, his body swinging side to side as he traded handholds for footholds with unerring grace and precision. He made it appear so easy. Almost as though the mountain itself was helping him.

"Yes," she replied faintly, "quite an adventure, for some."

"I thought you enjoyed taking risks. Or does Milady doubt that our quest will be successful?" Evan prodded her.

"No."

"No, you don't enjoy taking risks? Or no, you don't doubt the value of our quest?"

Laurel felt her father's arm snugging her shoulders. "It's all right, duckling. We're all a little nervous." She sensed rather than saw him give Evan a look.

A pause, then, "Does it help if I point out that one of the people making this climb is my grandda, who is at least four times our age and actually creaks when he moves? And if he can do it—"

Reilly heard him. "Hey! You'd better watch that kind of talk, young'un!"

Laurel appreciated their efforts to lighten her mood, but they couldn't stop the churning in the pit of her stomach.

Once Stephen had pulled himself over the lip of the ledge, he stood up and waved to the rest of the group. Then he disappeared from sight. Several moments later, his face came back into view.

"There's plenty of room," he called down, "and it's solid. I've anchored a pulley assembly up here, and I'm dropping both ends of a safety line. Mr. McQueen, if you'll handle that...? And Laurel, keep your shadow hands ready in case someone freezes up and needs a little help to keep going. You two will come up last."

"Wait a minute!" said Evan. "This isn't right. There has to be another way in, at ground level."

"What are you talking about?" McQueen demanded.

"Tim Klein isn't a climber. He's a telepath. And he was only a child when he came across his 'habitat'. If it had been this hard to get into, I doubt that he would ever have found it. When we were sending to each other earlier, he said he 'fell into the mountain'. It didn't make any sense to me at the time, but now that we're here…"

"The young'un is right," said Barrett. "If there's something inside that's expecting us, why make us work to find the entrance? More to the point, we came out here to test Tim's story. Thirty-eight years ago, he would have been a scared, tired, hungry child, begging the voices in his head to help him."

"And doing it telepathically," Peter pointed out. "If there's a way to get inside, it must be telepathically controlled. Evan, we need you to think to the mountain again. Ask it for a doorway."

"You people just don't want to climb," came Stephen's disappointed voice from overhead. Then, "Whoa! *That's* pretty," he declared.

It certainly was. Before the eyes of the six who still stood at the base of the mountain, a swath of the rock face shimmered for several seconds as though it was melting away. Then the shimmering stopped, and the wall appeared to return to normal.

"What just happened?" demanded Barrett.

"Let's find out." McQueen scooped up a fist-sized rock and lobbed it at the mountainside. It went right through the wall, not making a sound or even a ripple.

Half a dozen jaws dropped in unison.

Keeping his gaze riveted on the spot where the rock had disappeared, Peter said tersely, "Everyone, stay back from the wall! Stephen, you need to come down here, right now!"

"On my way, Dad."

"Evan, is that what I think it is?"

"It's a portal, Mr. Nyquist," the young'un confirmed. "And the only way to find out where it leads is to walk through it."

"Maybe not. Tim Klein fell through one of those and ended up in a sort of habitat. He said it gave him whatever he needed, correct?"

"Yes, sir."

"And at the time he went through it, what he probably wanted was to go home." Peter turned and gave Evan a piercing look. "When you ordered up this portal, what did you tell the mountain *we* wanted?"

Evan paused. "That we needed a door to get inside and

learn what it really is."

"What are you thinking, Nyquist?" asked Reilly.

"Based on what Evan just said, that it's most likely safe to walk through. If this is alien technology, there's still the chance that we could end up aboard a ship somewhere, or on another planet, but the odds are against it."

"Thanks for putting *that* thought into my head," McQueen grumped.

"Whatever we do, we have to do it as a group," Peter told them. "Otherwise, there's no point in bringing witnesses along with us. So we'll need to take a vote. It will have to be unanimous, and the young'uns have a say. If we're not all willing to take this risk, then none of us should. We'll go back home with what we've already learned, and there will be no hard feelings."

As Stephen came over to join them, looks passed back and forth among the members of the expedition. Evan opened his mouth to say something, but his grandfather put a hand on his shoulder and whispered something into his ear that made him change his mind.

"We've come this far, and I for one want answers, not more questions," said Barrett. "I vote we keep going."

"All those in agreement, raise your hand," said Reilly.

Laurel had a lump in her throat that felt an awful lot like her heart, but this was a mystery she could not walk away from. Evidently, everyone else felt the same way. A forest of hands shot up around her.

"I don't think we'll need the climbing gear," her father remarked. "Since this excursion was my idea, I'll go first." He turned toward the portal and put his arm through it up to the elbow. "There's definitely empty space in there," he told the others. Then he took a deep breath and stepped through the wall.

Silence. For several seconds, everyone stood frozen in place.

Then they heard his voice, sounding close by. "I'm in a large room," he called out to them. "It's quite comfortable, so feel free to join me."

Stephen and Laurel didn't hesitate. Pausing on the other side of the portal, Laurel glanced around and saw walls, a floor, and a ceiling, all apparently made of the same polished metal as Emma Nyquist's living room. This room, however, was devoid of furnishings. For just a second, Laurel's memory flashed back to the day she'd first entered the Sorensens' home, that feeling of being out of place until she caught a glimpse of something familiar...

"Huh!" said Stephen, pointing. "Where did *that* come from?"

Following his gaze, she saw the tapestry that Emma had woven—and that Greta Sorensen had displayed in her living room—seemingly attached to the far wall of this room inside the mountain.

All at once, an arm shot through the portal and past her head, close enough to graze her cheek. Annoyed, she reached out a shadow hand and yanked the rest of Evan Reilly into the room. "You nearly hit me!"

"You shouldn't stand so close to the door," he told her. His eyes were sparkling, and she looked away, just in time to notice and duck another probing forearm.

"He's right, it's a holographic illusion," said a voice from the other side, and a heartbeat later McQueen followed his arm through the portal. In short order, Barrett and Reilly entered as well.

"So, the mountain is hollow after all," remarked McQueen. He made a face. "A little sparsely decorated for my tastes, though."

At once, the air beside him was shimmering. With a collective intake of breath, everyone froze again, staring at the light effect. When it stopped, a piece of furniture had materialized—a brown upholstered chair with a plump seat cushion and generously stuffed arms.

McQueen's eyes looked in danger of falling out of their sockets. For a moment he struggled to speak. Meanwhile, Reilly let out a low whistle of appreciation.

"That's my chair from home!" McQueen finally managed to sputter.

"Tim said that all he had to do was think about what he wanted and the habitat gave it to him," Evan reminded the group.

"But Tim Klein is a telepath," Reilly pointed out. "McQueen isn't."

"I don't think it matters here, Grandda," said Evan.

"Well, I don't know about the rest of you," declared Barrett, "but I am now officially impressed. If Todd's chair wasn't teleported here, then this place has technology that can create things out of thin air."

"So did Mars before we left it," said Peter. "Holographic technology. I learned about it at the Technikum. That chair and the wall hanging are both holograms. And I'm afraid we're no closer to proving anything than we were before. Still… are the other telepaths witnessing this, Evan?"

The young'un gave him a grin. "They're all tuned in, Mr. Nyquist. And Nick Gorodin wants you to know that he's mightily impressed too."

"Good for him," said Barrett in a voice tinged with irony.

Something had begun gnawing on the corners of Laurel's mind. "Papa, are holograms real?"

"They're copies made out of light, duckling. If you mean are they solid, the answer is yes. Mr. McQueen can sit in that chair and it will feel the same as the one in his living room. If you mean, could he take that chair home with him and have two identical chairs…? No. It only exists in this particular space because of the light-projecting devices that I assume are positioned all around it."

"So, if I were hungry and the habitat gave me a sandwich, it wouldn't be real food."

He gazed at her thoughtfully. "Your stomach might feel full, but you wouldn't be getting any nourishment from it, no. And as soon as you stepped outside, your hunger would return."

Tears started in her eyes. "Poor Tim! When we saw him on the commons, he was skin and bones. Now we know why. The habitat must have been starving him."

Evan appeared at her side, a determined expression on his face. "Not true! The habitat realized it couldn't feed him, Laurel. Tim told me it stopped giving him human food after a while. Instead, it sent him out to find his own meals, and supplemented them with pills and some sort of biscuits, and all the water he could drink. The AI did what it could to protect him and keep him alive."

"But first it had to learn how," Peter pointed out. "It gave him what he asked for until it could figure out what he needed." A light seemed to turn on then behind her father's eyes as he added deliberately, "Because it didn't know what humans ate."

"So what is this place, exactly?" McQueen demanded. "What have we found, besides an empty room and a demonstration of hollow-whatever technology?"

"We've found an installation that's controlled by a very sophisticated artificial intelligence," Peter replied, adding, "which may or may not be within the capabilities of our scientists in the city. Either way, there has to be something more to it than just this room."

"Why don't we think about doing some exploring and see what the AI gives us?" said Reilly.

"What would be the point? Of the exploring, I mean," Evan explained. "The AI won't respond to our general thoughts. We have to be more specific about what we need."

"All right, then," Peter told him, impatience putting an edge on his voice, "how about this? We need information. We need to know whether this AI was put here by aliens before we arrived. And if it was, then we need to know what it knows about the founding of our colony."

Once again, the air shimmered, this time all around them. The chair and wall hanging snapped out of existence in twin flashes of light. The walls dissolved into sparkles with a sound like the crashing of waves against the Silver Cliffs. Moments later the air cleared, and the "explorers" found themselves standing in a circular space with a domed ceiling. In the centre of the room sat an object that resembled a large crystal ball, mounted on a pedestal that appeared to be made of pure energy. Everything else was shiny and metallic and looked absolutely pristine.

Gazing around her, Laurel felt as though an icy shower was tattooing her skin.

"Were we transported here, or did the AI just transform the room we were in?" Peter wondered aloud.

"A little of both, actually," Evan replied. "I'm in contact with the AI. This is the ship's information centre, and it has agreed to answer as many of our questions as it can. However, it's designed to communicate telepathically, so I'll have to act as a translator."

It was becoming more and more probable that the installation had an alien origin.

"So it *is* a ship," said Peter. "And it's programmed to provide creature comforts, so it must have had a pilot, or at least a passenger. Is that true?"

"It had three beings aboard, all scientists," Evan reported.

Barrett's eyebrows rose. "Scientists, eh? And where are they now?" he asked.

Evan tilted his head and looked pensive for a moment. "It says they belong to the land."

"Belong to the—?" McQueen's eyes widened with sudden comprehension. "They've been buried?"

"Are they dead, Evan?" Reilly wanted to know.

Peter chimed in urgently, "How long ago?"

"One hundred and one planetary years," Evan told them. "It says the land took them shortly after the intruders arrived."

"So I was right," Peter declared. "This world had already been claimed by another race before we got here."

"Evan, this is important," said Reilly. "How did they die?"

Another pause, then, "It wants to show you."

Instantly, a second sphere materialized in the air above the first one. Images shimmered into being deep inside it.

"This was recorded by one of the AIs," Evan told them. "The ships are connected telepathically, so they were all witnesses, and each one has a copy."

Staring at the globe, Laurel saw a small ship land on the planet's surface. Moments later five beings emerged, swathed in protective shells that included helmets with tinted panels at the front and sides. Facial features were impossible to discern, but all five looked to be about the same height.

"The measurers," she whispered.

"The guardians were alarmed," said Evan. "They couldn't let anyone land on the planet yet. They activated their personal shields and hurried out to warn the strangers away."

In a blink, the scene changed, giving the group their first look at the rightful owners of Manua. Their skin colours ranged from light tan to black, and each scientist had a different body type. They were quite different heights as well. A shiver trickled down Laurel's spine as she recognized some of their characteristics: the flattened noses and high foreheads of the city folk, the large eyes and long-fingered hands of the miners and manufacturers, the height and strong muscles of the farm folk from the Fingers.

Evan was continuing to narrate meanwhile. "The strangers didn't understand the warning. They could send but not receive telepathic communications, so the guardians had to resort to looking fierce and chasing them back onto their little ship to get them to leave."

He turned troubled eyes to the group. "The AIs recorded both what the measurers thought and what the guardians thought back to them. The humans kept asking whether the guardians owned this planet."

"And what did the guardians reply?" said Reilly.

They all knew what the answer was before Evan gave it. Laurel could tell from the expressions on the adults' faces.

"They said that a world was not a possession but a parent, and that once this one was ready, they would be her children."

"The farmer belongs to the land," murmured McQueen.

The picture shimmered and reformed as the scene changed again. Evan continued, "The strangers left, but they came back later and dug holes in the ground."

"My god," said Barrett. "It's a funeral. Those are human bodies."

"The colonists who'd died after getting the vaccine," Peter confirmed. "Ashes to ashes, dust to dust. They injected our DNA into the terraforming process, just as I theorized."

"The strangers were back, and they were poisoning the planet," Evan went on. "The guardians had no choice. They came from every ship and joined forces to drive the intruders off. Then—" His voice broke. "Just watch."

Laurel stood paralyzed with horror, wishing she could tear her gaze away from the globe, as the guardians rushed toward the funeral site. There were about twenty of them, each waving a short rod that glowed at both ends. Evidently, the humans thought they were weapons, for, without a word, six of them pulled laser pistols and proceeded to kill every guardian who was attacking them. Then, surrounded by alien corpses, the humans finished burying their own dead. The funeral completed, they picked up their shovels and dug another hole, large enough to hold all the remaining bodies on the ground. They slung the dead guardians into the mass grave and filled it back up. There was no ceremony, no respect, not even a backward glance as the humans returned to their shuttles and departed.

In a tremulous voice, Evan went on, "The next time the strangers came back to bury more of their DNA, there was no one left to oppose them."

With that, the videoglobe seemed to melt away, absorbed by the air above the spherical console. A leaden silence took its place.

For a long moment the seven humans remained motionless, listening to one another breathe. Then McQueen remarked with forced casualness, "Looks like you've got your proof, Nyquist."

"This explains everything," Barrett agreed. "Like how the water could have been safe for humans to drink after only two years. The antibodies and DNA we buried must have become part of the terraforming process."

"But so did the aliens' DNA," Peter pointed out. "Manua isn't just tailoring itself for human habitation, it's also tailoring *us*. Turning us into facsimiles of the people we murdered in order to steal their world."

"Murdered? That's a little harsh, isn't it?" said Barrett.

"No, Ken, it's not," Peter replied grimly. "It's an ugly truth that the Consortium has been keeping secret all these years. This colony with its high ideals of trust and equality began with a heinous criminal act, followed by a cover-up. It's no wonder things are falling apart."

"So now what?" demanded Reilly. "Do we make this public knowledge?"

Peter was frowning with concentration. Laurel could almost see him working his way through the flow charts in his brain. "Papa?" She put a hand on his arm, forcing him to look at her. "Wouldn't it be a kindness?"

In an instant, his expression cleared. "Yes, duckling, it would. Evan, did all the telepaths receive this information?"

"They did, Mr. Nyquist, and they're pretty shaken up by it. Now they're wondering what they're supposed to do with it."

"Tell them that for the moment, they're to do nothing. None of the murderers are alive to be charged with their crime, so there won't be a tribunal. However, I believe we now have the leverage we need to put the Consortium—and the colony— back on track."

CHAPTER SIX

Three weeks later, Peter Nyquist was standing on a wagon bed on the commons, along with the other six members of the mountain climbing party. They would be his witnesses, not only to this meeting but also to the existence of the alien ship and what it had told them. All six were primed to testify if necessary, but he didn't think it would come to that. The delegation they were expecting from the Consortium contained a member whose daughter and nephew were both telepaths.

"Here they come!" Stephen called. All eyes turned to watch the rainbow procession of cars now crossing the Palm from the city. A red car was in the lead, followed by blue, green, and yellow vehicles, in that order.

Reilly leaned in and murmured, "Four cars for four members. If electrical energy is in such short supply, shouldn't they be sharing one vehicle?"

"They are sharing, Sean," Peter murmured back, "with their respective security details. We've pried them out of their safe little corner in the city and forced them to come to a large open space to meet with giants. It's only natural that they'd feel vulnerable."

"You figure they'll have guns?"

Standing between them, Laurel stiffened immediately at the mention of weapons. She'd seen on the AI's spherical screen what a laser rifle could do, and she was wishing she could banish the image from her mind.

"I'm sure they will," Peter replied evenly. "That's why we'll greet them on the ground, not towering over them from up here. Don't worry, duckling," he added, placing a comforting arm around Laurel's shoulders. "I lived among the city folk for nearly three years. I know how they think."

"But that was before Axel was born, and things are changing so fast, Papa," she said, unable to keep the anxiety out of her voice.

"Not everything," he told her. "Some things simply refuse to budge. That's when you go round and about."

"The best way to a destination," she repeated, recalling their earlier discussion.

Smiling, he held her hand as she climbed down to the commons.

The cars approached in single file, pulled up alongside the wagon, and parked in a straight line, end to end. By then, all the farm folk were standing in a line as well, doing their best to show a welcoming face to their visitors.

Formality didn't come naturally to farmers. Everyone in their party would much rather have been conducting this discussion around a wooden table loaded with food and drink. However, Peter had insisted that the meeting take place without hospitality, on neutral ground. So, there they were.

As expected, the Consortium had chosen their four tallest members, all male, to form this delegation. They were dressed in identical blue suits with long-sleeved jackets. One of the men was carrying a device, most likely for recording the meeting. He glanced around in confusion for several seconds, apparently searching for a flat surface on which to set it down.

With growing amusement, she watched him dither back and forth. City cars had curved roofs, so that wasn't an option. A chair would have worked, but no one had brought any. He made a face. Clearly, the lack of furniture on the commons was an annoying inconvenience for him. He might have settled for the wagon bed, but there was the matter of the horse.

The Nyquists' was a Percheron, bred for size and strength, and city folk weren't accustomed to being around large animals. When Maisie swung her head to see what he was doing, then let out a snort right behind him, he nearly jumped out of his highly polished shoes. Eventually, he gave up and took his place at the end of the line, holding the device in his hands. In that moment, Laurel dubbed him Device-man.

Of the other three delegates, one had a moustache, one was wearing a hat, and one had a belly that stuck out below the bottom fastening of his jacket. Laurel gave them labels as well: Moustache-man, Hat-man, and Belly-man.

"What is this?" demanded Moustache-man. "I thought we were going to have a meeting."

"It's a negotiation," Peter corrected him pleasantly. "First, though, in the spirit of full disclosure, you should be aware that one of us is a telepath, and that this individual is currently in contact with every other telepath on Manua. They'll be witnesses to what is said and done today."

"You could be bluffing," Belly-man cut in.

"I could," Peter acknowledged in the same mild tone of voice. "And your friends in the vehicles might not be armed. Both sides are taking a risk here, gentlemen."

Hat-man was nodding thoughtfully. Laurel thought she saw a gleam of respect in his eyes. "All right, Mr. Nyquist, we'll make this brief. Your... invitation to this meeting mentioned newly discovered evidence relating to a serious crime committed a hundred years ago. Can you show us this evidence?"

The farm folk passed glances back and forth.

"Yes, we can, but you'll want to change your clothes. Those suits you're wearing aren't really practical for a hike in the mountains," Peter replied, then explained, "We found an alien ship buried in our eastern range, containing a visual record of what happened at the founding of the colony. There's no safe way to bring it out here."

"And you didn't think to record what you saw?" sneered Belly-man.

Peter's demeanour never wavered. "Actually, we did. The same telepaths who are monitoring this meeting also witnessed our expedition. Any one of them can provide a full account of what the AI showed us. You can compare it with the documents in the forbidden section of the library and see for yourselves that they match."

Three of the four faces fell in unison. Device-man was the exception. He was most likely the one with telepaths in his family.

"If you've already broken silence and the information is public knowledge," blustered Belly-man, "then why did you make us come out here? What is there to negotiate?"

Now Peter was beaming at them. "It's not public knowledge yet. The only ones who know the whole truth are the members of the expedition and the telepaths who were linked in at the time. And what we're about to negotiate... well, let's call it an exchange of kindnesses."

He received wary looks from four pairs of eyes.

"I was recently reminded that sometimes it's a kindness to withhold part of the truth," he continued. "A hundred-year-old crime can't really be tried, so there's no benefit to dredging that up. However, the rest of the story—the terraforming—

provides an irrefutable explanation for our rapid and diverse mutations. You just completed a fifty-year study of that very phenomenon. Now you can include our findings to validate yours and also prepare the colony for what's to come."

"Is this another threat?" demanded Belly-man.

"Not at all," Peter assured him. "It's a prediction. Eventually, those aliens will be arriving here in ships to settle their terraformed planet, and we'll need to be ready for them. Not to fight them off, but to negotiate a peace, telepathically. Otherwise, we could end up with a repeat of what happened a hundred years ago, only we'll be the ones who are slaughtered."

"Their technology is that much better than ours?" Device-man asked.

"Light years ahead," Peter confirmed.

"And the team and the telepaths will keep silent about the crime that our ancestors committed?" said Moustache-man.

"Correct."

Hat-man made a sour face. "And in exchange for this 'kindness', as you call it, what do you want from us?"

"It's three kindnesses, actually. Two of them I've just told you about. The third will become evident after you've done three things.

"First, you're going to do everyone the kindness of shutting down your ill-conceived memory experiment. You know the one I'm referring to. Loading up a rememberer's brain with data from the library? That was never going to work. All it's done is rip families apart and destroy people's lives. It ends immediately."

"That would be premature," protested Belly-man, making Laurel wonder whether the living memory chips had been his idea. "It's a long-term project. These rememberers, they're creating a network, sharing memories with one another—"

"They have a human condition called 'hyperthymesia'. It's not a recent mutation or an emerging talent. It's been around for centuries, and any scientist worthy of the title would have done the preliminary research and learned everything they possibly could about it before inflicting so much pain and grief on the residents of this colony." Peter had spoken softly and in measured tones, creating an air of genuine menace.

In response, Moustache-man drew himself up to his full

height (a futile gesture in these circumstances, Laurel thought) and demanded haughtily, "And just how do *you* know about it?"

"That's not the question you should be asking," said Peter, showing him a thin smile. "What you should be asking is: what positive things will happen as a consequence of the Consortium ending the experiment? Flow charts are a specialty of mine, so let's follow this to its logical conclusion.

"First, all the test subjects and children you've locked away will be returned to their families, who will be overjoyed to welcome them back home."

"They'll hate what was done to them," said Hat-man.

"Yes, and they'll blame the scientists for it, not you. The Consortium will be the ones who stepped in and ended their suffering. People will look favourably on you for that.

"Next, since you'll no longer be obsessed with identifying and collecting rememberers, you won't need to ban fiction anymore. You can therefore do us all the second kindness of repealing that law. By restoring access to works of fiction in the library, you'll be giving people back the fantasies that they enjoy so much. They will cheer your decision, causing your popularity to rise even further.

"Finally, once the law has been wiped from the books, it will no longer be a crime to write or distribute fiction. So, you can bestow the third kindness of dropping all pending charges and pardoning every reader or author who has been convicted and detained. Once again you'll be returning people to their families. Every citizen will appreciate your mercy and your wisdom. You'll sleep much better at night, and you won't need armed guards to protect you anymore. That assurance of safety is the third kindness that we offer you, in exchange for the ones I've just described."

Feeling trapped in the silence that followed his words, Laurel had to remind herself to breathe. Safety in exchange for safety. How could they possibly refuse an offer like that? Then she sensed her father's underlying tension and understood: he knew they could, and feared that they might. Dealing with city folk was evidently a lot more dangerous and complicated than she'd thought.

"You're asking us to do a great deal in exchange for you and your allies doing nothing," Hat-man pointed out. "It doesn't seem quite fair."

"On the contrary," Peter replied evenly, "we've already done a great deal. We worked hard to secure that information about the founding of the colony—information that you've possessed and have been refusing to share for a hundred years. And don't presume to lecture farm folk about fairness, please. As your dealings with us have amply demonstrated, you don't exactly have a claim to the moral high ground here.

"I've laid out our terms, gentlemen. Do you accept them? Or should we be talking to the governing council instead? We thought the Consortium was the seat of power in the city. Were we misinformed?"

Moustache-man stiffened. "No, you weren't. We're the ones to talk to, but there are fifteen in the Consortium. We'll need time to meet with the other eleven and consider your proposal."

Peter curved his lips in another mirthless smile. "How fortunate, then, that they've been listening in through that communication device," he said, pointing to it. "Go ahead and confer with your fellow members. Meanwhile, it's lunch time for farm folk. When we've finished eating, we'll be expecting your response."

With that, he turned and climbed up onto the wagon bed, followed by the rest of the expedition team. On Peter's instructions, Emma Nyquist had packed them a meal, filling a crate with sandwiches and four kinds of apples. It was enough food for three times their number. Laurel had waited for her mother to raise an objection. Strangely, however, Emma hadn't even questioned the order.

Now, as the seven explorers sat on the wagon, having a satisfying picnic within the sight and hearing of the city folk, Peter nudged Reilly and asked, "How many did you count inside those cars, Sean?"

"Nine guards altogether." He cast a glance over the side of the wagon. "I'll bet their stomachs are rumbling right now."

"I'm counting on it." Peter produced a sack and proceeded to fill it with nine each of the sandwiches and apples. "The young'uns need to do this," he said. "Evan, Laurel, go feed the guards. Not a morsel for the high foreheads from the Consortium, mind. They don't get to taste our hospitality until they've reached the right decision."

Evan flashed a wicked grin. "That's my department, I take it."

"It is. Don't chat them up. Just work your charm. When the guards thank you for their lunch, tell them they're welcome. If they ask why we're giving it to them, tell them this is the way farm folk like to do things."

Ten minutes later, Laurel scrambled back onto the wagon bed, with Evan close behind her. "They were so glad to see us, Papa!" she blurted.

"Especially when they realized all the food was just for them," Evan chimed in.

Peter beamed at the young'uns, then turned to the others and said, "And now we have nine new friends in the enemy camp."

"You've done this before, Nyquist," remarked McQueen.

"Yes, I have, twice. There's something to be said for having one foot in the city."

"Cameron says you're devious, but I'm beginning to think you're bloody brilliant," said Barrett. "The next time he opens his mouth about you at conclave, I may just shut it for him."

"Let Laurel do it for you, Mr. Barrett, with her shadow hand," Stephen suggested. "He'll never see it coming, and he won't know who to blame."

This drew chuckles all around.

Meanwhile, Laurel was watching the delegates from the Consortium. They were huddled together around the communication device, having an animated discussion. Belly-man had briefly noticed the two young'uns moving from car to car earlier and had tried to leave the group and challenge them, but Hat-man had reeled him back in. Arms were gesticulating now. Getting a workout. They were going to be tired when this was over. City folk didn't get much exercise, she'd heard.

"How *did* you know about that hyper-whatever that you were talking about, Nyquist?" McQueen was asking.

"From Colleen. She'd stumbled across it while researching for her graduation thesis and tried to bring it to the Consortium's attention. They didn't want to hear about it then, but everyone's going to be hearing about it now."

The huddle was breaking up. As the four city folk turned to stand facing the wagon once more, Moustache-man called out,

"We're ready."

The farm folk climbed down from the wagon bed to hear the Consortium's decision.

"We accept your terms as stated," said Hat-man, "provided there's a reasonable timeline for implementation."

"It takes time to wind down a scientific experiment like this," Belly-man informed him.

"Wind down?" Peter echoed softly. "I suppose, if you're talking about tabulating and analyzing the data you've collected and then preparing a report. Your alleged scientists can take all the time they want doing that. However, the word I used was 'end', as in 'stop the abductions and torture immediately'. And issuing and enforcing that order takes no time at all.

"So here's your timeline, gentlemen: the experiment is to be over by the time you reach the city gates from here. All test subjects and incarcerated children are to be returned to their families within three days. You have one day after that to repeal the law banning fiction."

Belly-man's eyes widened with alarm. "But—!"

"Shut up, Owen," said Hat-man. "We'll make it work." Addressing Peter, he added, "Go on."

"…and the three days following that to release from custody anyone who has ever been arrested, charged, tried, convicted, sentenced, or imprisoned as a consequence of that law being in effect."

"The governing council may not have enough staff to handle all that paperwork before your deadline," Moustache-man pointed out.

"Then they'll need to hire more," Peter replied. "I think it's safe to say that the work will go even more quickly if the new hires are family members of the prisoners awaiting release. And just to be clear," he added firmly, "every telepath in the city is now aware that we have a binding agreement. They will be monitoring. Any failure on your part to carry out its terms will be considered a breach of contract, freeing us from our obligation as well."

For the first time, Hat-man smiled. "Mr. Nyquist, you play a good game of hardball. Are you typical of the farmers in the Fingers?"

Straight-faced, Peter replied, "No. Most of them are

younger than I am." A beat. "And faster." Another beat. "And a whole lot smarter."

The other man laughed.

⌁

"They're coming! Dad just turned off the main road!" Stephen's voice rang out from the porch, pulling everyone in the compound away from what they were doing.

Emma had been stirring a huge pot of savoury stew. She dropped the ladle onto the counter and tore off her apron, then raced headlong for the front door.

Laurel had been supervising the children's afternoon lessons in the living room when Stephen's cry caused eyes to glance up and compupads to drop. She made eye contact with Marie, whose face had lit up like an incandescent bulb. The little girl was on her feet and running outside before anyone could utter a word.

By the time Peter had brought Maisie to a halt in the yard, the welcoming committee had grown to encompass the entire Nyquist clan, including baby Willem. The air practically sizzled with excitement. Emma was bobbing up and down on the balls of her feet, just like Sophia when she was itching to run.

The Bertrands would be the first new family to settle in the Fingers in nearly a hundred years. Laurel immediately recognized the trio of pale green chairs that lay atop their household goods in the wagon. Then she saw her uncle, sitting beside her father on the driver's seat.

Arrangements had already been completed for the new medical doctor to set up his practice. A half-acre of land with a cottage on it had been donated by the Sorensens, and every family in Central Valley had contributed labour and materials to prepare the building for tenants.

There was still plenty of daylight, as well as many pairs of willing hands. They could make short work of the move. But Laurel knew her mother would insist that Roger and his family spend their first night back together under her roof. It was the way farm folk liked to do things.

Peter and Roger climbed down to the ground on opposite sides of the wagon. It had been a long, tiring ride from the city.

Roger was still stretching his legs when Marie shot out from the crowd and bounced into his arms, nearly bowling him over.

Emma rushed to greet him as well, pulling up short when she realized someone was missing. "Roger, where is Annelise?" she demanded sharply.

Wordlessly, he pointed behind him to the blanket-wrapped form on the rear-facing passenger seat. "She's exhausted. She was up all night, packing for the move. I think she was afraid that if she fell asleep, she might wake up back in her cell."

"Well, she's safe now," Emma declared with tears in her voice. "You all are."

Working quickly, the Nyquist men took care of Maisie and Annelise. They unhitched the horse and put her into her stall, and they carried the human into the spare sleeping chamber to finish resting. They threw a canopy over the wagon to protect its contents overnight. Then Mama Nyquist shooed everyone into the house to wash up for dinner.

Besides the stew and biscuits, there were apple pies for dessert, with milk for the children and warm cider for the adults and young'uns to wash it all down. When plates had been emptied and the table had been cleared, the children and their parents retired to private quarters for the night. Meanwhile, Laurel and Stephen went to the kitchen to wash the dishes. They worked quietly in order to listen in on the elders' conversation behind them.

"There are two kinds of gifts identified in the report," Roger was saying. "The physical ones—strength, speed, equilibrium, and agility—those are human traits, amplified genetically instead of through practice. The mental skills are largely human as well: high intelligence, organizational planning, keen eyesight or hearing, a special affinity for animals or machines, even hyperthymesia. There's nothing particularly alien about any of them, other than the fact that they've been dialed up so high and so quickly."

"What about the telepathy and telekinesis that have begun to emerge in our young'uns?" asked Peter.

"That's the really exciting part. Putting that together with what you told me about terraforming, and about the aliens being telepathic, I've come up with a theory."

"Are we going to like it?" Peter asked, only half-joking.

"It depends. How do you feel about human evolution?"

"Evolving as humans, or evolving into aliens?"

"Both." His voice becoming animated, Roger explained, "A fertilized egg in the womb goes through all the stages of evolution. It begins as a single-celled organism, and it gestates, growing increasingly more complex. At various points, it could be mistaken for the developing young of a fish, a reptile... for a while, it even has a tail. At the end, a fully-formed infant is born, with twenty-three pairs of chromosomes that have taken genetic contributions from two different sources.

"What if that is what's been happening to us? What if the terraforming process is causing us to gestate like a fetus in the womb, only we're going through all the evolutionary stages of an alien race?"

"And when the terraforming is completed, we'll be born?" said Emma doubtfully. "As what?"

"No idea," Roger told her. "But with luck, we'll be something the aliens are willing to accept as belonging on this world."

Remembering what her father had told the delegates on the commons, Laurel nearly dropped a plate. The aliens would be coming. They would download the records from the AI's memory and watch their guardians being murdered by human intruders. And then they would decide what to do about it. *With luck,* she thought, *we'll be different enough from those trespassers that the aliens won't kill us all outright.*

Meanwhile, Roger was continuing with growing excitement, "Just imagine the directions medical research will be taking over the next few generations, especially brain research. You said that the alien ships appear to be networked together, and that our telepaths are networked as well. If this trend continues, Manua may be preparing us for a first contact with the race that built those vessels."

"More like second contact," Stephen murmured beside her. "Are you ready for another adventure, story lady?"

She stopped what she was doing to reflect for a moment.

Laurel remembered every waking moment of her life from the age of nine. She recalled negotiating the maze of service corridors in the city on the day they'd rescued Marie, and the way her stomach had clenched at the prospect of climbing a mountain for the very first time. Danger was exhilarating in small doses, she decided. Adventure made for an interesting life, which made for a good story.

And Laurel loved a good story.

"Sure," she replied, smiling as she reached for the next plate on the pile. "Why not?"

Born and raised in Toronto, Arlene F. Marks found her storytelling muse at the age of 6, and she has been writing and sharing her imaginative tales ever since. She is also a retired educator and veteran teacher of the craft, having authored two literacy programs for the classroom, as well as *From First Word to Last: The Craft of Writing Popular Fiction*. During her life, she has worked as everything from a travel agent to a fashion consultant. However, her first love and current obsession is writing speculative fiction. *Imaginary Friends* is her debut short fiction collection.

Arlene lives with her husband on the shore of beautiful Nottawasaga Bay. She spends an inordinate amount of time following her characters around the universes in her mind, but she can be lured away from them by dark chocolate... and interesting owls to add to her collection.

www.thewritersnest.ca

www.ingramcontent.com/pod-product-compliance
Lightning Source LLC
Chambersburg PA
CBHW020800190726
48285CB00006B/2116